"Come here," Virginia heard herself say.

Cameron lay full upon her, their loins nestled. Against her leg, she felt his desire, insistent and boldly male. As she lay beneath him, a decade of failed hopes and tarnished dreams vanished like the stars at dawn. A volley of sensations exploded in her mind, and when her hands circled his neck and discovered the drumbeat of his pulse, the rhythmic pounding found an echo in her woman's core. He tilted his head to the side, opened his mouth on hers, and sought entry. She let him in, and the gentle stabbing of his tongue matched perfectly the thrusting motion of his hips.

Desire rang in her ears and thrummed in her belly. Her hands curled into fists.

"Ouch!"

She'd pulled the hair on his chest. At the surprised look in his eyes, she said, "Have I hurt you?"

His smile turned shy, knowing, and he lifted his brows.

"Yes, and I know just the treatment. Come with me."

Before *TRUE HEART*, there was *Beguiled* and *Betrayed*. . . .
Turn the page to read rave reviews!

BETRAYED

The First Enchanting Novel in the Clan MacKenzie Trilogy

"A terrific book. . . . Delightful. . . . A wow of a read."
—Merry Cutler, Annie's Book Stop

"A wonderful, witty story. Sarah and Michael will capture your heart. . . . If this first book [of the Clan MacKenzie trilogy] is an indication of what's to come, we are all very lucky readers!"
—Patti Herwick, *The Paperback Forum*

"Betrayed is a delightful example of Ms. Lamb's wonderful writing style. The dialogue is razor sharp and sassy, the characters are lively and entertaining, and the story holds your interest from start to finish. I can't wait to read about the next MacKenzie sister."
—*Rendezvous*

"Arnette Lamb captures the era with fine strokes and rich colors. *Betrayed* is a truly charming romance brimming with familial love and romantic sentiment."
—Kathe Robin, *Romantic Times*

"Arnette Lamb's *Betrayed* is fantastic! Five bells! She's got herself a real winner."
—Donita Lawrence, Bell, Book and Candle

"Arnette Lamb just gets better and better."
—Denise Smith, Aunt Dee's Book Bag

Books by Arnette Lamb

Highland Rogue
The Betrothal
Border Lord
Border Bride
Chieftain
Maiden of Inverness
A Holiday of Love
Betrayed
Beguiled
True Heart

Published by POCKET BOOKS

ARNETTE LAMB

TRUE HEART

POCKET **STAR** BOOKS

New York   London   Toronto   Sydney   Tokyo   Singapore

This book is a work of fiction. Names, characters, places and incidents are products of the author's imagination or are used fictitiously. Any resemblance to actual events or locales or persons, living or dead, is entirely coincidental.

An *Original* Publication of POCKET BOOKS

 A Pocket Star Book published by
POCKET BOOKS, a division of Simon & Schuster Inc.
1230 Avenue of the Americas, New York, NY 10020

ISBN: 0-671-88217-1

First Pocket Books printing February 1997

10 9 8 7 6 5 4 3 2 1

POCKET STAR BOOKS and colophon are registered
trademarks of Simon & Schuster Inc.

Cover and stepback illustrations by Lisa Falkenstern

Printed in the U.S.A.

For Ron Dinn,
who is my own True Heart
and the love of my life

Acknowledgments

Thanks to Marie Sproull and Millie Criswell for sharing their knowledge of tidewater Virginia and for trusting me with their research books.

Thanks also to Pat Stech. I'd list the reasons, Pat, but they'd fill a book.

TRUE HEART

Prologue

Rosshaven Castle
Tain, Scottish Highlands
Spring 1779

"You didn't for a moment think I believed you asked me into the stables to show me a new horse."

Even after all these years, Juliet brought out the rogue in Lachlan. He took her hand and pressed her palm against his cheek. "What I have in mind is infinitely more entertaining than a foal."

Her interest engaged, she lifted her brows. Her fingers traced his mouth. "Which is why you brought me to the loft."

Her familiar scent softened the robust aroma of freshly mown hay. Her touch did more earthy things to his sense of decorum. "Why I brought you up here is a surprise."

"I see." She licked her lips. "You *intended* to wrinkle my dress and muss my hair?"

"Aye. The first before I ravished you, the second *while* I ravished you."

Always the grand skeptic, she said, "A husband cannot ravish his own wife . . . unless . . ."

She had more to say, but she'd make him wait. His patient and practical Juliet had helped Lachlan raise Agnes, Sarah, Lottie, and Mary. But respect and love for his four bastard daughters only scratched the surface of her fine qualities. She'd given him four more daughters and an heir. He loved Juliet more today than when she'd placed his son in his arms. At sunrise next, he'd love her more still.

Talking with her was a gift he'd forever cherish. Touching her was a pleasure he couldn't deny himself now that they were alone. "In the event you've lost the essence of the conversation, my love, you were holding forth on the issue of whether a husband may ravish his wife."

"True. But the word *holding* distracts me." She glided her hand down over the placket of his breeches and made a carnal image of the ordinary word. "Will you hold forth on why there is a satin pillow beneath the hay?" She flicked her gaze to the spot where roof met wall.

Lachlan chuckled. "If you hope to tease me with conversational detours, you'll go wanting for that. Not even a bolster of gold could distract me at the moment."

Her supple fingers began an arresting rhythm, and her voice softened to an enticing purr. "Pondering two things at once is surely manageable for a man of your considerable resources."

Desire thrummed in his chest and rang in his ears. "As I did when you interrupted my civic duties to show me Mary's painting of Lottie, barefoot and astride a draft horse?"

"Lottie was beyond mortification over it. You were more interested in what our good sheriff Neville Smithson had to say about tariffs. But this is different." She put that thought to action.

Excitement quivered in his belly. On a shallow breath, he said, "You, on the other hand, are not completely captivated."

With her free hand, she cupped his neck and pulled him closer. "I've been captivated since the winter of '68."

The occasion of her entry into Lachlan's life and the genesis of his true happiness. For hours he'd anticipated this time alone with her. Their eldest and his first child with Juliet, ten-year-old Virginia was betrothed this very day to Cameron Cunningham, a lad they favored. Their youngest, Kenneth, would one day foster with Cameron's parents, Suisan and Myles. Lachlan's elder daughters were seventeen years old and planning their own futures.

Lottie would wed David Smithson later this year. Sensible Sarah had begun to tutor the children of Tain. Mary planned to move to London to apprentice with the artist, Joshua Reynolds. Agnes was busy breaking every rule of society. Lily, Rowena, and Cora were still in the nursery with their three-year-old brother.

For now, time alone with Juliet was a luxury to Lachlan, but in a few years he'd have her all to himself. This afternoon's tryst was a rarity he intended to savor. Teasing her was a part of their love game.

He plucked a straw from her hair. "But coherent thought is ever your constant companion, nay?"

"Not always."

3

"Let's see about that." Gaze fixed to hers, he kissed her. Her brown eyes glittered with pleasure, and desire smoldered in their depths. A sense of belonging swamped him, and as he deepened the kiss, he wondered for the thousandth time what goodly deed he'd done to deserve this woman. With a sweetness that always thrilled him, she returned his ardor and heightened it with her own.

In the distance he heard the happy sound of childish laughter. Juliet heard it too, but that was the way of mothering with her. Even in the crowd at Midsummer Fair she could discern the voices of her own children.

Lachlan broke the kiss. "Which of our brood is so joyous? Cora?" He spoke of their youngest daughter.

"Kenneth. Agnes must be tickling him."

"I'll be glad when his voice changes. Let's hope that occurs before Lottie's wedding, else I'll have him strewing rose petals instead of bearing the wedding band."

"He squealed with laughter today when he saw Virginia's betrothal ring."

"Do you think they are too close?"

"I think Cameron and Virginia have a special need for each other."

Lachlan couldn't deny that a deep bond existed between his daughter and his fosterling.

"Put any doubts from your mind, Lachlan. Cameron and Virginia are perfect for each other."

"Aye, as perfect a pair as Lottie and David."

"Will you rejoice when Agnes flies the nest?"

"Aye and nay. But 'tis dear Sarah I worry over more."

"Sarah's too sensible to choose a poor husband. I'll

wager my new carriage that you'll grieve when Virginia weds."

His first daughter with Juliet was unlike any of his other children. Outspoken and adventurous, Virginia had been strongly influenced by her four older sisters. From Lottie she'd learned grace and stitchery. At Mary's hand Virginia had perfected stubbornness and an artist's skill. From Sarah she'd gained a love for books and philosophy. From Agnes she'd learned too much cunning and bravery.

Cameron had been Virginia's special friend since she'd spoken her first word. He'd taught her to string a bow. He'd looked after her when everyone else was too busy. Five years hence, he'd become her husband. Lachlan felt a pang of loss at the thought of giving Virginia to another, even if Cameron was both perfect for her and the man of her choice.

"Now who's distracted?" Juliet teased.

Lachlan pressed her back into the soft hay. She winced and shifted.

"Uncomfortable?" he asked.

She gave him a look of tried patience. "No. But a pillow would be nice."

That mysterious pillow again. An odd jealousy stabbed him. He couldn't own her every thought, never would, but independence was also a part of her allure. Now she was curious about the pillow and wouldn't leave the subject alone. He reached for the item in question and held it so they could both inspect it.

Embroidered in golden thread were a halo and the words We love you, Papa.

Juliet said, "Only Lottie's stitches are so finely done."

Lachlan eased the pillow beneath her head. The shiny embroidery thread paled beside the glow of Juliet's fine complexion. "Never will I understand the female mind."

"We are cerebral creatures, even in our stitchery."

They'd plowed this conversational field often over the years. "Cerebral." He pretended to ponder it as he stared at the message on the pillow. The sentiment of the words filled him with pride. "For a thinker you're doing some very earthy things with your other hand."

"Then I'll allow you a moment to gather your priorities."

"Gather holds great appeal." Which is what he did to her skirts, exposing her legs and moving his hand up her thigh. He found bare skin. "No little silks? You're bold, Juliet."

She fairly preened. "The last time you lured me into the stables you took my underclothing and wouldn't give it back. Agnes made a show of returning the garment to me on the occasion of the vicar's next visit. Virginia spilled her tea and soiled her best gown."

Two months to the day after Kenneth had been born, Lachlan had enticed his wife into the loft. They'd spent the day loving, laughing, and napping in their pursuit of happiness. She was the sun to his day. The moon to his night. The joy to his soul. The love in his heart.

He worked his hand higher. "We were also interrupted that day."

The interruption had come when she'd asked him to give her another child. He'd refused. She'd respected his wishes.

"'Twas a rough argument 'tween us." She mimicked his Scottish speech, but beneath the mockery lay regret, for she'd carried his children with ease and birthed them with joy. Five babes of her own had not been enough for his Juliet. Counting his illegitimate daughters, nine children were plenty for Lachlan.

"You're wonderful," he said.

"I thought I was the moon to your night."

"Aye, you are."

"The rain in your spring?"

"And the skip in my step."

She pretended to pout but spoiled it by chuckling. "The thorn in your side?"

He blurted, "The hope of this loving if you laugh like that again."

She giggled low in her belly, more dangerous than full-out laughter. Still in the throes of mirth, she said, "Do you recall the morning I seduced you in Smithson's wood house?"

Lachlan did. "Hothouse better describes it. Actually I was remembering the time you tied me to the bed at Kinbairn Castle."

"You made a delicious captive except for that one request you refused me."

Had she been cunning, Juliet could have gotten herself with child that day, for she had ruled their passion. "I prevailed."

"A winning day for both of us, but—" Something caught her attention. "Look." She pointed to the ceiling.

Craning his neck, Lachlan saw a piece of parchment secured to the rafter with an arrow. Printed on parchment in Sarah's familiar handwriting were the words We love you, Mama.

Fatherly love filled him. Knowing he'd bring Juliet here, the lassies had left the pillow so he could see the affectionate words. Mary, the best archer of the four, had secured the note in a spot where Juliet couldn't miss the loving words. Even though she wasn't their mother, they thought of her that way. But the positioning of the messages left no doubt that the girls knew Lachlan and Juliet would be making love in the loft today.

On that lusty thought, he burrowed beneath her skirts and feasted on her sweetest spot.

Too soon she tugged on his hair. "Please, love."

He growled softly, triggering the first tremor in her surrender to passion. The beauty of her unfettered response moved him to his soul. But when she quieted, he eased up and over her, wedging himself into the cradle of her loins. His own need raging, he entered her, but not quickly or deeply enough, for she lifted her hips and locked her legs around him.

Lust almost overwhelmed him. "Say you're wearing one of those sponges." The sponges were the second most dependable way to control the size of their family.

Her slow smile struck fear in his heart. She wasn't wearing the sponge. If she moved so much as a muscle below the waist, he'd spill his seed, weighting the odds that she'd conceive again.

With his eyes he told her no.

Juliet's smile turned to resignation, and she mouthed the words, "No ill feelings, love." He didn't need to hear the sound of the words, he'd heard them many times in the last three years. She waited until he'd mastered his passion. Then she reached into her bodice and retrieved a small corked bottle. With a flick of her thumb, she sent the cap sailing into the hay. The smell of lilac-scented water teased his nose.

To tease her, he pulled the wet sponge from the

bottle. "Excuse me for a moment." He put the sponge between his teeth, leered at her, and again burrowed beneath her skirts.

Primed, sleek, and ready, she awaited him. In his most inventive move to date, he inserted the sponge, then brought her to completion a second time.

"I want you now," she said between labored breaths.

Obliging her came easy to Lachlan. Just when he'd joined their bodies again and began to love her in earnest, voices sounded below.

"You must let me go with you," said a very disgruntled Virginia MacKenzie.

Lachlan groaned. Juliet slapped a hand over his mouth.

He knew to whom Virginia was speaking: her betrothed, Cameron Cunningham. Hoping they wouldn't stay long, Lachlan returned his attention to Juliet.

Praying for patience, Cameron followed Virginia into the last stall. "You cannot go with me."

She stopped and folded her arms. "Why not?"

The greatest adventure of his life awaited Cameron. For the first time he would command the family ship, the *Highland Dream* himself. With MacAdoo Dundas as his first mate and Briggs McCord as his mentor, Cameron would sail to China. Years from now, after he and Virginia were married, he'd sail around the world with her. For now, reason seemed prudent. "Your father will not let you go."

"He needn't know until we are under way. I'll leave him a note."

"Well, then, it wouldn't be proper."

"Proper?" Her dark blue eyes glittered with temper,

and her pretty complexion flushed with anger. She pointed to the sapphire and pearl ring he'd given her earlier in the day. "We're betrothed. That should be reason enough. Papa knows you will not ravish me. I haven't even gotten my menses yet."

From another female the remark would have sparked outrage, but Cameron had known Virginia MacKenzie since the day of her christening ten years ago. His ears still ached when he remembered how long and loudly she'd cried. He'd been eight years old at the time. He'd fostered here at Rosshaven. He'd learned husbandry from Lachlan MacKenzie, the best man o' the Highlands. The announcement earlier today of Virginia's betrothal to Cameron had been a formality. Their marriage, five years hence, would mark the happiest day of his life. She was his special friend, his conscience. Once, she'd saved his life; a dozen times, she'd saved his pride. Their parents heartily approved, for the union would unite the families.

He told her a lie and the least hurtful refusal. "You cannot go with me to France." He was actually sailing for China. She'd learn that truth from her father on the morrow.

"Lottie says you're going for manly pleasures, but she will not tell me what that means."

"Lottie's making mischief." Lottie MacKenzie was one of the duke's first family of children. In 1761, Lachlan MacKenzie had gone to London to convince the Hanoverian king to give back the lands and titles Lachlan's father had forfeited after the Jacobite rebellion of '45. Less than a year later, Lachlan had returned with the ducal coronet of Ross and four illegitimate daughters: Lottie, Sarah, Mary, and Agnes. A year younger than Cameron, the girls had each been sired on a different woman. They had been born within weeks of each other. The duke of Ross had raised his daughters himself. He'd also spoiled them.

Cameron had learned that lesson the hard way. "Pay Lottie no mind."

A blush of uncertainty stained Virginia's cheeks. "You haven't noticed my new dress. Don't you like it?"

Cameron had heard that coy tone often. "Aye, but I don't like you mimicking Agnes's wily ways."

"What ever do you mean?"

With three sirens and a scholar for mentors, Virginia had always seemed older than her age. But Cameron knew her better than anyone. In the company of her family, she behaved as a proper daughter and role model for her younger siblings, Lily, Rowena, Cora, and Kenneth. When alone with Cameron, the adventurous Virginia came to life.

He used a method that had worked successfully in the past. "I'll bring you back a surprise."

"I want no more surprises. I have a trunk full of trinkets, pretty cloths, and flowery perfumes. You took me to Glasgow last year."

"My parents sailed with us."

"I want to go to France."

"Not this time, Virginia."

"But everything's formal now, and I've made us a symbol of our own." From the fancy wrist bag that matched her blue satin dress, she produced a white silk scarf. "See?"

Fashioned after the ancient clan brooches, the design stitched on the cloth featured a ring of stylistic hearts with an arrow running through.

"The arrow is from the badge of your mother's people, Clan Cameron. The hearts are in honor of our friendship and love, which will be timeless." No flush of embarrassment accompanied the declaration. "It took me ever so long to think it up and a week of nights here in the stables to stitch it. 'Tis a secret. I wanted you to see it before everyone else. I've saved all of my money. In France, I'll have it set in gold or silver."

Cameron voiced his first thought. "'Tis feminine for a man to wear hearts."

Her eyes filled with tears. "That's a wretched thing to say. I've made it just for us and our children."

Immediately defensive, Cameron stood his ground but murmured, "Oh, I'm sorry then. I was surprised is all."

"Then don't disappoint me again. Take me with you."

"Nay."

Now desperate, she looked around the stables, as if a better argument hid there. She found it. "Go without and I'll let Jimmy Anderson kiss me."

Cameron's temper flared. Virginia MacKenzie was his; no other man would have her. "Do and you'll be sorry." He could have kissed her, but she was too young yet; intimacy between them would come later.

"I'll cancel the betrothal if you leave me here."

His pride stinging, Cameron tucked the scarf into his sleeve and headed for the door. "Cancel it if you wish. I only agreed to please my parents."

"Liar! You said that to hurt me because you're a coward."

She spoke the truth, but if he didn't make an exit now, she'd probably talk him into taking her and in the doing gain the substantial wrath of her father. "You cannot come with me, and your father is only part of the reason."

Virginia gave up the fight. Cam didn't mean those hurtful words; he just wanted another manly adventure. But she was tired of hearing his tales of visits to exotic ports of call. She wanted to see them for herself with him. He was always flitting off to France or to the Baltic. But this time was different; the precious sapphire ring on her finger stood as proof of that. She would not be left behind.

In preparation, she'd convinced Sarah to teach her French. Lottie had tutored her on etiquette. Agnes had explained French currency. Mary had given her an appreciation of the artisans of France. She'd make Cameron proud, and she'd help him sail his ship.

As she watched her best friend leave the stables, Virginia didn't need to argue the point. By the time Cam's ship sailed tomorrow, she'd be tucked securely in the hold of the *Highland Dream*. Or perhaps she'd stowaway in the crow's nest. She liked to play up there.

Papa would be very angry, but with Lottie's wedding approaching, he wouldn't come after Virginia. Not if she were with Cameron.

Chapter

1

❦

Glasgow Harbor
1789

Cameron swung a canvas bag onto his shoulder and stepped onto the quay in Glasgow Harbor. No one awaited him, only an elegant residence with loyal servants. When compared to his youthful expectations, his life was empty, and the realization saddened him.

Pain no longer accompanied memories of Virginia. Only a deep sense of loss. Hours after his departure on that first trip to China almost ten years ago, Virginia had disappeared without a trace. Thinking she might have sailed with Cameron, her father had sent a ship after the *Highland Dream*. Upon learning of her disappearance, Cameron had wanted to turn back and look for her, but the duke of Ross had forbidden him to cancel the costly voyage. The duke had been certain that he could find his missing daughter.

They'd failed of course, and Cameron had learned to live with a soul full of regret.

"I'll wager a quid Agnes has another son," said his companion, MacAdoo, speaking of Lachlan MacKenzie's firstborn daughter, who had married the earl of Cathcart five years before.

They walked side by side, same as they had in ports throughout the world. Six years older than Cameron, MacAdoo Dundas was his oldest friend and best confidant. They'd been raised together at Roward Castle, the ancestral home of Cameron's mother's people, the Lochiel Camerons. They'd spent a year at the English court. They'd wenched and adventured together. They'd grieved over the loss of Virginia. They gambled on almost everything.

Cameron was ahead in the wagers. "My quid says she'll give Cathcart a lass this time."

MacAdoo hefted his own seaman's sack, which contained his prized possession: bagpipes. With a skill even the old Highlanders envied, he could woo a hesitant lass or bring tears to the eyes of the crustiest seaman.

Grinning, MacAdoo said, "That's because you let that comely shopgirl in Calais talk you into a pretty doll rather than a set of soldiers."

The gift was stored in Cameron's bag along with his own special keepsake: the silk scarf Virginia had given him so many years ago. Other than constant regret, it was his only remembrance of her. The cloth had yellowed and frayed with age, but Cameron's memories of the girl were still fresh.

The image of Virginia's brooch rose in his mind as vivid as the day he'd first seen the delicate ring of hearts with an arrow running through.

Cameron stopped in his tracks and blinked. The picture became real. Before him loomed a wall of

16

hogsheads. Burned into the wood of one of the barrels was the symbol created almost a decade ago by Virginia MacKenzie.

His heart pounded, and the ale he'd drunk with his crew just moments ago turned sour in his belly. No one else had seen the hallmark before Virginia's disappearance. She said it had been her secret gift in honor of their betrothal. By candlelight, she'd embroidered the scarf for him. After her disappearance, when Cameron had relayed to her father the details of that last meeting in the stables at Rosshaven, the duke of Ross confessed to being in the loft at the time. He had overheard their argument, but he had not seen Virginia's hallmark.

Cameron had thought never to see her symbol again.

"What's amiss?" MacAdoo said.

With a shaking hand, Cameron pointed to the design.

"Sweet Saint Ninian," MacAdoo whispered. "Isn't that a match to your scarf?"

Cameron put down his burden and peered closer at the design. With only a slight variance, a common heraldic crown over the top, the symbol was the same. The hearts were more perfectly drawn, as if a woman rather than a lass had fashioned them.

From the ashes of certainty, a spark of hope flickered to life.

Virginia could be alive.

The thought staggered him.

MacAdoo grasped Cameron's arm. "What's wrong? Have you gone light in the head?"

Mouth dry, hands shaking, Cameron leaned against the stack of tobacco casks. Past disappointments warned him to take caution. But what were the odds of another person combining the arrow of Clan Cameron, his mother's Highland family, with the heart of love in this exact fashion? No coincidence appeared before him; Virginia was alive and this drawing was proof. Or was it a cry for help?

"Stay here," he ordered.

Stuffing the hogshead under his arm, he located Quinten Brown, captain of the merchantman.

"From where did this hallmark come?"

Brown swept off his three-cornered hat and tucked it under his arm. His hair reeked of the fragrance of pine, a favorite scent among seamen. "Why would you be asking, Cunningham?" he said in his clipped English speech. "Ain't the brandy trade enough for you?"

In his place, Cameron would also be protective of his livelihood; any businessman would. To allay the man's worry and loosen his tongue, Cameron fished a sack of coins from his waistcoat. "I've seen this design, and it's very important to me. I've no intention of heeling in on your tobacco trade."

Satisfied, Brown pocketed the gold. "'Course you ain't. What would you want with my trade when you got all them friends at court. Rumor has it you've talked the Cholmondeleys out of their daughter."

The Lady Adrienne Cholmondeley had never been farther from Cameron's mind. "Tell me what you know about this cask."

"I know all of the tidewater plantations."

The cask had come from Virginia. How ironic. "What about the plantation where this cask originated?"

"I'll tell you what I know o' the matter. The cooper at Poplar Knoll—Rafferty's his name—always favored the plain crown, even after the colonies was lost to us." He traced the design. "This girlish mark, the hearts 'n' arrow on that barrel, I ain't seen it afore now."

"Then how do you know this tobacco came from there?"

"The new mistress herself come aboard to pay her respects to me." Rocking back on the heels of his bucket top boots, the seaman clutched his lapels. "Her husband, Mr. Parker-Jones, bought the plantation more'n a year ago. I tell you true, Cunningham, the slaves 'n' servants o' that place are praising God. The old owner and his wife were devils and more."

Cameron had scoured every port in the British Isles, the Baltic, Europe, and even the slave markets of Byzantine. He'd searched Boston, the cities on Chesapeake Bay, and even the Spanish-held New Orleans. "Where is this plantation?"

"Poplar Knoll? The tidewaters of Virginia."

Cameron had sailed those waters but not in many years. With his father serving in the House of Commons, Cameron now favored the shorter European trade routes. "On the York River?"

"No. The James, just west of Charles City."

"The south or the north shore?"

"South if I'm remembered of it. Fine dock with lovey doves carved into the moorings. Yes, south side."

At the least, the person who'd crafted this hallmark had some knowledge of Virginia. If she were on an isolated plantation, that would explain why he hadn't found her. For years after her disappearance, the lost war with the colonies had limited shipping traffic, and little news traveled out of tidewater Virginia.

Anticipation thrumming through him, he thanked the captain.

"Keep the cask, Cunningham. You paid good coin for it."

Rejoining MacAdoo, Cameron made his way to Napier House, home of Virginia's sister, Agnes. Now the countess of Cathcart, Agnes was the only family member who still believed that Virginia was alive.

Dear God, he prayed, *let it be so.*

Chapter

2

Poplar Knoll Plantation
Tidewater Virginia

Planting would be upon them soon. From dawn's first light until sunset or rain forced them to stop, the indentured and the enslaved would hunker in the tobacco fields.

Virginia shifted on the bench, her back aching at the thought. Across the weaving shed, the strongest of the slaves dismantled the looms used to weave book muslin, the fabric of necessity for slaves and bond servants. Everyone, even the pregnant females, worked in the fields until harvest. At first frost, the looms would come out and the weaving would begin again.

Life at Poplar Knoll would continue for another year. But three harvests hence, Virginia's indenture would end. The old bitterness stirred, but she stifled it. This was her home for now, and she'd make the best of it. She'd tried escape once, nine years ago. For penalty, three years had been added to her servitude.

21

For punishment, she'd been shackled at night until her twelfth birthday. Freedom would come. Three years from now, she'd have money in her purse, new shoes and a traveling coat, and passage to Williamsburg. From there—

"Duchess!"

Noise in the room ceased.

Virginia looked up. Merriweather, the smartly dressed butler from the main house, strolled toward her. Past sixty years of age, Merriweather had snow white hair, which contrasted sharply with his thick black brows.

"Wash your hands and face, Duchess. Mrs. Parker-Jones wants to see you."

No one addressed Virginia as Virginia. They hadn't believed her story about who she was and how she'd come to the colonies almost a decade ago. When she'd proclaimed herself the daughter of the duke of Ross, they'd laughed and named her Duchess. She'd been a frightened child of ten.

Anniegirl, a slave with blue eyes and pale woolly hair, slapped her hands against her cheeks. With too much drama, she said, "Oooh, Duchess. Maybe Mr. Horace Redding himself has come to call on you—his most ardent disciple."

In his essays styled for the ordinary man, Horace Redding had struck a balance between the conservative and the liberal philosophers of the day. Many considered Redding's first pamphlet, *Reason Enough,* the moral cornerstone of the revolutionary movement in America. Once a Glaswegian harnessmaker, he had been immortalized in song and script and dubbed the freedom maker. To Virginia, his words served as the voice of logic and a link, although weak, to Scotland.

She chuckled. "If Redding has come, shall I beg one of his handkerchiefs for you?"

Anniegirl's sister, Lizziegirl, older by two years and dark like their mother had been, dropped the yarn she'd been winding. "An' a lock of his hair if you please."

Merriweather cleared his throat. "That's enough sauce from the two of you."

At eleven and nine, the girls squirmed with the need to defy any order. Their mother, a slave, had befriended Virginia. Their father was a beast named Moreland, the former owner of Poplar Knoll. He'd never touched Virginia, but her skin crawled at the thought of him and his wife and the misery they had made of her life.

Their brother, Georgieboy, laughed. "You're in trouble."

Lizziegirl stuck out her tongue. "The master'll sell you to mean ol' Mr. Pendergrast."

Georgieboy paled and shrank back. The neighboring planter whipped his own slaves rather than leave the task to his overseer.

"Silence!" Giving the girls a final warning, which had the desired effect, Merriweather ordered Georgieboy out, then turned to Virginia. "You've done nothing wrong, Duchess. The mistress hastened me to say so."

Virginia put aside the hatband she'd been tooling for the wagonmaster. Since Mr. Parker-Jones had purchased Poplar Knoll almost two years ago, Virginia had spoken to the mistress only once. Did this summons also involve the design Virginia had branded, without permission, into one of the hogsheads? Hopefully not, for she'd come away from the meeting with a small victory and an apology from the mistress, who assured her the matter was ended. To replay the woman's kindness, Virginia had painted a river scene, carved a frame, and presented it to Mrs. Parker-Jones.

Encouraged, Virginia went to the table and washed her face in the bucket of clean water. Her fingers were stained from the dye she'd applied to the leather hatband before tooling, and the soap had no effect. She untied her apron and took the comb from her basket. She'd carved the comb herself.

As they left the shed and made their way through the servants' hamlet, she combed her hair and tied it at her nape. Just past her shoulders, her hair would have to be trimmed before summer, else she'd swelter in the sun.

"She'll not be seeing you in the front parlor, Duchess." No rancor hardened Merriweather's words, and Virginia smiled. She might be a bond servant, but never had she been a sloven.

Over the years, her footsteps had helped keep the paths worn smooth. Half-a-dozen trails led from the hamlet, which consisted of ten wooden houses with earthen floors. A vegetable patch to the south of the buildings provided enough food for everyone, even those in the main house. To the east lay the henhouse and the pigsty. Firewood from the forest to the west was plentiful.

The Parker-Joneses preferred slave labor to indentures. As the only female bond servant remaining at Poplar Knoll, Virginia now lived alone in one of the houses. She slept on a pallet stuffed with straw, and her few possessions wouldn't even fill a hatbox. But she would not feel sorry for herself; she'd hold her head high and think of the day when she'd be free.

She paused at the herb garden, pinched a stem of mint, and stuck it in her bodice. The clean smell masked the odor of leather and strong soap.

"What's gotten into Lizziegirl?" Merriweather asked.

"Georgieboy told her that Mr. Moreland was her father, too."

His mouth turned down in disgust. A Cornishman, Merriweather had emigrated to Virginia after the surrender at Yorktown. He'd been a reader of the news by trade, and the old master had taken such a liking to him he'd offered Merriweather the esteemed post of butler. Although Merriweather didn't precisely gossip, he managed to keep the servants at the plantation aware of the important goings-on at the main house. Virginia returned the favor.

At the rose trellis, he plucked a dead blossom. "The old master should have done something about those children of his besides turn his back on them."

Few social issues stirred Virginia's ire as this one did. "He should have left their mother on her pallet in the slave quarters, where she belonged. As if she had a choice, though."

Merriweather waved to the gardener, who conversed with the cook near the parsnip patch. "Sinful practice, taking a slave girl into his bed."

If adultery was the greatest of Moreland's sins, naming his illegitimate offspring after the kings and queens of England was the lesser of his cruelties. His own children were slaves. God curse him for selling them with the land.

Virginia echoed a familiar sentiment. "Things are better now. Mr. Parker-Jones doesn't take slaves to his bed."

"Neither is his wife jealous of you."

25

That topic was too distressing. "Do you know what the mistress wants with me?"

"Could be the matter of that cask again. Captain Brown was here this morning."

Regrets again plagued Virginia. She'd be free in three years, and she'd risked it all and maybe more on the vague hope that Cameron or someone in her family would recognize the symbol on one cask among a shipment of hundreds.

Cameron. Sadness dragged at her, but gone was the longing and the despair. She'd overcome those feelings ages ago. With the passage of time, events blurred, faces faded, and she often distrusted her memory of the life and people she'd left behind in Scotland. Surely they'd buried her memory long ago, at least that's what she told herself when melancholy came upon her.

"I put the newspaper in the springhouse for you."

Merriweather's kindness reached out to Virginia. Bond servants had few rights and fewer entitlements. For years he'd secretly passed the newspaper on to her. Had he not, she knew she would have lost the ability to read. Through those papers, she'd come to know Horace Redding. In him, she'd found someone to admire, and that was important to her. Admiration for her fellow man was another practice of people who were free. She'd vowed not to lose the traits, both good and bad, that she'd been taught as a child.

"Thank you, Merriweather."

He smiled, and she knew what he'd say next, so she said it for him, mockingly. "If anyone sees you reading the newspaper, the trouble is on your back."

Clasping his hands behind his back, he slowed the pace. "North Carolina's to become a state."

Virginia fought the urge to skip down the path. "It's

not in the paper, else you wouldn't have said it. Who told you?"

"Captain Brown."

Except for salt, some tools, and fineries for the home house, Poplar Knoll was self-sufficient. News from the outside world had always had a soothing effect on Virginia. Without it, she would have gone mad or thrown herself in the river. "That will make twelve states in the Union. Tell me more."

"I'll tell you this, Duchess. You would have made a fine newsreader yourself if—"

"If I had been a man." She chuckled. "By my oath, Merriweather, had I been born my father's son, I would not be here."

His mouth pinched with mirth. "No, you'd be in the House of Lords, your grace."

Virginia laughed outright. She felt no animosity at the fate that had brought her here.

"The wheelwright gave me a message for you."

Virginia couldn't hide a blush. "What did he say?"

"Only that he'd be back in a fortnight and hoped to see you again. What have you done with him, Duchess?"

"I said hello, shared a ladle of water with him, and showed him the way to the smithy." She'd been helping the head gardener prune the roses. The wheelwright had flirted shamelessly with her.

"I thought as much—or as little, that being the case."

"Did he tell a different tale?"

"No, but when next he visits, he'll have courting on his mind."

Courting. Romantic rituals in tidewater Virginia bore no resemblance to the social customs Virginia had grown up with. Prior to the Parker-Joneses purchase of Poplar Knoll, Virginia would not have been allowed to speak to a visitor, let alone share common niceties.

"What will you do?"

She chuckled. "I shall try to keep my wits if and when Mr. Jensen returns."

She was still smiling when Merriweather ushered her into the back parlor. Mrs. Parker-Jones was reading a book.

Virginia guessed her age at past fifty. Her hair had once been black, and although she did not pamper herself, she took pride in her appearance. From Merriweather, Virginia had learned that wealth had come hard and late to them. A childless couple, she and Mr. Parker-Jones would often be seen taking refreshments in the formal gardens in the evening. They smiled often in each other's company. At planting last year, the mistress had driven a cart herself and brought cider to everyone in the fields. It was the first such kindness anyone at Poplar Knoll could remember.

Virginia thought it sad that pox scars marred Mrs. Parker-Jones's complexion, for she seemed an unblemished soul.

Closing the book, she waved the butler away. "Shut the door on your way out if you please, Merriweather."

Although she'd never been in this room, Virginia refused to gape at the fine furnishings. She'd seen better at Rosshaven. The mistress's dress was another matter. Virginia had forgotten what it was like to wear a fabric as soft as velvet against her skin. Book muslin was good enough for servants and slaves.

Mrs. Parker-Jones had something on her mind, and

from the way she toyed with the bindings of the book and stared into the cold hearth, the subject troubled her.

"Take a seat and tell me about yourself." She indicated the facing chair. "Where are you from, and how did you come into servitude?"

Caution settled over Virginia, and she stayed where she was. She knew a bond servant's place. Getting too close to those in the home house had been disastrous for her. Her skin crawled at the thought of the last mistress and the degradation she'd heaped on Virginia. "Three years remain on my indenture, ma'am. I want no trouble."

She sighed, her lips pinched in distress. "You have not been mistreated since our arrival here. I want the truth. Are you Virginia MacKenzie?"

Something in the tone of her voice alarmed Virginia. She gripped the back of the chair. "Why do you ask?"

"I'm curious. Where are you from?"

Virginia knew she should tell the tale that everyone believed: the lie Moreland had told. She did not; she could not lie to Mrs. Parker-Jones. "I am from the Highlands of Scotland."

"How did you come to be here?"

"When I was ten years old, I trusted a ship's captain named Anthony MacGowan. May he rot in hell." Virginia would go to her grave with a curse on her lips for that swine.

"Won't you please sit down?"

"Thank you, no."

As if holding on to a weak belief, she stubbornly said, "Mr. Moreland swore your father sold you into bondage. We paid him for your indenture."

"Mr. Moreland and I saw it differently."

"You ran away from Poplar Knoll once. They found you on a raft in the river."

She'd tied fallen limbs together with vines. She'd been so brave then, so desperate to get back home. "Yes, and I paid the price."

The mistress grew sad. "Again I apologize for what Mrs. Moreland did to you."

"Thank you, but it wasn't your fault. You needn't mention it again." At least Virginia hoped she'd drop the disgusting matter.

Mrs. Parker-Jones strummed her fingernails on the book. "Are you the daughter of the duke of Ross?"

Not in years had Virginia spoken of her other life, and every time she had told the truth, she'd regretted it. Mistrust came easy. "Why do you ask?"

"Please tell me the truth. I swear it will not be used against you."

Virginia had received more humiliating treatment for reasons other than her birthright. For no reason at all, save her sex and the color of her skin, she'd been forced to endure humiliations that still chilled her to the bone when she thought of them.

"Is the *sixth* duke of Ross your father?"

How could Mrs. Parker-Jones know the specifics of Papa's title? Unless this interview was not a trick.

Virginia swallowed back apprehension. "With all due respect, Mrs. Parker-Jones, may I know why you are asking?"

"Do you know a sea captain named Cameron Cunningham?"

Cameron.

Images of her youth swam before Virginia. Then she saw nothing at all.

* * *

"Virginia!"

Through a curtain of confusing thoughts, Virginia heard her name. No, not her bondage name. She must be dreaming of her childhood, of Papa tossing her atop the haywagon, of Agnes showing her how to spit straight, of Lottie teaching her to pee standing up without soiling herself or her clothing, of Cameron taking her to the Harvest Fair and buying her sweetcakes—

"Duchess!"

Acrid smoke from a burned feather seared her nose. Batting the air, she turned away.

"Duchess."

Merriweather's voice. Poplar Knoll. Servitude. Virginia opened her eyes. Two chandeliers wavered overhead. When the images converged, she felt a hand on her arm. She drew back, longing to return to the dream.

"You fainted . . . Virginia?"

Virginia. Her given name spoken by the mistress of a tidewater plantation. Curiosity pulled her fully from the swoon.

Mrs. Parker-Jones knelt beside her. "Have you hurt yourself?"

"No," Virginia was quick to say. She felt hemmed in, befuddled.

"Then you know this Cameron Cunningham?"

"Aye." Hope thrummed to life inside her, and she prayed that she didn't embarrass herself. "He was always Cam to me."

"Sweet Jesus. Merriweather, fetch the brandy." Mrs. Parker-Jones held out her hand. "We both need fortification, don't you agree?"

Ignoring the offered hand, Virginia pulled herself up and sat in the chair. The spring cushion felt odd, and the smooth wood of the chair arms were cold against her skin. Her mind whirled like a top. Cameron. Cam. The boy she'd pledged to marry. The man who'd sailed to France without her. After all these years, Cameron had—had what? "Cam saw the cask."

"Yes. He recognized that design of yours."

The unthinkable had come to pass.

She couldn't form questions fast enough. "Where? Where did he see them? Is he here?"

"He saw them in Glasgow."

A world away.

"Moreland's account says you were a thief, and your father despaired of turning you from a life of crime. At your sire's bidding, Moreland paid your fine." She frowned. "Which happened to be the price of a ten-year indenture before the war."

Virginia couldn't stop thinking about Cam. Absently, she recited an old truth. "Moreland lied. He bought me from a hellish man, Captain MacGowan."

"You must have been terribly frightened."

By the time Virginia had been herded off the ship in America, she'd been beyond fear. But the horrors of that voyage paled beside what had come later. "May we talk of something else?"

"Certainly, Virginia. Do you know the name of Cameron Cunningham's ship?"

She'd never forget it. "The *Highland Dream.*"

"No. It's named the *Maiden Virginia* now."

An old memory stirred. She and Cameron stargazing on the roof of the stables at Rosshaven Castle. He'd promised to name his ship after her. He'd vowed to take her around the world. She looked at her hands, stained and workworn and devoid of the lovely ring he'd given her.

But she'd worked hard to forget the past, to dodge the heartache. The pain returned and, with it, the most important question. "Will he come for me?"

Looking like the one with a great secret, she said, "Captain Brown says yes. He sailed from Glasgow before your Captain Cunningham and arrived yesterday. He came to visit this morning."

"What did he say about Cameron?"

"He believes that with fair winds, the *Maiden Virginia* could dock in Norfolk today or tomorrow."

Relief robbed Virginia of breath. Her plan had worked. Cameron had seen the cask and remembered the symbol. Cameron hadn't forgotten her. "On his way here."

"Yes."

"What did Cameron say to Captain Brown? Tell me every word."

"Their conversation was brief and very confusing to me."

"Tell me every word just as it was spoken."

"Cameron Cunningham was curious about the design on the cask. Captain Brown explained to Captain Cunningham where the cargo came from and gave him our location. The next day, from a member of Cunningham's crew, Captain Brown learned that Cameron visited the daughter of the sixth duke of Ross, who lives in Glasgow. Someone they knew had drawn a similar symbol as the one you put on that cask. They are looking for that person. Brown also found out that they planned to sail for Norfolk as soon as possible."

They were sailing here, right now, to fetch Virginia. But who was "they"? Who was coming with Cameron? Tears pooled in her eyes and her heart soared. "I first drew the design years ago."

"What will you do now?"

Deciding for herself on anything but the most elementary actions was as unnatural to Virginia as sleeping on a soft bed. One thing was certain: She'd throw her arms around Cameron Cunningham and cry her heart out. Mrs. Parker-Jones needn't know that. "I'm not sure what to do. When you said 'they' were sailing, whom did you mean?"

"I don't know."

Merriweather returned with a silver tray. He poured two glasses of brandy. Mrs. Parker-Jones took them both and handed one to Virginia.

Had she ever tasted brandy? She couldn't remember, and strong spirits weren't poured at table in the servants' hamlet. Unsure of the proper way to drink the brandy, she waited and watched. When Mrs. Parker-Jones took only a sip, Virginia did the same. The liquor burned a path to her stomach, and she almost choked.

"Drink it gently." Clutching her own glass in both hands, Mrs. Parker-Jones took another sip. "I wish you had told me who you were."

Virginia almost huffed in disbelief, but habit prevented her. "Would you have believed me?"

"I do not know, but I like to think I would have written a letter for you."

Compared to the former owner of Poplar Knoll, Mrs. Parker-Jones was a saint. But the Morelands' cruelty was a part of the past. Cameron was on his way. Virginia would be free again. At the thought, her hands shook and she gripped the small glass until her hands grew numb.

"Please believe that I would have helped you."

Acknowledging the mistress's kindness seemed of

great importance to Virginia. "Saying that you might have helped me is enough."

"Merriweather, have—" Turning to Virginia, she said, "Is miss the proper address for a duke's daughter?"

Class distinctions were one of the reasons the colonies had fought and won their independence from England. Virginia had spent her youth beneath the banner of revolution. Could she adjust to the social structure of her homeland? Not immediately.

By way of explanation, Mrs. Parker-Jones said, "My family was from Pennsylvania—rather provincial, you see. So I haven't any experience with the gentry."

A reply to that honesty was easy. "The proper way is my lady, but I'd like to be called Virginia."

"Then Virginia it is. Merriweather, have Virginia's things brought to the guest room facing the river. You'll need dresses, hats, and shoes. Everything. They cannot see you as you are."

Reality set in and, with it, the second most defining statement Virginia had every heard. The first had been on the deck of Anthony MacGowan's ship. His words still had the power to wound. *Get to the galley or I'll chain you in the hold until we dock in Norfolk. If you tell anyone on this ship who you are, I'll throw you overboard and say you fell.*

Merriweather left. Virginia put aside thoughts of Anthony MacGowan and the fear he'd instilled in her. "Please tell me everything that Captain Brown said about my family." A cruelty struck her. "Are my parents alive? My sisters, my brother?"

"I'm sorry, but he said nothing about them. He did say that one of your sisters lives in Glasgow." She demurred. "But I've already said that part."

"Which sister?"

"She is the countess of Cathcart. How many sisters do you have?"

"Seven that I know of. My brother, the youngest, was only three when I . . . left."

Plaintively, Mrs. Parker-Jones said, "What happened, Virginia?"

The answer sat like a rock in her belly. As a child working in the tobacco fields, she'd falsified her life. With each passing season, she imagined a new past for herself. But the truth had always been there, looming like a great shadow over her head. Eventually she'd settled for the truth. "A foolishness too great to tell."

"I hope you do not hold Mr. Parker-Jones or myself responsible."

How could she? Along with the plantation, the tobacco fields, and the slaves, they'd purchased her indenture and those of the other bond servants. It had been a business transaction for them; no malice had been involved. "No, I do not."

"We acted in good faith."

"I know, and for their sins, MacGowan and the Morelands will pay in hell."

"How can I help you?"

Virginia couldn't settle on any one thing, for she wanted the impossible. She wanted her childhood back. She wanted to wake up in her bed at Rosshaven Castle on the morning of her tenth birthday. "At the moment, I'm not sure what to ask for."

"Your vocabulary doesn't need much work, but I'm afraid I can't teach you Scottish. Or do you remember how to speak it?"

She'd avoided dredging up old memories; now she must sift through the imaginings and call up the true past. "In the MacKenzie household, both English and Scottish are spoken." She almost mentioned her mother's heritage, but why should Mrs. Parker-Jones care about that irony?

"Good. Will you tell me about your siblings?"

"There's Lily, Rowena, and Cora. They were nine, eight, and six when last I saw them. And Kenneth, my father's heir. He was three." She remembered a laughing fair-haired boy, they called Gibberish because he talked too fast.

"What of your other four sisters? You said you had seven."

"They're older." The addition came easily; Virginia had practiced that ability, too, since coming to Poplar Knoll. "They are seven and twenty years old now."

Mrs. Parker-Jones frowned. "All of them are the same age?"

With the calling up of those memories came a sense of peace and love. "Papa's very handsome. He went to court and fell in love with four women at once. When they bore his children, he took Agnes, Lottie, Sarah, and Mary from their mothers and raised them himself—until my mother came to Scotland."

Mrs. Parker-Jones opened the book. "This was written by the earl of Cathcart. 'Edward Napier.' She spoke his name with the proper respect due the nobleman who invented tools for the common man. "He names his wife in the dedication."

"It must be Sarah. Papa always said a blueblooded lord would woo her, and she's so very beautiful and as bright as any Oxford scholar."

"No, it's not Sarah."

The oddity of the conversation baffled Virginia but in a pleasant way; she was discussing her family with someone who believed her. "May I read for myself?"

Embarrassment brought a flush to her scarred cheeks. "I did not know you could read."

A prevarication popped into Virginia's mind. She would not endanger Merriweather for the kind gift of sharing the newspaper with a lonely girl. Then she remembered that she needn't make excuses for herself any longer. She took the book and traced the golden letters on the binding. *Plows for Field and Farm,* by Lord Edward Napier, earl of Cathcart. Virginia knew the Napier name. Every plantation and farm used the tools he'd invented. The Napier plow was as common as the Morgan rake.

With a shaking hand, she turned the pages. On the dedication page, she found the words, "For my children, Christopher and Hannah, and for dearest Agnes, who has made us a family again."

Agnes. Fondness choked Virginia. Agnes, the trouble finder, as Papa used to say. Agnes had fallen in love and married an important man. Bully for her.

"You remember Agnes fondly?"

"Fondly? Of course. She's my sister."

What other great events had occurred in Virginia's absence? Was Papa alive? Mama? The possibility that they might be dead was too wretched to contemplate.

Virginia clutched the book to her breast. Surely her family had lost hope of finding her. She remembered the exact moment she'd given up hope of finding them. It had been her fifteenth birthday. But by putting away the past, she had bettered the present. From that day forth, her life at Poplar Knoll had become livable. With one exception. But she wouldn't think about those dark times. Not now.

"What are you thinking, Virginia?"

"They gave me up for dead."

"Not anymore."

If that was true, if Cameron and her family now expected to find her, what regrets would they bring with them? How had they dealt with her loss?

"I'm sorry. But I've said that to you before. When I learned about what Mrs. Moreland had done to you, I could not fathom a deed so cruel."

The darkness of denial blanketed Virginia. Never again would she visit those evil times. "I don't want to talk about that."

Mrs. Parker-Jones shivered in revulsion. "No, I don't suppose you do." Composing herself, she continued. "I wasn't blessed with children, but I do come from a large family. We lost a brother once. I'm certain your loved ones were bereft at losing you."

Bereft. She thought of the funerals she'd attended with her family. Cameron standing beside her, helping her place a rock on the cairn in tribute to a family friend. Save Cameron's strong presence, the memories were vague. Had the MacKenzies constructed a cairn in memory of her?

"Imagine how happy they are now."

Mrs. Parker-Jones looked so distressed Virginia felt bound to comfort her. "All will be set to rights when Cameron comes for me."

"What will you tell him of your life here?"

Dread chased away her joy. How could she look her family in the face and tell them the truth?

"I do not know."

Chapter

3

Everyone had given up hope of finding Virginia. Everyone except Agnes MacKenzie. For the first five years, Cameron had kept the faith. He'd searched the world and yearned for the girl he had planned to grow old with. When he'd finally accepted defeat, he'd done so with the help of her father, Lachlan MacKenzie. That had been five years ago. Five years of peace with himself, years of accomplishment and restful nights. He couldn't start believing again. But the closer he traveled to America, the greater the battle.

Three weeks and four days out of Glasgow, her hold perfectly weighted with stone, the *Maiden Virginia* eased into the James River. Cameron stepped aside and allowed Quinten Brown to take the helm. Never had anyone other than Cameron's father or his crew piloted his ship. Cameron had sought out Brown in Norfolk. The man assured Cameron that he could steer a man o' war safely up the James River. To

Cameron's disappointment, Brown had no knowledge of who had created the hallmark, only that it had come from Poplar Knoll. Rather than hire another man's ship to sail the unfamiliar waters of the James River, Cameron had hired the man.

The crew went about their tasks, but their attention was fixed on the English captain at the wheel. MacAdoo Dundas was more blatant in his unease, for he noisily hammered an extra horseshoe into the mast.

"She's a fine one, Cunningham," said Brown, loud enough for all to hear. "I'll not run her aground, so you can belay that scowl."

Cameron tried to stand at ease but could not.

Beside him, Agnes MacKenzie laughed. "Well said, Captain Brown."

Agnes had married Edward Napier, earl of Cathcart. She'd even shunned Highland tradition and taken his name. But she'd always be Agnes MacKenzie to Cameron. More than a friend to him, she was the true believer he could never be. She'd pledged her dowry and her life to finding Virginia. Cameron's efforts paled by comparison, but Agnes had yet to deal with the guilt she felt over the loss of Virginia. Perhaps now she would be spared that pain.

She'd been out of the birthing bed only two days when Cameron had arrived in Glasgow and spied the cask. Upon seeing the hallmark, she'd packed a bag and sent messengers to every member of her family. Then she'd demanded that they sail immediately for America.

That's when her husband had stepped in. Edward Napier had lost his first wife to an Atlantic crossing, yet he could not refuse Agnes this voyage. As her physician, he'd insisted that she stay abed for at least a week. She had compromised and rested for three days.

Amazed at her resiliency, Cameron watched her sway easily with the motion of the deck. A year older than she, he couldn't remember a time when he hadn't known Agnes MacKenzie and her three sisters. Then Virginia had come along, and Cameron's life had forever changed.

"Do you think Virginia will favor Papa or Mama?" she asked.

MacAdoo politely excused himself, but his sour mood was evident in the stiffness of his gait. He'd taught Virginia to climb the rigging.

"Cameron, are you listening? How tall do you suppose she has grown?"

Cameron gritted his teeth, lest he give in to temptation and begin to hope. Virginia was dead. The hallmark on that cask was a coincidence. Some smitten cooper with courting on his mind had created the romantic design.

Agnes clutched his arm, her brown eyes narrowed in determination. "She's alive, and I say she favors Father."

On the subject of Virginia, Agnes had always spoken succinctly, but a new conviction now fired her belief. She'd sailed with Cameron to China and spent a year learning the weaponless fighting skills of the emperor's best. She could bring any man to his knees with one well-placed blow. Garbed in bright yellow wool, her golden hair twisted into a shapely do, she looked like a helpless noblewoman. A contradiction. A foolish assumption.

Cameron couldn't help but smile.

Her brows flared. "Are you mocking me, Cameron Cunningham?"

He held up his hands as if to ward her off. "Never."

"Are so." She smoothed the fit of her butter yellow gloves. "But then I suspect you are anticipating the uncomfortable conversation you must have with Adrienne Cholmondeley."

The problem of Adrienne was his affair, and he made a practice of never speaking with Agnes about his love life. How could he when she believed his betrothed was alive and any romance he enjoyed was a betrayal of Virginia?

He knew the way to deal with Agnes. "On the matter of whom Virginia favors, I say one MacKenzie female with your father's temperament is quite enough."

She fairly preened, for she knew he was speaking of her. "I meant to say that Virginia will favor the MacKenzies in physical appearance."

She knew when to retreat. Cameron grinned. "In that event, I pray she favors Lady Juliet."

The humor faded from Agnes's eyes. "I pray she has Mama's strength."

She meant fortitude, and she referred to Lady Juliet, Virginia's mother and the woman who had raised Agnes. Even Lachlan MacKenzie knew better than to cross his duchess. But Virginia had been closer to her father. He'd taken her everywhere, taught her to ride as soon as she could stand. He'd formally given her to Cameron on her tenth birthday. He'd also given her up for dead.

"If you truly believed she is dead, why have you kept that tobacco cask?"

Too late Cameron realized Agnes had tricked him into thinking casually about Virginia. He also knew when to retreat. "You should rest," he said. "I promised your husband you wouldn't tire yourself."

43

"I'm fine, but I will leave you to fret over your future and Captain Brown's helmsmanship."

Brown stiffened formally. "You needn't have a care about that, my lady. I know this river as well as I know the buttons of my shirt."

She turned on the charm. "I fear that's not enough to assuage poor Cameron and his crew, but the MacKenzies are indebted to you, sir."

As the object of her attention, Brown almost groveled. "You will remember me to your father, Lady Agnes," he said. "Best man o' the Highlands is how Lachlan MacKenzie's known."

"That he is. You can be sure I'll tell him that you led us to Virginia." She slid Cameron a challenging glance, but her attention was fixed on Brown. "I believe, however, that he'll thank you himself. He cannot be more than a day or two behind us."

As a result of her three-day forced bed rest, the messenger had surely reached her father at his home in Tain before Cameron had set sail. Lachlan MacKenzie would make haste to follow. The rest of the family had probably already arrived in Glasgow, for the hallmark was the strongest lead to Virginia they'd had in over five years.

Brown acknowledged a passing ship, but his interest clearly lay with the conversation. "Every Scot in the Chesapeake will turn out for a chance to see the Highland rogue in the flesh."

Cameron had to say, "What if she isn't here, Agnes?"

Her smile faded and stone would have melted beneath her gaze. Without a word, she strolled across the deck and down the companionway.

Cameron said, "She's yours, Brown."

"Oh, no. I know better than to rile that MacKenzie female. They say she took a bowshot to save Edward Napier."

Cameron had been speaking of the ship, but Brown had a point. "She did indeed save his life, but her husband swears he prevails in their disputes."

"Smartest man in the isles ought to know his way around MacKenzie's firstborn lass."

"Aye, Agnes and Napier are well paired."

They shared an agreeable glance, then Cameron moved to the bow.

In the ship's wake, waterfowl took flight, and deer dashed for safety in the lush landscape. Rain clouds hovered in the northern sky, moving westward and leaving the James bathed in sunshine. Riverboats stacked high with hogsheads of tobacco lumbered past. Swift passenger ships and slave sloops scurried around the *Maiden Virginia* like skitterbugs on a smooth lake. In the distance, an occasional chimney fire streamed upward, the smoke clinging like a beard to the face of the forest. The sails snapped in the breeze. The damp air smelled ripe with spring.

Anticipation sat like a stone in Cameron's belly, and he gripped the bulwark to push the feeling away. But no matter how hard he tried, he couldn't stop thinking about the past. He remembered a girl who'd despaired because her younger sister, Lily, had gotten a love letter first. He thought of the spring they'd found a wounded badger and nursed it back to health. She'd stood beside him in this very spot. He'd been a brash and cocky youth. Virginia had been reasonable and honest but not always truthful, he corrected, recalling the time they'd dressed in servants' garb and gone to the docks without permission. Her father had caught them, and when the duke accused the older Cameron of corrupting Virginia, she'd looked her father in the eye and sworn the fault was hers. What the duke could not see was her hand and the odd fist she made when telling a lie. Only Cameron knew about that habit of hers among many others.

The old ache seeped into his soul. On its heels would come hope. Then disappointment more bitter than before.

Virginia Mackenzie had been the joy of his youth and often his savior. If he fell asleep in church, she always awakened him. She'd been the perfect friend for a headstrong lad with more swagger than sense.

That she would one day become his wife had been a foregone conclusion. They'd even picked out names for their children.

"Look a port bow, Cunningham. Poplar Knoll, ho!"

A newly refurbished dock came into view, the piers carved with doves. A brick path, laid out in herringbone design, led to a gabled mansion as fine as any he'd seen on the river.

"It's another ship, Virginia," said Mrs. Parker-Jones.

They were upstairs in Virginia's room. The mistress of Poplar Knoll stood at the window. Virginia sat in a chair, her back stiff and straight, a result of the new stays. She rubbed a tender spot beneath her breasts and wondered why free women abided the things.

"Virginia, how many ships is that today?"

Virginia went back to the dress she was hemming. "I've lost count."

She'd been treated with every kindness since moving to the main house. Before leaving this morning for Richmond to attend the tenth anniversary ceremony of the moving of the capitol, Mr. Parker-Jones had apologized again and wished her luck should her family arrive before he returned. She'd asked him to give her back her indenture papers and the twelve pounds, sixteen shillings she was due. He'd signed the document and, to her surprise, given her one hundred pounds. She'd contemplated leaving—going to Williamsburg or Norfolk in anticipation of Cameron's arrival. But he must not learn the truth of her life here. Those years and the private hell that accompanied them were hers alone.

"The ship's docking, and it—" Mrs. Parker-Jones gasped. "Sweet Jesus. It bears your name."

Virginia sprang from the chair, her mind suddenly blank with fear. For three days she had vacillated between joy and melancholy. For three nights, she'd walked the floor.

"Will you come down with me?"

As if to emphasize the moment, the plantation bell pealed, announcing the arrival of visitors. Pain squeezed Virginia's chest, but she forced herself to choose a path.

Moving to the window, she looked at her hands. Her nails were now groomed, but the dye stains had not faded. There'd been no time to sew gloves and Mrs. Parker-Jones's hands were much smaller than Virginia's. Her old smock had been given to another servant, and she had altered several of the mistress's dresses. The feel of soft cotton against her skin should have given her confidence; it confused her more, for it was a constant reminder of how mean her life had been.

"Will you come downstairs with me?"

"Yes. No. I don't know."

In the sunlight, Mrs. Parker-Jones looked younger

than her years and deeply troubled. "They are not strangers, you know."

But Virginia was a stranger to them. For ten years, their lives had been as different from hers as cold to warmth, freedom to servitude. If they knew the details of her life, her family would hold themselves responsible.

The blame and the burden were hers alone to bear.

On that fateful day ten years ago, when she'd learned that Cameron had already sailed, she'd willingly boarded MacGowan's ship. She'd believed his lie about taking her to France and Cameron.

Sparing her friends and family grief was also within Virginia's power. She had changed. Would they recognize her? Would they pity her?

As other questions rose in her mind, she watched the dockmen moor Cameron's ship. The *Maiden Virginia* rested at her doorstep. How many times in the early years had she pictured his ship sailing around the bend, her knight come to rescue her? Too many times, and that fanciful notion sobered her to the reality of the moment.

When the gangplank was secured, she strained to better see the two men and one woman who moved to disembark. The woman wore a yellow gown and matching gloves. Fair and light on her feet, she came first. She couldn't be Cameron's sister; Sibeal had red hair. Had Cameron married? Virginia had often imagined that. The knowledge would hurt more now, for it would prove that he'd forgotten her, but not by any fault of his own. He'd take her to her family and go home to his own. Virginia would embark on a new life.

But as God was her witness, she would not allow Cameron or anyone else to pity her.

Next onto the quay was a man she remembered well. MacAdoo Dundas's flaxen hair was unmistakable. An instant later, Cameron Cunningham stepped into view. Virginia drank in the sight of him. Beneath a tricorn hat with a red plume, his blond hair was tied with a cord at the nape, and he carried the tobacco cask she'd branded.

Tall and slender, he wore the lively red, black, and white tartan of his mother's people, the Lochiel Camerons. Only in portraits in his family home had Virginia seen the colors of his clan. Worn in the old style, the tartan was pleated and belted at his waist, with one end of the cloth thrown over his shoulder and pinned there with a brooch. Virginia knew the story of his mother's sacrifice to save the plaids. But wearing—even possessing the tartans or their patterns—was outlawed as a treasonous offense. Did Cameron defy an order of the crown, or had England forgiven the Jacobites?

Where was Papa? Her gaze flew back to the ship. Ordinary seamen roamed the deck. Lachlan MacKenzie had not come. Her mother had not come. What if they were dead?

The cruelty cut too deeply, and she turned her attention to the woman beside Cameron. She couldn't be Sarah, for Sarah had always been tall like Cameron. They moved onto the brick path leading to the front door, which faced the river. With energetic strides, the woman easily kept pace with her male companions.

"Who is she?" asked Mrs. Parker-Jones.

Virginia's childhood had been surrounded with females. Faces she could no longer recall. Cora's hair had been fair. Lily's too. And Sarah and Agnes. But this woman didn't look seven and twenty, the age Agnes and her sisters would be. It was so long ago, and this woman could be Cameron's wife. "I do not know."

"She's beautiful, and if that man carrying the cask is Cameron Cunningham, you are lucky indeed. He's very handsome."

Virginia's heart swelled with pride. "He's Cam."

"Then we'd better greet them."

Pain squeezed Virginia's chest. Assuming Cameron had taken a wife, he'd probably feel guilty. All of Virginia's family would, especially if they knew the truth about her life the last ten years. She'd spoken of that often with Mrs. Parker-Jones during the days of waiting.

Virginia forced herself to chose a course of action. "Tell them what we discussed yesterday at supper." They had discussed so many possibilities, Virginia had grown weary.

Resignation saddened Mrs. Parker-Jones. "If you are sure that is what you want me to say to them."

If poor choices were wealth, Virginia was rich beyond the counting. "They must not know the truth, not the whole of it. Will you go along with the story?"

Their eyes met. Virginia smiled encouragingly. "It's best all the way 'round."

"I've no talent for the dramatic. What if I bungle it?"

"You'll do fine. It's better they think Moreland died."

On a sob, Mrs. Parker-Jones hugged Virginia. "So will you, Virginia MacKenzie."

Just as she moved to step away from the window, Virginia saw the woman in the yellow dress stumble.

* * *

50

Cameron steadied Agnes before she could fall, but almost dropped the cask, so discomfited did he feel. If asked why he'd brought the hogshead, he wasn't sure he could give a reasonable answer. His mind saw it as proof. His heart told a different tale. Since finding it, he'd taken odd comfort in keeping the thing near.

Agnes held onto him. "My stomach's all aflutter, and my wits have gone praying."

"She was only a lass, and it's been ten years," MacAdoo said.

Climbing the steps, Cameron counted off just how long it had been.

MacAdoo adjusted his waistcoat. "She probably won't know us."

"I hadn't considered that." Agnes looked up at Cameron. "What will we do?"

Think the worst. But Agnes wouldn't follow that advice. Thanks to her constant discussions about Virginia, neither would MacAdoo.

Shoring up his courage, Cameron took the last step. "What will we do? Beyond wondering why there are no poplar trees in the yard at Poplar Knoll, I haven't a notion."

"Cameron!" She elbowed him in the ribs.

He winced and rapped the doorknocker, a fine casting of doves in bronze. Seriously, he said, "We'll keep our horses *before* our cart."

"She's here. I can feel it in my soul."

A white-haired, very poised butler opened the door. "Welcome to Poplar Knoll. My name is Merriweather. May I be of service?"

Cameron shifted the cask. "I'm Cameron Cunningham. We've come seeking information about this design if the master of the house will see us."

Agnes said, "We haven't an appointment, but our

mission is of the utmost importance. We've come from Glasgow."

Blinking at her boldness, the butler nodded and stepped back. He spoke to Cameron as he waved them inside. "Mr. Parker-Jones is away in Richmond, but the mistress is here. Come in please. May I take your hats?"

Cameron removed his. MacAddo shuffled his feet and murmured, "Forgot mine."

Agnes said, "I'm certain Merriweather will not hold it against you."

"We are not so formal in America," the butler said, smiling.

In the entryway, a footed silver bowl, engraved with the dove motif, graced a table fashioned in the style made popular during the reign of Queen Anne. Straight ahead, a long hall led to the back of house. Without carpet, the oaken floorboards gleamed from a recent polishing. A potted palm and a standing screen with thin lace panels cast shadows in the narrow corridor and blocked the view of what lay behind it.

They were led into the first room on the left, a formal parlor. On the inside wall, a gilded mirror faced the front windows, bringing more light into the room. Unlike most such rooms, Cameron found this one inviting and the chairs arranged for easy conversation. Had Virginia sat in this room?

"Excuse me," said the butler. "I'll tell Mrs. Parker-Jones that you are here."

Cameron put the cask on the floor at his feet. Agnes sat but not for long. Nervously, she walked around the room and examined the three paintings on the wall.

"This is clever." She indicated a small picture beside the window. On canvas, the artist had reproduced the exact view of the front lawn and the river as seen from this spot. Instead of a frame, a small windowsill surrounded the view. Only in this rendition, towering poplar trees in full bloom flanked the brick path. Agnes peered closer. "The artist has an interesting name . . . Duchess."

On either side of an arched doorway, the other two paintings were portraits, a man and a woman. From the style of their clothing, the work had been done some years ago.

Tension rippled through Cameron, and just when he thought he could bear it no longer, they were joined by a woman about fifty years of age. She wore a green linen dress with modest panniers and only a little lace. Her dark hair was liberally streaked with gray, and her complexion bore the deep scars of pox. She had either suffered the disease as an adult, or the artist had been kind in his depiction of her in the portrait, for she was the same woman, albeit older and her cheeks now scarred.

She smiled nervously and extended her hand. "I'm Alice Parker-Jones."

"I'm Cameron Cunningham, and with me is Lady—"

"Please, Cameron," Agnes interrupted. "No ceremony."

Cameron began again. "With me is the ordinary Agnes MacKenzie Napier and a gentleman of Perwickshire, MacAdoo Dundas."

How-do-you-dos were exchanged. Seats were offered and declined.

Polite conversation was the last thing on Cameron's mind. He managed to say, "You have a beautiful home."

"Thank you. It's rather new to us. My husband

53

purchased it two years ago after the previous owner passed on."

She was certainly forthcoming, which boded well.

"Merriweather said you are from Scotland. You had a pleasant voyage?"

Agnes, a master of rhetoric, dawdled at adjusting her gloves.

Cameron said, "Very pleasant, and I'm sure you're wondering why we've come. We're seeking information about the design on this hogshead which, I understand from Quinten Brown, comes from Poplar Knoll."

She didn't spare a glance at the cask. "Yes, it does. What is it you wish to know?"

Beside him, Agnes squirmed with the need to take control of the conversation, but he knew that good manners would prevent her from interrupting again.

He took a deep breath and asked, "Who drew the design?"

"Our housekeeper did. She's very talented."

"May I speak with her?"

"May I know why?"

Cameron had made the speech hundreds of times in dozens of countries. The words came easy. "She may be someone we know. Someone lost to us ten years ago."

"Ten years, you say? My sympathies." She smiled sadly. "You are welcome to talk with her, but I'm sorry to say she has no memory of her life before Poplar Knoll. A fall from a horse, I believe."

An awful possibility struck him. "You mean her mind is damaged?"

"No, not like that. She's bright and resourceful. She simply cannot remember where she came from or how she got here."

"How long has she been here?"

"I'm not sure. When the previous owner . . . died . . . we asked her to stay."

"What age is she?"

"About twenty, I would say."

Agnes expelled a breath.

Hope stirred to life in Cameron. But past disappointments demanded caution. If Virginia hadn't contacted him because she'd forgotten the past, how had the hallmark gotten on the cask?

"It's Virginia," Agnes said. "I know it is."

"Virginia?" their hostess repeated. "Yes, that is her name, but I understand it was given to her because she did not know her own, and she was found in Virginia."

Mrs. Parker-Jones seemed unaffected to Cameron, as if she were prepared for the conversation. Odd. He thought she'd be surprised. According to Brown, his visit to Poplar Knoll upon returning from Glasgow and speaking with Cameron had been brief and the conversation with Mrs. Parker-Jones uninformative. Perhaps she was merely protecting a member of her staff.

"Fetch her," Agnes commanded.

"Please," Cameron rushed to say. "And if you will be so kind, we'd like to speak privately with her."

She glanced wearily at Agnes. "Very well, but remember, you are strangers to her."

If their hostess were subtly conveying advice, Agnes was having none of it, for she'd assumed what Cameron called her "countess mien." Mrs. Parker-Jones looked away first, as did most people when faced with a determined MacKenzie female.

Leaving the room, she entered the long hall he'd noticed upon their arrival.

Silence filled the parlor, but if expectation were a sound, the noise was deafening. Could this colonial housekeeper be Virginia? A memory loss explained why she had not contacted them years ago.

Cameron allowed the thought to sink in. Virginia, with no memory of Scotland. Virginia, alive and well.

Agnes threw her arms around him. "I knew we'd find her."

MacAdoo collapsed into a chair but bounded to his feet again. Cameron felt ready to bolt through the door and find Virginia himself. The moment of truth was upon them.

Let it be her, he silently prayed. *Please, God, let it be Virginia.*

When Mrs. Parker-Jones did not return immediately, he moved to the doorway and peered into the long corridor. About half the distance down the hall, two females were silhouetted behind the lace screen. He recognized Mrs. Parker-Jones's heavier, shorter form. The taller, slender woman beside her was a mystery, a willowy shadow. They were conversing, but from so far away, Cameron couldn't hear their words. He'd bet next year's profits that the mistress was telling her who they were and explaining what had occurred.

The older woman moved away and disappeared into the doorway nearest the potted palm. The form behind the screen bowed her head. The poignancy of her stance, the importance of the moment, filled Cameron with hope. He went still inside. To every saint he made a promise of favor.

"Will she never come?" Agnes railed, throwing her arms in the air. "What's taking so long?" Fabric rustled. "Do you see her?"

Cameron turned. Agnes was moving toward him. He thought of the woman behind the screen and the turmoil she must be feeling. More, he knew that he had to be the first to see her. She belonged to him.

Hiding his resolve, he shrugged. "Nay, I don't see her, but 'tis a large house."

"I cannot bear a moment more of this waiting."

"Of course you can. She'll come when she's ready."

"'Tis easy for you to say. You gave her up for dead when Papa did." She gasped. "Hoots, Cameron. I'm sorry. You must feel wretched."

She didn't mean those hurtful words; she was just impatient. "Blessed better suits me."

"I may go mad in the waiting."

"I'll see what's keeping them."

"I'll go too," she said.

MacAdoo started to rise, but Cameron signaled him to stay put. To Agnes, he said, "I must also find the necessary. Will you go there with me as well?"

All impatient noblewoman, Agnes huffed and turned away. "Just be quick about it."

Congratulating himself, Cameron started down the hall. The stately form behind the screen had not moved. As he approached, he considered what he would say. Logic told him that if she was Virginia MacKenzie, he should offer her solid proof. Then he remembered the one item that had linked them together so many years ago.

Heaven help her, for Virginia couldn't make her feet move. It was too late to change her mind. Mrs. Parker-Jones had already told them the story of a memory loss.

Them.

Virginia's heart soared. Cameron, Agnes, and MacAdoo awaited her in the front parlor. She had truly been rescued at last. Life among her family awaited. The beautiful woman in the yellow dress was Agnes, the older sister who'd always told Virginia to look to her wits in times of trouble. She couldn't have survived without Agnes's good advice. She remembered the dedication in Napier's book. Agnes was now the countess of Cathcart.

What of everyone else? In moments, she'd know. All she had to do was pick up her feet.

Footfalls sounded in the hall. A heartbeat later Cameron peered around the screen. The moment he saw her, he breathed a sigh.

Staring up at him, she felt a burst of pride. No longer gangly and cocky, he cut a powerful figure in his Highland garb, and the kindness in his brown eyes reached out to her, same as always.

Smiling, he moved closer. "I saw your shadow and thought you might be frightened."

He hadn't forsaken her.

Now she must pretend to have forgotten him.

She recalled her blackest moments at Poplar Knoll. With those horrors in mind, she could easily conceal her thoughts. "I'm somewhat overwhelmed."

"Then we'll go slowly, but the sum of it is, we're all happy to our souls to have found you."

Regard for others was not new to him, she decided and felt tears fill her eyes. "I'm very glad that you've come for me."

"Good, then I'm safe until you remember what I gave you on your sixth birthday."

She had to duck her head. Oh, Lord. She felt ready to crack apart inside. He'd given her two badger's teeth on a string to replace her own front teeth. She hadn't talked to him for an entire week she'd been so angry.

Gathering strength, she looked up. "You're certain I am who you think I am?"

He gave her a smile that weakened her knees. "Aye. You're Virginia MacKenzie." Reaching into his sporran, he retrieved the scarf she'd given him in the stables at Rosshaven Castle on the day of their formal betrothal. "You stitched this for me a long time ago."

She didn't have to pretend surprise; she hadn't expected to see that piece of silk and girlish vanity again. It brought back a flood of memories. At first sight of the hallmark, Cameron had shamed it for a silly design. But he'd been young and brash and more eager for manly pursuits than for tending the feelings of a love-struck girl.

How did he think of her now? "It was special to you?"

"Very special, and see, you haven't forgotten everything." His kind eyes gleamed encouragement. "You remembered the symbol."

"But not apurpose. I thought I'd just thought it up."

"The rest of your past will come back to you. Just give yourself some time."

The rest would come. An hour ago she had decided to wait a week or so, then suddenly regain her memory. But that plan was faulty and might arouse suspicion. Unknowingly, he'd given her a way out of the lie. Each day she could pretend to remember a little—a person here, an event there. Yes, that was a better plan.

But she must move cautiously, start in the logical place. She'd made a list of questions a person with no memory would ask. With those queries in mind, she gave him back the scarf. "Are you Cameron Cunningham? Mrs. Parker-Jones said that was your name."

Assuming a military stance, he clicked his boot heels together and gave her a formal nod. "At your service, my lady."

The title brought her up short, but she had wits enough to ask a question. "Why do you address me so?"

"Because your father is the duke of Ross, and that makes you a lady."

He spoke of Father in the present tense. Papa was alive. What about Mother? Why hadn't they come with him? Apprehension clutched her heart. "You know my parents?"

"Of course, and you'll be reunited with them soon."

Virginia felt a relief so deep she closed her eyes to savor it.

His hand gripped her arm. "Will you swoon?"

Euphoria made her giddy. She looked up at him and smiled. "I pray not. I'm just more overwhelmed by the moment."

"Of course you are, but take heart, Virginia. We're in uncharted waters too."

Her name rolled off his tongue like a lullaby. Never again would anyone call her Duchess. Henceforth she'd sleep in a bed and wear soft clothes. She'd read any newspaper she chose, and books. She'd acquire enough books to make a fine library. She could travel at will, go in any shop. She was free.

"Good," he said. "I can see you've cornered the gist of it."

She wanted to ask him how soon they would set sail

but decided against it. Another, more personal question begged to be asked. "Would you have known me? Do I look the same?"

He grew pensive, but his gaze never left her. "You're very beautiful, but all of the MacKenzie women are."

"I was not seeking flattery."

"Very well. You're much taller than I expected. Sarah will rejoice at that."

"Sarah?"

"One of your sisters, and speaking of that, if I don't take you in to see Agnes, she'll have you redefining the word *overwhelming*. Trust me, you wouldn't wish that event on your meanest enemy."

Take heart, she told herself. She took his arm first. He had skillfully skirted the question about differences in her appearance, but she had plenty of time to glean the answer. She had a lifetime. "I'm ready."

As they walked toward the front of the house, he said, "Do you still favor lemon tarts?"

No chance of finding exotic sweets on the menu in the servant's hamlet. The idea of catering to a bond servant's whim was laughable, but she must respond reasonably. Another excuse presented itself. She held up a stained hand, hoping he would accept a lie. "The spring berries here are delicious and bountiful this year."

He examined the fingers on her left hand. "In that respect, you haven't changed. You always were one for doing a job yourself rather than ordering the servants about."

Thank the saints, he didn't know the irony of that statement, and if Virginia had her way, he never would. She had a right to her pride and her privacy.

Sparing her family and Cameron the truth about ten years of servitude and eight years of hell must surely be the kinder method. She gladly chose that path. She put behind her the cruelty of the Morelands and prepared to start her new life.

But at the thought of coming face-to-face with Agnes, her courage waned.

Chapter

4

〜

Cameron stopped before they reached the open door to the parlor. "Stay here." Taking hold of her hand, he moved an arm's length away and peered into the room.

Virginia gladly accepted the delay; her stomach was flip-flopping. Ten years of wishes were about to come true, and as was the case in all of the most important moments in her life, Cameron held her hand.

To the occupants of the room, he said, "In her own words, Virginia MacKenzie is somewhat over-whelmed. Go gently with her, Agnes."

The heat of embarrassment rushed through Virginia, but with it came the joyous familiarity of days gone by. He had always played the cavalier. The difference lay in manly allure, which he now possessed in abundance.

"Oh, bell heather, bring my sister in."

The cheerful impatience in Agnes's voice drew Virginia. Cameron's strong presence gave her courage. Somehow she'd repay them for the deception, but until she could find a place for herself in the world of the free, she must act the stranger.

Shrouding her heart, she stepped into the room.

Agnes hurried forward. Her dress wasn't merely yellow. On a background of buttercup wool floated a sea of tiny golden thistles embroidered in silk thread. The modest panniers allowed the fabric to drape rather than hang. Her brown eyes glittered a welcome. "I'm one of your sisters. Agnes is my name." She swallowed back a sob. "Do you not remember me?"

Not as she was, for Agnes had always been taller than Virginia. Now she stood almost half a head shorter and as poised as a queen. The honest plea in her voice shamed Virginia.

Wishing she could answer truthfully and knowing she could not, she plucked up a story. "I'm sorry. I fell from a horse a very long time ago."

Agnes nodded, not in confirmation but acceptance, for her lips were set with scorn. "Leave it to a colony of Englishmen to ignore your Scottish accent and think you are better off with them."

Agnes had always cursed the Brits, or Loyalists, as they were called in Virginia. "I haven't a Scottish accent."

"Not after ten years in the colonies, but you did as a child. Any decent person would have recognized your Highland speech and looked for your family."

Virginia's heritage hadn't mattered to Anthony MacGowan. Much as she hated to admit it, selling her into bondage had been one of his more humane acts. Those and the more unsavory of her experiences were Virginia's secrets to keep.

Now she must offer comfort to Agnes. "I have lived with decent people." The Parker-Joneses and her friends in the hamlet certainly counted as that.

Cameron drew her farther into the room. "Good, because Agnes brought twelve pounds, sixteen, in case you'd fallen into indenture and had to be bought out."

"Cameron! You promised not to tell that."

"You promised to put the coins in a sock and cosh the colonial scoundrel with it before you rescued her from his clutches."

Agnes waved him off. "Thank goodness we haven't that to deal with. But I shudder to imagine the consequences of a ducal MacKenzie in bondage."

Virginia congratulated herself; she'd made the right decision in keeping the truth to herself.

"I don't suppose you remember speaking Scottish," said Agnes, an apology in her voice. "But you were the best at mocking Papa."

"No, I don't," Virginia answered, staring at Agnes's fine gloves and amber jewelry.

"Mrs. Parker-Jones says you are her housekeeper." Agnes swiped the air with her hand. "No more. Our father is a wealthy man, a peer of the realm. We're taking you away from here."

"Easy, Agnes," Cameron said. "You'll frighten her off. But it might be a gift to us all that she doesn't remember your bossy ways . . . if a doubt still remains with her."

MacAdoo stepped forward. "Do you remember nothing of Scotland, lass?"

He'd broken his nose since Virginia had last seen him. He'd aged more than the others, but he was six years older than Cameron. "I'm sorry. You are also sure that I am Virginia MacKenzie?"

"I'd've known 'twas you," said MacAdoo. "Your MacKenzie blue eyes tip the odds."

Cameron's hold on her hand tightened. "And you still have your mother's fine complexion."

Agnes smiled up at her. "You also have Juliet's hearty spirit."

Did she? What a delightful thing to say, especially when Virginia wasn't sure she could recall her mother's face. She hadn't recognized Agnes.

Regretting it more by the moment, Virginia dredged up a question from her list. "Who are you?"

MacAdoo rolled his eyes. "Pardon my bad manners, lass. I'm MacAdoo Dundas. I had my first taste of ale on the night you were born. When you were braw enough, I taught you to patch sails and climb the rigging."

Cameron leaned closer. "MacAdoo came with me from Perwickshire. My mother and your father were close friends. That's how I came to foster with the MacKenzies."

Were Cameron's folks still alive?

"Now who's confusing her?" Agnes taunted.

Virginia said to MacAdoo, "Then you are not related to me?"

He folded his burly arms across his chest. "Nay, lass. We share no common blood. We were friends and will be again."

"Yes, I hope so, MacAdoo." She hadn't spoken his unusual name in so long the word stumbled off her tongue.

"Let's sit." Cameron led her to the only couch and sat beside her. He pointed to the hogshead. "When I made port in Glasgow and found that cask, I went straight to Agnes. She lives there, too. She sent word to all of your family."

Virginia said a silent prayer that others in her family had survived. But who? "Tell me about them."

Agnes stripped off her gloves as she spoke. "We are nine siblings counting you. Only one lad, thank the saints. I'm the eldest of your four older sisters—Lottie, Mary, and Sarah. Unusual as it is, we are all the same age, and we are not"—she slid a glance at Cameron—"a litter, as some trolls say we are. We all have different mothers. Father raised us alone until your mother, Lady Juliet, came to the Highlands. We were six years old at the time. You were born the next year."

"Careful, Agnes," Cameron said. "If that's not confusing, nothing is."

One thing was certain to Virginia, legitimate or not, Lachlan MacKenzie loved all of his children equally. He'd found Agnes a very important earl.

Ignoring Cameron, Agnes continued. "Then there's Lily, a year younger than you and wed to Randolph Sutherland. She's so modern she delays childbearing. Next is Rowena. She's eighteen, truly accomplished, and studying music in Vienna. Cora is sixteen, and she intends to catch a prince at her coming out. Our brother, Kenneth is thirteen and making an occupation of being a dreadful boor."

Virginia rejoiced. Her sisters and brothers were alive, and they had fulfilled their dreams, except for Kenneth, and he'd been too young to know what he wanted. Agnes loved them too. She had always been direct in her manner, but the affection in her voice shone clear.

The most important question begged to be asked. "Where are my mother and father?"

Tears pooled in Agnes's eyes. She dried them with her gloves. "A few days out of Norfolk. They sailed shortly after us. Hoots, it's wonderful to see you again, Virginia."

Virginia couldn't sit still. Not stopping to consider the right or the wrong of it, she rose and embraced Agnes. As her favorite older sister squeezed her tight, Virginia wondered how many times she'd prayed for a moment of Agnes's company. Reliable Agnes, who smelled of lilacs. Loyal Agnes, the only one who had not laughed when an eight-year-old Virginia had declared her undying love for Cameron Cunningham.

Virginia said the first thing that popped into her mind. "I'm very lucky."

"Aye, and so are we all." Drawing back, Agnes offered Virginia a glove to dry her tears.

"Oh, no. I couldn't. I'll soil your fine—" Virginia stopped. She was speaking like a servant.

"Here, take it," Agnes insisted. "They're only gloves. I've dozens of them."

They were ordinary to her. As a bond servant, Virginia was fortunate to have a pair at all. But Agnes must never know about that.

In her struggle to contain her wayward emotions, Virginia counted her blessings. Her brothers and sisters thrived. Mama and Papa were alive and on their way to Poplar Knoll. Cameron, Agnes, and MacAdoo were here at last. They would take Virginia back to Scotland.

Cameron said, "Agnes tricked the earl of Cathcart into marrying her."

"I did no such thing."

Ignoring her, he went on. "They have two children from his first wife. Agnes has a son, Jamie, and a new daughter who is named Juliet for your mother."

Virginia hoped Edward Napier appreciated his

good fortune. "What of the other three sisters, Mary, Sarah, and Lottie?"

Staring at Cameron and waving the glove, Agnes smiled broadly. "See? Contrary to what you say, I did not confuse her."

How could she forget her older sisters? They had enriched her life, and Agnes had come with Cameron to rescue her.

"Stop preening," Cameron scoffed and pulled Virginia back to the couch. "Your sister Lottie married David Smithson, who is now the earl of Tain. She has too many children to count."

MacAdoo chuckled and slapped the chair arm. "Three lads and a sprite of a lassie."

Agnes stiffened her neck, thrust up her chin, and said to the room at large. "Never were brighter, more attractive, well-bred children born of a mortal womb." Placing the back of her hand to her forehead, she added, "Travails though they were."

Cameron and MacAdoo laughed at her mimicry. Virginia smiled. Lottie had always been a priss, and Agnes had always mocked her for it. "Um . . . Mary?"

Agnes sighed and made a task of smoothing out her skirt. "Wed at last to that English scoundrel, Robert Spencer, the earl of Wiltshire. Her daughter Beatrice is four, and I trust a son has brought her to bed as we speak."

To an impressionable girl, the four sisters had been mentors and, on occasion, menaces. "Then you all are countesses?"

"Not Sarah. She married a viscount, but Michael Elliot is as distinguished as my own Edward."

She spoke with pride, as well she should. Every man

with a plowshare or a flail had Edward Napier to thank for his modern tools. If Sarah's husband were as admirable, Virginia would cherish knowing them both.

Cameron said, "Sarah has twin sons and her daughter has yet to take her first steps. They make their home in Edinburgh."

Someone rapped on the doorknocker. Merriweather hurried to answer the door. "Welcome, Captain Brown. May I help you?"

A broad-bellied man wearing a dark gray coat and knee breeches over a red waistcoat stepped inside and doffed his hat. So this was Captain Brown, the man who'd led Cameron to Virginia. Mrs. Parker-Jones had told Virginia about him. He looked like a robin, and he peered into the parlor at Virginia as if she were a fat worm.

"Aye, I'd like to speak to the mistress if she'll spare a moment or two."

"Of course. She's expecting you. Please follow me."

"Don't bother. I know the way."

Brown started down the hallway, his shoes sounding loudly and probably scuffing the floor. With bittersweet humor, Virginia realized that she knew more about cleaning a house than running one. But they wouldn't be here long enough to discover that lie. Her bag was packed. She was ready to resume her life.

Merriweather moved into the doorway. "Shall I serve refreshments?"

Everyone looked to Virginia. Food was the last thing on her mind. But as a respectable member of the household, the comfort of the guests was her responsibility. Had they noticed her lapse? *Bless Merriweather,* she thought. "Please serve tea and some of the berry tarts." She remembered the brandy Mrs.

Parker-Jones had given her. "Unless Cameron and MacAdoo would like something stronger?"

As if the movement were natural, Cameron draped an arm around her shoulders. "Tea and berry tarts will be perfect."

Virginia felt sheltered, even in the casual embrace, and the covetous way Cameron admired her made her heart beat fast.

Merriweather stood there, waiting for something else, but what? Virginia had no inkling.

"Shall I also have rooms prepared?"

Rooms? No. They were leaving right away.

"Not for me," said MacAdoo. "I'll stay aboard ship."

"A hot bath and a soft bed would be lovely," said Agnes.

Virginia almost choked on her own selfishness. Cameron, Agnes, and MacAdoo were surely tired after the long voyage. They would want to rest. A meal must be planned. The table set. Napkins folded. Silver polished. Dozens of other things. Mrs. Parker-Jones must have instructed Merriweather to offer the hospitality of Poplar Knoll to their guests. It was up to Virginia to learn their preferences. But how?

An old image of Lottie came to mind, and Virginia acted accordingly. "I'll have the porter fetch your bags from the boat. Have you brought servants, Agnes?"

"No. My maid only travels with me if Edward or the children come along. I'd be grateful if someone could press my gown before we dine. Unless you do not dress for dinner?"

Cameron stretched out his legs. "I'd fancy seeing you wield an iron, countess."

Agnes flipped the glove again. "We are offered this

71

observation from a man whose wardrobe consists of a shirt, a strip of tartan cloth, and his Highland pride."

To Virginia's surprise, Cameron blushed. "I told you Agnes was trouble."

Virginia envied their easy camaraderie. She'd been a part of that friendship once and would again, but only when she could join in comfortably as an equal. In some circumstances she might have been called to freshen the gown of a visitor. She needed help from the mistress. If she didn't gather her wits and perform the duties of housekeeper, they'd see through her ruse. Pity would follow, and she couldn't bear that thought.

"Watch yourself, Cameron," Agnes warned. "Virginia doesn't remember you either. I could weave her some juicy tales."

"Weave away. I've nothing to hide from Virginia, and she knows better than to believe your lies."

But she had hordes of things to hide from him, from them all.

She rose to tell them what she'd learned in three days on the subject of the evening meal.

Cameron and MacAdoo shot to their feet. That little courtesy was new. Slaves and bondsmen did not rise in the presence of their female counterparts. What other niceties occurred in polite society? She couldn't recall.

To Agnes, she said, "We do wear our best dresses, and the cook serves at nine o'clock this time of year."

"Must you go?" Agnes asked. "You haven't told us a thing about yourself."

Once they were safely away from Poplar Knoll, Virginia would be free of those who could expose her. She thought of a truth and cloaked it in humor. "If I don't instruct the staff, you'll be sleeping on a pallet and dining on corncob soup and Tuesday's bread."

Agnes laughed. "You always were one for a good jest, Virginia. Wasn't she, Cameron?"

"The very best." Cameron took her wrist and, bending from the waist, kissed her hand. Years ago, the first time he'd performed that courtesy, he'd turned her hand over and spit in her palm. She'd been six and mortified. Now she was curious and moved by him in a very adult way.

Curling her fingers around the kiss, she held it. The look in Cameron's eyes turned absolutely joyous, and when he sent that gaze on an exploration of her, from the coil of her hair to the hem of her dress, she grew warm inside.

He lifted his brows in some sort of approval, as if he knew how affected she'd been by his touch, and, with a knowing grin, promised more.

Discomfited to her toes, she excused herself and went in search of Mrs. Parker-Jones. But she learned that the mistress was still behind closed doors with Captain Brown. In the pantry, Virginia helped Merriweather assemble a tray.

"Thank you for rescuing me. I would have left them to collect dust in the parlor."

"Don't fret, Duchess . . . pardon me, Virginia."

"Oh, Merriweather. I shouldn't have lied to them."

He examined every glass and fork as he set them on the silver tray. "I doubt they'd be pleased to know that you bathed in the river and plucked chickens."

Shame at labor she'd performed paled in comparison to the despair and loneliness she'd suffered. Those heartaches were hers to bear, but they were also at an end. "They mustn't know."

"Nor will they. You haven't gotten by all these years on luck."

"What would you have done? Would you have told them the truth?"

Pausing, he leaned on the sideboard. "You mean, had I your family?"

"Yes."

A casual shrug and a huff gave him a noble air. "I cannot conceive of such a happening, but . . ."

His faraway look enticed her to say, "Tell me."

"I think you will have a remarkable life. Were I you, I would rejoice at the prospect."

Viewed in a positive light, the unexpected events in her life took on a different meaning. Henceforth she vowed to see them that way.

"Remember this, Virginia. You've kept yourself bright and respectable. You no longer cower as you did when the Morelands were here. You hold your head high."

"But what *about* the Morelands and what they did to me—"

"Shush. That was the worst of your plight, and you came away from it with good character. You counseled the slave children. You gave them dignity and taught them to care for their personal needs. You're obedient, but never have you cowered."

"I shall miss your good counsel."

She asked him to offer her excuses to Cameron, Agnes, and MacAdoo. Then she located the porter in the garden, cutting a bunch of spring lilies.

"Are those for Lizziegirl?" she asked.

Georgieboy nodded. "Little sister's pouting because I told her that Moreland was her father, too."

Perched between two races and accepted by neither, the old master's slave children had a rough go of it. More often than not, this rawboned lad was more sensitive than his younger sisters.

"I believe she was bothered at the *way* you told her, not by the knowing."

"I just said out the words."

"Now you must tell her you're sorry. After that, and do not tarry, will you please go to the ship and bring back our guests' luggage?"

"Ain't 'spose to *ax* me, Duchess. Tellin's the freeman's way."

Bond servants and slaves took orders and asked permission—sometimes for the most personal things. "I'm making a mess of it, Georgieboy."

"It'll come along to you a little at a time." He pulled a flower from the bouquet and offered it to her. "You lookin' the proper lady in your fine dress and done-up hair. Fronie says you're wearing them laces."

Saffronia was the midwife in the slave hamlet. "Most ladies of quality have mastered wearing stays before the ripe old age of twenty."

"Fronie says white women stupid in their ways."

"She and the others must keep my secret."

"She will. But the dockmen said that ship's named for you. You gotta worry about Rafferty."

The cooper. Months ago, when he'd caught Virginia branding the cask, he couldn't run to the main house fast enough to tattle. Then he'd told everyone in the hamlet that she'd gone mad and would have ruined his entire shipment of barrels had he not stopped her. He'd tormented her, belittled her in front of the whole village. Now he was bitter.

"I'm safe then. My family has no need to visit Rafferty's shed or the hamlet."

Chapter

5

〜

After dinner, over a bracing glass of cider, she sought advice from Mrs. Parker-Jones. Later she made her daily visit to the servants' hamlet. On her return to the main house, she saw Cameron in the formal garden.

The damp air was sweet with the smell of night-blooming sallies. Moths swirled around the lanterns that cast a golden glow over the stone benches and statuary. Before today the garden had been just a pretty place; now it felt cozy and inviting.

"You were very quiet at dinner," he said, patting the place beside him on the bench.

It had taken all of her concentration to get through the ceremony of the meal without embarrassing herself. Cameron had tried to engage her in conversation. Even when she'd observed the others, he'd watched her. "I enjoyed hearing you and Agnes speak about the MacKenzies."

"The MacKenzies?"

She did feel like a stranger to her kin. Sitting beside him she thought of what Merriweather had said. "I'll get used to it all."

"Have you been trysting with a beau?"

Her first response was to laugh. Women might be outnumbered five to one in tidewater Virginia, but for servants on an isolated plantation, odds didn't matter. Rules did, and breaking them, even for love, led to more bondage. "I've been on a quest for new shoes."

He picked up one of the slippers. "Your cobbler made these? They're very fine."

They were her first slippers in ten years. Serviceable boots or bare feet were the footwear of bond servants. "We make everything here. We weave our cloth, grow our food, and in winter we pay the Indians to hunt for us."

"You have a silversmith?"

Tripped up again. "No. Of course not."

He plucked the newspaper from her hand. "What have you there?"

"The *Virginia Gazette.*"

He held the slipper in a delicate way. "Are you interested in politics?"

On this subject she could converse comfortably, even if he was distracting her with the way he caressed that shoe. "I'm interested in what Horace Redding has to say."

"Are you?" With his thumb, he traced the slight heel. "Burke names him a purveyor of pandemonium."

"Burke disdains any progress beyond a snail's pace."

"Paine claims Redding is the voice of unrest."

"Perhaps, but I dare say we'd still be crowning the trunks of our trees and carrying the weight of an Englishman's yoke without the words of Horace Redding to inspire us."

"Us. So your mother says. She can still bring fire and brimstone when the subject turns to British rule."

The oddest irony of all was the fact that Virginia's mother had been a bond servant from Richmond before traveling to Scotland and marrying the duke of Ross. The very place Virginia had been named for had become her prison.

But she was free now and eager to reacquaint herself with Cameron Cunningham. Dinner had been too brief and Virginia too hesitant. "How do you see Horace Redding?" she asked.

The subject pleased him, for he turned sideways on the bench and faced her. "He always has an entourage around him. He's a bit of a braggart, and he can't drink two pints and keep his chin above the table."

Shocked, she ignored the hand he placed on her shoulder and said, "He's no drunkard, and how would you know?"

He shrugged. "'Twas all the gossip at Christmas last. He returned to Glasgow then."

"Do you visit Glasgow often?"

"Aye, I have a house there."

Both he and Agnes lived in Glasgow. By visiting her sister, Virginia could be close to Cameron. She could also find a way to pay her respects to Horace Redding.

Drums sounded in the hamlet, and the slaves began to sing a favorite song about a lowly weaver's son who slew a tiger and became king of his tribe.

Cameron took her hand and held it tenderly. "I've something to tell you, Virginia. 'Tis of some importance."

Apprehension engulfed her. He had married. Now he would tell her. From the wariness in his voice, the subject troubled him.

"I'm listening."

He stared at his hand, which still rested on her shoulder. "We were very close as children." He traced the neckline of her dress, which was modest by a parson's standard. "You might think that odd, me being eight years older and a lad, but . . . there you have it."

He looked uncomfortable, and she knew she would ease his way. That might be best, though, for she had much to do before she took her place among her family and friends. Until that day came, frankness would serve her best. "If you tell me I lost above one hundred pounds abetting with you, I will not pay it. A memory loss should absolve a gaming debt." He, in fact, owed her twenty pounds.

"Will it dissolve a formal betrothal?"

The beautiful music became a buzzing in her ears. "We are betrothed?"

"Aye, on the day before you disappeared."

She wasn't supposed to know. It followed that she should not care. But she did. Her heart ached at the thought of him taking another. "Do you wish it to be dissolved?"

"Do you?"

She couldn't let him get away with that. "That's an unfair question. I cannot answer today for a pact made when I was ten." She also couldn't tell him that she'd given up hope. He was Cam. Her Cam. She couldn't tell him that either.

"We needn't belabor it now. I just wanted to tell you myself before Agnes blurted it out and embarrassed you."

Embarrass her? How? "You're certain she will speak of it?"

"She'll wage a bloody war to see that the decision is yours. She proved that when Mary refused to wed Robert Spencer even though she carried his child."

Poor Mary. Mary, the artist who could paint a flower so real you expected it to smell. Mary, who forgot time and worked day and night when inspiration came upon her. Agnes had always made excuses and defended Mary. But why would he speak of Agnes's opinion of Virginia's betrothal unless the contract stood? Her dowry had been substantial, she recalled, papers and books had been signed, but the particulars were long forgotten.

"I gave you a ring."

Anthony MacGowan had kept it as a souvenir.

"I must have lost it. I'm sorry." Gathering gumption, she said, "Then you have not wed?"

"No."

She felt relieved but confused. "Because of the betrothal?"

He leaned back and studied the stars.

Instinctively she knew that at some point he'd broken the promise of the contract with her. After a fashion she'd done the same, or at least the result had been the same. In one respect, life for Virginia had stopped on the morning of her fifteenth birthday. It should have been the day she spoke her wedding vows to Cam; instead she'd huddled in the springhouse at Poplar Knoll and made a promise to herself. So long as she lived in bondage she would not think of the future. From that day forward, she planned nothing beyond the moment her indenture would end.

When he remained quiet, Virginia realized her mistake. She'd asked an artless question and gotten the answer she deserved. But she still had her pride and her freedom and the world awaited her. It should have been enough for one who had required little in the way of personal gratification. With sad acceptance, she now understood that dashed hopes and broken dreams were not solely the province of the enslaved. Cam had suffered too.

To end the uncomfortable moment, she pretended nonchalance. "I'm not so naive to think you've been pining the loss of a ten-year-old who stitched girlish symbols and expected you to wear them."

He frowned. "How did you know that I refused to wear it?"

Be bold, she told herself. "Did you? You don't seem the prideful sort."

He smiled, his teeth a white slash in the dark. "You were always naive, Virginia."

He did seem more worldwise than she, and why not? But she had skillfully avoided trapping herself. "Have you turned roguish?"

"Oh, nay. The gentry have sole rights to that."

He had no title; his mother's people had lost everything in the last Jacobite rebellion. By an act of Parliament, the descendants of the Lochiel Camerons were forever stripped of their nobility. His father was an English sea captain. "Are your parents living?"

"Aye, my father won a seat in the Commons. My mother loathes London but endures the session for him. I have one sister, Sibeal, who is two years younger than you. She met an Italian at court and married him. They live in Venice."

Sibeal and his parents prospered. "That's wonderful, Cam."

"Only you, of the MacKenzies, addressed me that way—Cam."

81

She'd almost given herself away again. She must be more careful, but she'd blundered without thinking. He'd always been Cam to her. "Mayhap it's a good sign, but I've had no great revelation of the past if that's why you are smiling."

His grin broadened. "I was smiling at the *way* you talk—all soft vowels and Virginia drawl."

Even her speech was different, but that would also change. She was learning new things every day.

"When Lottie hears you talk, she will threaten a swoon. Then she'll summon a tutor at your father's expense."

"I thought Agnes was the more loyal Scot."

"She is, in all matters except you." His voice softened. "She blamed herself for what happened to you that day."

"She does?"

"Aye, she gave you a penny and sent you away so she could meet a beau."

The diversion had allowed Virginia to look for Cameron's ship. When she'd learned that he had already sailed, she grew frantic. Moments later she made the biggest blunder of her life.

"You don't remember any of that day?"

She'd spent years trying to forget her folly. "No. Does everyone else in the family blame her?" An unfair burden in any circumstances.

"Nay, but it's driven a wedge between her and your father. They can come to peace with it now. We'll all have that to be thankful for."

An unfortunate turn of events, for Agnes had worshiped Papa. "What else has occurred as a result of my . . . absence?"

"Nothing else that I can recall or reveal in mixed company." When she chuckled, he went on. "Have you questions of me? Where you lived? The things we used to do."

Failing to ask those questions was another mistake on her part. Learning her past would be foremost to one without a memory. But the expression in his eyes and the feel of his hand on her neck distracted her. "Yes. Tell me."

"You were born at Rosshaven Castle in the northern city of Tain. Your birthday is May 17, 1769. Your father has another estate in the Highlands. 'Tis Kinbairn, and we often summered there. Lachlan does not sit in the House of Lords. He abhors London, but he governs his dukedom fairly and it prospers.

"You were a bright child and well behaved until you got your first horse. You grew independent after that."

"I did?"

"Aye, you took your responsibilities seriously, and you boasted that you would one day breed the finest horses in Scotland."

"Sounds rather pompous of me."

"You were confident." He touched the newspaper. "'Tis good you kept up your education. Your family values that."

Were it in Virginia's power, she'd make certain they never learned how hard she'd worked to keep and build upon the small knowledge she'd acquired by the age of ten. Leaving Poplar Knoll was vital if she expected to succeed.

"When and to where will we sail?"

"To Glasgow first, but I had hoped to stay until your father arrives. Unless 'twill inconvenience the Parker-Joneses."

Even though Mrs. Parker-Jones had ordered the house staff and the slaves to keep quiet about Virginia, someone could let the truth slip. And there was Rafferty.

Now that Cameron had come for her, she must convince him to make a hasty departure. "I should like to see Scotland." Even Norfolk held great appeal to her now.

"Are you unhappy here?"

"No."

"Good. We all feared that you had been enslaved and held against your will. I'm relieved that you haven't lived in bondage to more than the loss of your memory." He shivered. "How degrading that would be."

His revulsion bolstered her courage. "Everyone here is treated well."

"Brown said the old owner was cruel, but he must have gotten that wrong, too, for he insisted that Moreland sold the plantation. Mrs. Parker-Jones said Moreland had died."

What else could Virginia say but, "Captain Brown meant well I'm sure." Quickly, she changed the subject. "Why do you suppose I drew the design?"

"You do not know its significance, do you?"

She wasn't supposed to. "Tell me."

"My mother is Scottish—of Clan Cameron. I was named for them. My father is English and has no coat of arms. The MacKenzies have a long history and tradition, but you wanted a hallmark for us and our children. So you combined the arrow from the Cameron badge with your own symbol, the heart of love."

"I was a romantic?" Looking at Cameron Cunningham and feeling his warmth, she could easily become one again.

"Aye, the hearts prove that." He took her hand. "Virginia . . . we parted badly. 'Twas my doing. I was rash and selfish."

Here was the guilt she dreaded. She gave his hand a little squeeze. "You found me. Let us call it even and return to Scotland." The longer they remained, the greater the risk of discovery. As if to remind her of her change in circumstances, the stays pinched that one tender spot beneath her breasts.

"If that is where you wish to go."

"Where else would I go?"

"Anywhere you like. I'll take you myself."

The intimacy in his words startled her until she looked up. He wanted to kiss her, and curse her for a tawdry wench, she wanted him to. But desire was another emotion she must battle. "You have a question in your eyes."

He seemed to shake himself. "Why are there no poplars at Poplar Knoll?"

To cover her disappointment, she laughed. "When the Morelands refused him firewood for his troops, General Arnold felled the trees."

"Arnold. Aye." Despite his agreement, he sounded distracted. "Tell me about the Revolution. What was your life like then?"

Save rationing and handed-down clothing, those in bondage had not been affected. Through the newspaper, she'd kept abreast of the war. "No battles were fought here, but soldiers often tramped through."

"It doesn't speak well of soldiers or the men of Virginia."

"The men of Virginia were elsewhere. Would you have them forsake the cause of freedom?"

"You're passionate about it."

"Why wouldn't I be?" Her heritage was Scottish, but she could not maintain that for more reasons than pride.

"I meant to say that I thought someone would have snatched up a beautiful woman like you."

It was a poor choice of words but a logical statement that demanded a reasonable reply. "I always knew I would remember my past, and I feared my family might have been villains or worse." She congratulated herself on a fine turn of the conversation. "How could I present a husband to a band of thieves or knaves?"

"Or to me?" A lifting of one brow accompanied the gentle challenge. He meant to himself in the sense that he was her betrothed.

"What would you have done had that occurred?"

"Had you presented a husband to me, your betrothed?"

"Yes."

"Oh, I would have been cordial before I called him out."

"What if I loved him?"

His smile was quick, rakish. "Never would that occur, so rid yourself of that notion. As to your family being knaves or thieves, your father is the best man o' the Highlands, and your mother is a goodly soul. The MacKenzies are loyal to their own. Agnes stands as proof of that. They'll rejoice, hold a ball in honor of your return, and, if Lottie has her way, you'll be presented at court."

Virginia couldn't go to court, not when she didn't know a viscount from an underbutler. Even if a person of noble birth had visited Poplar Knoll during the last ten years, Virginia would not have been introduced. She'd left the grounds only once on an ill-fated raft. Only rarely did she leave the hamlet and then only for the fields. If she tried now to mingle in proper society, she'd make a fool of herself. She'd probably knock over tables if she attempted to wear the panniered skirts popular today. And she'd embarrass her family. She'd refuse and have them think her stubborn before she'd risk it. "I'll decide when and if I go to court."

Rather than be surprised by her reaction, he nodded. "You'll have to stand up for yourself or Lottie will manage your life."

How oddly wonderful to hear him speak so casually about Lottie. "The rest will come."

"Aye."

She didn't know she'd spoken aloud.

"Pity you cannot recall the name of the demon who brought you here."

She'd mulled that over often since learning of Cameron's imminent arrival. By trying to step back into her old life and sparing her family more heartache, she forfeited gaining revenge on Anthony MacGowan. In return for a judgment against him, she must tell the truth to the world outside Poplar Knoll. She couldn't. Never could she admit that bathing had been a luxury and toilettes a flight of fancy.

She grew melancholy. To hide her feelings, she played the coward and pretended to yawn.

"I've tired you."

Would he think her frail? A day of backbreaking work in the field exhausted her; polite conversation with the enchanting Cameron Cunningham inspired her. Tired? She could dance a jig down the rutted road to Richmond.

She sat straighter. "Not at all. I'd like to see your ship."

"The easiest of requests to grant." He rose and pulled her to her feet. "Wait," he said. "You barely spoke at dinner, and I still know little about you. Tell me about your life here."

"Another time."

His assessing look discomfited her. "If I agree now, will you expect me to—"

"I expect you to be a gentleman."

"There is also a time for that."

Arm in arm they strolled down the path to the dock. High in the sky, a quarter moon provided little light, but Virginia knew the way. Glowing lanterns placed at the stern, the bow, and the topmast formed a triangle of signal lights.

At one time in her life, he'd held her hand to steady her coltish steps. They'd lost so much, missed the opportunity to share so many small maturities, like the moment she'd understood the roundness of the earth by watching the path of the sun. The occasion when she'd truly understood the depths of man's cruelty to his own. The second in time when the truth of conception and birth had become clear. But to share those experiences now, she would have to reveal the loneliness that had accompanied them.

As soon as she stepped on deck, her spirits soared. Before Cam had mastered command of the ship, his father had often taken them sailing. One summer they'd sailed around the Orkney Islands. In her queenly way, Lottie had declared the *Highland Dream,* as the ship had been called then, their personal water conveyance.

Cameron had replied by telling Lottie to find some other minion to do her bidding. He'd taken Virginia's hand and announced to Lottie that he was going sailing.

He'd stood up to Lottie as no one else.

"What amuses you?" he asked.

From her heart, she said, "I was thinking that you must be very proud of this ship."

He stood taller.

Crewmen roamed the deck, some dressed in ordinary seaman's clothes, some in colorful tartans. Virginia longed to ask Cameron how it was that they were allowed to wear their plaids, but that too would have to wait. Several of the men doffed their caps or raised a hand in greeting. In the dim light, she couldn't match faces to memories. "Should I know any of these men?"

"Only MacAdoo and the cook. One voyage to China was enough for my father's crew. They preferred the shorter voyages."

Worldwise perfectly suited him. "You've been to China?"

"Aye, that is one of the reasons we parted in anger. I told you I was going to France, but I lied and made the first of many voyages to the East."

The information settled like a blanket over Virginia, and the strangest thought captured her. All those years ago, she'd learned French for nothing.

" 'Twasn't humorous, Virginia."

Her reaction and his was the kind of honest exchange they had shared as children. He, with his dreams of owning a fleet of ships, and she, with her grand idea of becoming the greatest cartographer of their time. If shown a map of America today and asked to point out the location of Poplar Knoll, she would have failed.

The rest will come.

She stared up at the crow's nest. "I think that I am still rather naive."

He chuckled low in his throat. "Enough of Agnes's company and *that* will change."

He'd certainly changed. That once skinny neck was thick with muscles, and his voice was full and rich with a man's confidence. "Agnes is your favorite of the MacKenzie women."

"Nay." His gaze moved to her mouth, and he smiled. "You have always been my pick of the litter."

By force of habit, she hadn't included herself. Cameron had, and the sweetness of his words went straight to her heart. The smoldering look in his eye affected her in a much more earthy way. "I could tell Agnes you said that . . . about the litter."

"Not you." His attention wavered and settled on a spot behind her. "Never have you tattled on me. We were always loyal to each other."

They were joined by a man she did not recognize.

"She's river right, Captain."

"Forbes, meet Virginia MacKenzie."

"A pleasure, my lady."

The respect in the man's tone gave her confidence. "It's mine, I'm sure, Mr. Forbes."

"Carry on then." Cameron guided Virginia to the bow.

She went willingly, his romantic declaration echoing in her ears. She had stood here in this very spot, on the port side, a carefree child. She'd sat on a coil of ropes and charted the coastline of Dornock Firth.

"Do you remember something of the past?"

From out of the sky swooped a merlin falcon, its pointed wings beating a strong steady path above the plane of the river. Holding onto the rail and watching the river rush toward the sea, she experienced her first true taste of freedom. "Just a joyous feeling."

More than joy filled her. Volition and independence awaited her.

"Many an afternoon did we pass on this brig. You mapped the Orkney Isles until your fingers turned blue with the cold. My father made you go below."

"Where are those maps?"

"Agnes has them."

"You named your ship for me."

"Aye, and looked everywhere for you." He frowned. "I promised that I would."

Loyalty to her or to the youthful pact they'd made troubled him. Had he given his heart elsewhere? Staring up at him, at his strong profile limned in pale moonlight, Virginia felt an envy that pierced her heart. Other women had admired him, had been courted by him, had shared moments such as these. But he was to have been hers, her partner in love, her companion for life.

A shiver of longing spread through her. She thought of the years they'd missed, of the times to come, and when he maneuvered her behind the ship's lifeboat and kissed her, Virginia thought she might swoon again. She'd fainted at the sound of his name. She had no defense against the security of his embrace. Captured completely, his mouth moving tenderly on her, she felt sheltered and protected and melancholy. This was to have been her place in life, this man her own. But they'd missed so much.

Pain, hot and heavy, squeezed her chest, and when tears threatened to burst, she clung to him. She couldn't let herself cry; once begun, the tears might never stop. What would be left of her then, save the shattered remnants of a foolish girl's pride?

Much better that she put her mind to her first kiss,

given by the man who had always been hers and shared on the deck of his dream ship. Other memories flooded her, but the images were innocent and playful, not this yearning that strummed deep in her belly, the need of a woman for her man.

Drawing back, he whispered against her temple. "I cannot get close enough to you."

She couldn't hold back a sob.

He squeezed her tighter, and the pain of longing ebbed, replaced by a desire that had nothing to do with childhood promises and everything to do with a woman's need for her man.

" 'Twas your first kiss."

Pride drove her to say, "No."

His fingers skimmed down her arms and to her hands. A frown marred his forehead.

"Why are you looking at me that way?"

He squeezed her left hand. "Because you always held your hand just so when you told a lie."

He'd remembered her secret fist, and before that, her inexperience had been obvious. Now she had to scramble for an excuse or tell him the truth. "I did? I'm encouraged by that."

Cameron studied her. Those blue eyes had once gazed at him in friendship; now they shone with a lover's desire. He had expected her to grow into a beauty; she had her mother's fine brow and lush femininity. From the duke, she'd gotten her elegant nose and proud chin. But from where had the hesitance come? MacKenzie women were known for their independence and forthright manner. But more than that, he noticed a stillness in Virginia, a direct contrast to the lively girl she'd been. When he'd spied her shadow behind the lace screen, he'd been too anxious to take notice of it. He'd also been intrigued by her feminine form.

Women were scarce on this side of the Atlantic. How had a horde of colonial men left so beautiful a woman alone? Cameron didn't know. "Why would you be encouraged by an old habit?"

"Because it tells me I did not lie often or you would have known it."

"I'd've known anyway, so close were we."

He put action to the words and pulled her close. She wanted to yield, to explore the feelings his kiss inspired.

"That's a lass."

He'd read her lusty thoughts. That wouldn't do. She drew back.

"What's wrong, Virginia?"

"I hardly know you."

"'Tis the easiest of matters to change. And a task I fairly relish. Put your arms around my neck, Virginia."

She did and rose on tiptoe. He had a moment to consider the propriety of his actions. But convention didn't count where this woman was concerned: She was his, and when their lips touched again, time spun away. She followed his lead, but that had always been so. He traced her feminine curves and wondered why she bothered with a corset. Picturing her without it, with no clothing, sent his passion higher.

"Let her go, Cameron."

Agnes's voice sliced the silence, and Cameron tensed. He wanted to nestle Virginia beside him in his bunk as a prelude to making love to her.

He broke the kiss but held Virginia near. "Be gone, Agnes."

"Nay. May I remind you that now is not the time to dust off your betrothal to my sister. She doesn't know you, and you cannot take advantage of that. Other *matters* must first be settled or dissolved. Isn't that so? You haven't forgotten those other matters?"

She was speaking of his longtime affair with Adrienne Cholomondeley. "The only thing I'm certain of is that I'd like to strangle you."

"I'm surprised you would risk that with Virginia looking on."

Damn Agnes for being right. "For Virginia, I will risk much."

"Wait for Papa."

"Wait for what?" Virginia asked.

"For ravishing of any kind."

Virginia gasped, and Cameron cursed. "Ravishment is not foremost in my mind," he said to Agnes.

"No?"

"No. I think Virginia will steal my heart before she ravishes me."

Virginia laughed. "May I sleep on the ship tonight?"

"Virginia!"

Holding tightly to him, she faced her sister. "I'm sorry. I meant, may I stay here alone in one of the cabins. I'm not a woman of loose morals, I swear I'm not. But I don't recall ever sleeping anywhere except Poplar Knoll. Maybe being here will help me remember the past."

Several scented letters from Adrienne and a miniature were among the papers in his cabin. He couldn't let Virginia find it. "I'll settle her in MacAdoo's cabin."

Agnes stood her ground. "I'll settle myself in yours."

"Oh, I couldn't inconvenience either of you."

Agnes laughed, but Cameron knew the humor was feigned. "Truth to tell," she said, "the bed in my room is too soft. I've spent weeks aboard this bucket. Now that I've had a bath, I rather miss this ship."

Cameron gave up the argument. Kissing Virginia had stirred a mighty need in him. He knew he couldn't sleep. So he excused himself and walked to the gardens.

A stranger slipped from the shadows.

"Who are you?" Cameron demanded.

"Rafferty, my lord. Best cooper in the tidewater."

"What do you want?"

"Only to tell you that I was here the day they brought her up river. No taller'n my shoulder she was."

"She?"

He tipped his head toward the ship. "The one you came for. For a price I'll tell you things she don't want you to know."

Chapter

6

⤴

Virginia remembered everything. No fall from a horse had stolen her past.

Cameron paused on the stairs, his mind still reeling from what he'd learned from Rafferty, the cooper, the night before. Until Quinten Brown had delivered the news that Cameron was on his way to America, Virginia had lived in the slave hamlet. Until Cameron had set foot on this wretched land, she had worked in the fields.

The design on the cask *had* been a plea, not a silent signal, but a calculated risk and a cry for help. His legs suddenly weak, Cameron sat down and leaned against the banister. Unless the cooper had lied. According to Rafferty, the then ten-year-old Virginia had told them who she was. Moreland, the prior owner, hadn't believed her. With the entire population of Poplar Knoll looking on, he had laughed and cruelly named her Duchess. Duchess, a mockery of her heritage. The painting in the salon was her work.

What had driven her to lie? Cameron didn't know, couldn't think of a logical reason for the deception. She disavowed all knowledge of her heritage and lied about the life she'd lived here in Virginia. Did fear or pride or both lie at the heart of it? Surely so.

A door closed in the hall, and footsteps sounded. Knowing how odd he appeared, his long frame sprawled on the stairs, he sprang to his feet and descended to the first floor.

Mrs. Parker-Jones appeared in the hallway and moved to the front door. Using a key from the bulky ring at her waist, she unlocked the door and opened the drapes in the entryway.

Housekeeper's work.

Virginia wasn't the housekeeper. Not until recently. She'd worked the fields. Had Cameron not seen the cask and come for her, she would have served another three years. Would she have come to him then, or would he have received a message from Lachlan MacKenzie saying that she had been found? What turns would Cameron's life have taken in that time? He stared at the rug and contemplated the monumental mistake he would have made in marrying Adrienne.

"Captain Cunningham?"

Turning, he saw Mrs. Parker-Jones in the doorway, her hands behind her back. Until recently, this woman had not only kept her own house, she had ruled Virginia's life. Mrs. Parker-Jones, a keeper of slaves, an owner of souls.

"Are you ill, sir?"

Cameron swallowed back revulsion and gathered

his wits. "I'm fine, Mrs. Parker-Jones. How are you this morning?"

"Thank you, I'm well. Will you take coffee or tea before breakfast?"

Taking her to the river and tossing her in sounded appealing. But her injustice to Virginia was in the past. The sin of her other immoral practices was hers to bear. Now this woman aided Virginia. Why? Did she fear the wrath of the MacKenzies? Probably.

Let her worry. He put on a smile he didn't feel. "Where's Virginia?"

"In the kitchen giving the servants their orders for the day."

"I'll have coffee there if you'll direct me."

She almost dropped the keys. "The kitchen?"

He took great pride in saying, "We Scots do not stand on ceremony as our English neighbors or our American kinsmen do."

"My apologies." She flushed but did not look away, a result he surmised of her position of authority over so many people. "Our kitchen is outside . . . in a separate building. I'll show you the way."

He followed her, taking particular notice of the way she tried to hide those keys. For a certainty, she disliked playing the accomplice.

"Virginia said she slept on your ship last night. Planting started today, and we in the house have gotten a late start."

Did she disapprove? Her days of passing judgment on Virginia MacKenzie were over. Quinten Brown had said the Parker-Joneses were a blessing after the old owner. Rafferty had called her softhearted. What the cooper had said about the Morelands' treatment of Virginia made Cameron's blood boil.

He summoned civility. "You needn't apologize. You'll be forced to find a new housekeeper."

"That had not occurred to me. I am happy you've found Virginia."

"As are we. One of her sisters is a portrait artist. For a souvenir I had hoped to bring Mary that small painting in your parlor."

She stopped, suspicion narrowing her eyes.

He assumed an innocent pose. "Unless you are duly fond of it? Mary studied with Sir Joshua Reynolds. She collects art."

"You may have it."

"Where is Lady Agnes?"

She started walking again. "Still aboard your ship. Virginia said her sister had recently given birth and hesitated to awaken her."

"'Tis true, Lady Agnes was but days from her travail when we left Scotland."

"Virginia is very fortunate."

"She said you had treated her decently."

"Of course. We are the new owners of Poplar Knoll and not responsible for whatever misfortune brought her here."

Or the misfortune the Morelands had visited on Virginia, whatever those were. Rafferty hadn't known the details, only that the former mistress had been overly cruel to Virginia. But what had Mrs. Parker-Jones done for her? "You've seen to it that Virginia attends church?"

She faltered, and Cameron felt a flicker of retribution.

"We don't often go to church ourselves."

A nonanswer. "You did not give Virginia a choice?"

"Of course we did. She just could not go unescorted."

Not only did she aid Virginia, she worked at it. Cameron's curiosity grew. With a little effort, he could pry the truth from this woman. Would he? No, he wanted Virginia to tell him herself.

Outside, she led him through the kitchen garden and into the orchard. The absence of both servants and noise surprised him. A plantation this large should be bustling with people. He questioned her about it.

"Planting's begun." Slowing her steps, she lifted her skirts. "Excuse the poor repair of the walkway. We need everyone, even the mason, in the fields."

He shouldn't toy with her, but he couldn't help himself. "Sunrise to sunset?"

Halting, she turned and faced him squarely. "We must show a profit, sir. Mr. Parker-Jones hasn't a family from which to inherit."

Against his will, Cameron felt a measure of respect for her. "We will not inconvenience you for long."

"You're leaving?" Relief softened her features. "I thought the duke of Ross was coming. Captain Brown said Virginia's parents were on their way."

Lachlan would have to know the truth and who better to find the bastard Scot who'd brought Virginia to America and sold her to Moreland. While Lachlan was occupied with revenge against Anthony Mac-Gowan, Cameron could turn all of his attention to Virginia. She needed a friend, and since childhood, Cameron had been her closest companion. Yet she purposefully disavowed any knowledge of their long-time affection for each other.

In his heart he hoped her reasons for the ruse were honorable, but he didn't know this Virginia MacKenzie. He would, though. The woman who'd melted in his arms last night and kissed him with unbridled passion was his. She'd always belonged to Cameron, and in his youth much of his ambition had been predicated on that very fact.

"Have events changed?"

In more ways than he could readily count, but Alice Parker-Jones mustn't know that Cameron had happened upon the cooper and learned the truth. Neither would Virginia know.

"Events remain the same. Carry on." He waved her ahead, his thoughts turning to strategy.

A smoking chimney identified the kitchen among a grouping of small stone buildings. Cameron had to duck to enter the small structure.

The cook, two slave girls of mixed heritage, and the butler faced Virginia, who stopped in midsentence. Startled, she almost dropped the cup she was holding.

Mrs. Parker-Jones hurried to Virginia's side and handed over the keys. "Captain Cunningham insisted on taking coffee with you. I unlocked the front door."

"Allow me to serve Captain Cunningham," said Merriweather, moving to the kettle. "I'm certain you'd rather visit with your friend."

She was thinking about the kiss they'd shared; he could feel her regrets. That wouldn't do. If she wanted to deny what had passed between them, she was in for a surprise, but she wouldn't get it here, with an audience. "You slept well, Virginia?" he asked.

"Oh, yes." Her eyes glowed with pleasure, and Cameron thought again of how much she resembled her father. But more than MacKenzie blue eyes linked them.

She wiped her hands and addressed the servants. "You all know your jobs. The Parker-Joneses expect you to do them proud."

Merriweather handed Cameron a steaming cup of

coffee but spoke to Virginia. "Your evening report to the mistress will be brief and glowing, my lady."

"Thank you, Merriweather."

Getting her alone was Cameron's primary concern. Ignoring the intense scrutiny of the slave girls, he sipped the strong coffee. Over the rim of the cup, he said, "Do you still ride?"

Virginia slipped the key ring over her wrist. "Ride where?"

The slave girls snickered.

"Quiet," Merriweather ordered. "If Lady Virginia wants to go riding with Captain Cunningham, that's her affair."

The girls laughed louder.

Merriweather rolled his eyes.

For a moment Virginia looked bewildered. Then she rallied. Clapping her hands, she told the girls to get back to work. To Cameron, she said, "Pardon them. What were you saying?"

"I've never seen a plantation. I hoped you would show it to me."

Mrs. Parker-Jones was quick to say, "I'm sorry, but all of the horses are in the field."

Looking to the mistress, Virginia said, "There's the pony. We could take the cart."

One of the slave girls guffawed. "Gentry don't ride in a cart."

Merriweather rounded on the girl again. "Mind yourself, Lizziegirl."

Cameron should have known that they hadn't let Virginia ride. He put down the cup. "We'll have a walk then."

She almost ran to the door. "Would you like to see the dogwoods?"

"Of course." He'd agree to tour a workhouse to have her to himself.

She snatched up her shawl and preceded him out the door.

Looking up at him, she quietly said, "I wasn't completely honest with you last night."

He held his breath, anticipating a confession. But she must have had second thoughts, for she said no more.

"Here are the dogwoods. Aren't they lovely?"

His patience fled. "You were going to say?"

At his sharp tone, her gaze flew to his. "I'm no walkabout girl if that's what you were thinking."

"Because you kissed me."

"Ha!"

Overnight she'd found gumption, but he wouldn't allow her to make light of the passion they'd shared.

"I was not embarrassed that *you* kissed *me.*"

"You kissed me back."

"I will not fall into your arms like a ripe plum."

"Not if I pluck you from the tree first."

She fluttered her fingers in a dismissing gesture. "I've given that up."

She'd always been a bold child, quick to plant her feet and stand for her own, even if it was an event so minor as who was first at the well. Her father had affectionately called her Scrapper, an endearment often accompanying the tending of an injury such as a sore scalp from having her hair pulled. With four older sisters, she'd learned early to fight back.

"Affection for me will come back to you in time."

"Me and any other woman who strikes your fancy."

Agnes had been talking to her. He'd deal with Agnes when the time was right. "We'll see."

She pointed a finger at him. "If, and I say that with

great conviction—if I fall in love with you, it will be after I discover who I am and where my life will go."

He believed her. Other truths would have to wait and patience he had in abundance. No more careless remarks like he'd made in the garden last night when he'd expressed relief that she hadn't been in servitude. Agnes had voiced a similar view. But wasn't Virginia bringing it on herself by not telling them the truth? As long as she denied her servitude, hopes spoken in innocence by the ones who loved her had the power to wound. Expressing strong emotions toward injustice was a way of life for her family, for any honorable person, and the MacKenzies of Ross were quality to the core. It was natural for her loved ones to want the best for her, and no one loved her more than he.

"You mustn't be frightened of the future."

Her anger had cooled. "I'm not frightened, not precisely. I'm just . . ."

He willed her to unburden herself. "Just what?"

She stopped at an arbor covered with white blossoms. Bees swarmed the flowers. "I honestly feared you'd think me a wanton after that kiss."

Virginia, a tart? Awareness gripped him.

"You look odd," she said. "What's amiss?"

He told her the truth. "I keep expecting you to answer as the trusting lass I remember, and I'm sorry that I could not watch you grow up."

Lowering her hand, she curled her fingers. "I'm sorry that I have no recollection of our childhood."

That hurt. Even phrased as an apology and punctuated with her special fist, the lie wounded him. She remembered perfectly well. "Virginia?" When she did not look up, he raised her chin. " 'Twas always our plan that I would be the only man to kiss you."

"You've kissed many women?"

He wanted to look away, but he could not. He grasped her still-fisted hand and prayed she'd drop the pretense. "Define many."

She gave him a smile he'd seen hundreds of times, but the mature glimmer in her eyes was all teasing woman. With a twist of her wrist, she slipped her fingers into his. "Two."

He felt flattered, petted by her, and holding hands brought back fond memories of their past. "Are you flirting with me?"

Shyness cloaked her. "Not with any success. You did not answer me."

Rather than rejoice, he grew melancholy. He was saddened at the years they'd missed, and he grieved for her, for the suffering she had endured. "Artless questions are not allowed."

She began walking again; he fell into step beside her. They strolled into a forest lush with hardwoods and ferns.

"There's little to do here," she said. "You're probably bored."

"If you think holding hands with you is tedious to me, you lost more than your memory when you fell from that horse."

Her throaty laughter disturbed a fat squirrel in a nearby oak. Tail twitching, the aggravated creature barked back. "You've crossed an ocean to amuse a tree rodent."

"We pledged our lives to each other. I came for you, Virginia, to honor our promises." She grew so pensive, he said, "Do you recall something?"

"No."

Gaining her trust was like climbing a sand dune. If he moved too quickly, he'd lose ground.

"A pity we cannot sneak aboard the *Maiden Virginia* and sail today."

Sneak? His senses sharpened. "Just you and I?"

"Yes."

Her palm had grown damp against his. Although he knew the true answer, he asked her anyway. "Why so soon?"

The moment he'd spoken, he regretted it. Asking her a direct question was the same as soliciting a lie.

"I'd like to see Scotland."

It was his turn to take up the pretense. *Encourage her,* his heart said. *Shower her with fond memories.* "Your father swears that he suffers when he leaves the Highlands."

"I've not suffered," she said much too quickly.

"Are you frightened of meeting your parents?"

"Intimidated better suits my feelings—except when I am with you."

Cameron ignored her reasons and accepted the remark as flattery. "Good, but what about MacAdoo? I need him to help pilot the ship."

She squeezed his hand. "Teach me. I'm a very fast learner, and I'll make you proud."

Stating qualifications was normal for a servant, and beneath the fine trappings of a noblewoman, a glimpse of the forlorn girl shone through. As much as he wanted to please her, he owed her honesty. "If we sail without a chaperon, your father will force a wedding between us."

"We wouldn't . . ." Flustered, she let go of his hand and stepped back. "I promise not to let you kiss me again. You aren't obligated to me because of a promise you made as a boy."

Had Agnes told her about Adrienne? Cameron had worried about that before meeting the cooper. The affair was a mutual convenience. He'd explain to Virginia but not until she bared her soul to him. "The voyage is enough, and I cannot leave Agnes here."

She nodded in acceptance. "You must think me awfully selfish."

Dappled sunlight sparkled in her hair and accentuated the fineness of her complexion. Years ago, freckles had dotted her nose and cheeks. *Forget the girl she had been,* he told himself, *and think about the woman.*

"Selfish? Nay. I *know* that you are overwhelmed."

"Yes, I am."

And burdened. "If you like, we can go to Norfolk and await your parents there."

"Oh, Cam." She threw her arms around him. "May we please?"

Until that moment, he hadn't understood how much she wanted to get away from Poplar Knoll, but it made sense. Perhaps she could leave her demons at the dock. Once they were away from here, she might feel free to confide in him. He held her tighter, breathing in the clean scent of her hair, reveling in the miracle that he'd found her at last.

"Gather your things and say your good-byes. I'll tell MacAdoo we're leaving. Will you need help with your belongings?"

Against his shoulder, she said, "No, I haven't much."

He cursed himself for a heartless fool; he knew she possessed little more than her clothing.

Releasing him, she stood back. "I'll have the housemaid pack up Agnes's trunk and yours."

Her efficiency gave him pause. The cooper had sworn she seldom set foot in the main house. How had she learned to direct authority? "Very well, but first you must answer a question."

She cocked her head to the side, and a question rose in her eyes. "Are you blackmailing me?"

He liked this confident, teasing Virginia. He grasped the opportunity to entertain her with the past. "I have before."

"When?"

The game was on. If he made up a story, she'd show confusion. She'd also think him a liar. By telling her a favorite truth, he could watch her closely and see if she remembered the moment fondly. "When you were nine, you hid in the manger to watch a stallion mount a mare."

"You discovered me?"

"Aye. In exchange for my silence, you had to groom my horse for a fortnight."

Wistfully, she said, "We were great friends."

Not a question. He rested his hand on her shoulder. "We still are." He should tell her something she didn't know. "Mary gifted me with a new painting of us as children." Actually it was a painting within a painting. Mary had thought up the concept. Virginia, in the role of Duchess the bond servant, had used a version of the technique in the painting that hung in the parlor of Poplar Knoll.

"Agnes said she is a great artist."

"Aye. She'll want you to come to London. Her home is Lottie's greatest achievement in design."

"Lottie designed Agnes's dress—the one with golden thistles. She said Lottie would make one for me."

"Everyone will ply you with gifts and fond memories."

"It's rather daunting to have everyone remember only the best of me."

"Being glorified holds no appeal to you?"

"Should I question their accounts?"

"Yes, but never mine."

"Agnes said you could beguile the arrogance from the French."

"Agnes locked Mary and the earl of Wiltshire in a tower."

"Why?"

"Because they are too stubborn to admit that they love each other."

"What happened? When did she let them out?"

"She freed them on the night Wiltshire delivered his daughter."

"They were prisoners for nine months?"

"Nay. Four months."

"Four?"

"They knew each other well."

"But they are happy now?"

"Aye."

Tears filled her eyes, and he knew she was thinking fondly of Mary. To cheer her, he said, "You must be stern with Lottie. If you let her, she'll begin with your wardrobe and take over your life."

Breathing deeply, she mastered her sorrow. "Truly?"

"When I told her I'd bought an empty house in Glasgow, she descended on the estate and furnished it."

"Were you pleased?"

He'd always wanted Virginia for himself. With that desire had come acceptance of her family. Now he thought of them as kin. "I was and am flattered."

She stopped at a fence covered with barren berry vines. "Agnes said my happiest times were with you."

Cameron couldn't have resisted kissing her again,

not if his life had depended on it. "'Tis true." Drawing her close, he cupped her face in his hands and touched his lips to hers.

His imaginings had fallen far short of the mark. Putting his heart at her disposal came as naturally as steering into the wind. But the hot spur of passion that fired his loins was new. He'd cherished her with a lad's affection. Now he needed her with a man's desire, and if the way she kissed him back was any sign, she felt the same.

He worked out the motions required to lay her on the ground and strip away their clothing, and he cursed himself for not wearing his tartan. With a ready blanket and an hour's privacy, he'd ease the physical ache and in that lovely doing, tear down one of the barriers she'd erected between them.

Not breaking the kiss, he eyed the ground around them. The well-worn path meant others often came this way. Heavy undergrowth offered shelter, but at what price?

Faced with poor choices, he stifled his need and drew back. "Much as I want you, this is not the place."

"Much more of that and you'll learn all of my secrets."

Was she tempted to end the ruse? He longed for that day, but until then he'd pressure her. So he said the first thing that popped into his mind. "You kept only one secret from me."

Her skin was flushed with passion. "I did?"

"Yes."

"I'm not sure I want to know."

"Yes, you do. You did not tell me of your plans on the day you left us."

She studied her hands.

Did she blame him for what had befallen her? In the event she had not thought through the deception, he said, "A pity you cannot remember, for now you cannot seek justice against those who wronged you."

She stared into the distance. "If I did remember, my heart would be filled with anger."

Only that? He suspected other deeper emotions held Virginia MacKenzie captive and kept her silent. "Tell me what occupies your heart now?"

"Is that your blackmail demand?"

"Yes."

A flock of sparrows darted overhead. She followed their flight. "Thoughts of you. Agnes was very forthcoming last night."

Agnes had been Virginia's foremost champion; she'd say nothing to hurt her. "What did the trouble finder tell you?"

"Many things. Interesting details about your life."

"Believe none of them."

"She said you are responsible for the lifting of the ban on tartans and bagpipes. You're a hero to many."

The subject always made him uncomfortable. At the time he'd begun the quest, he'd done so because he needed a purpose in life. He'd been rudderless without Virginia. "We half-Scots must work harder to make a place in the Highlands."

"You're being modest. Agnes said you were."

"Agnes talks too much, especially on the subject of Scottish politics."

"I'm half Scottish, same as you."

"Say that in front of your father and you'll regret it."

"Agnes brought me a MacKenzie plaid."

111

Virginia's coloring would make pale the most festive of all the Highland tartans. "We'll fly it atop the mast . . . in case we pass your father on the river."

"Agnes also said she went with you to China. You met the Emperor."

"We were looking for you."

She turned and headed back the way they'd come. "I'm glad you found me."

Now that she'd relaxed, he said, "Do you think you ran away?"

"I do not know, but I have faith that it will all come back to me in time." She lifted her brows and shot him a warning glance. Cheerfully, she said, "You will find yourself at the disadvantage then."

What moment would she choose to end the charade? "I think I have always been at the disadvantage with you."

She laughed at his flattery, but her tone was serious when she said, "What made you think I ran away from home?"

Bittersweet humor filled him. "You asked me to take you with me, and when I refused, you accepted it too easily. I should have known at the time that you were up to something."

She looked away. "You could have taken me with you."

Not *should,* but *could.* Another unspoken message; she did not blame him. In their youth, he'd always known what she was thinking. Now he must listen in a different way.

"No, I could not, I'm sorry to say."

"Don't be sorry. We're leaving. All will be well."

He smelled bacon frying just as the house came into view. He thought of the long voyage to Scotland, the private places aboard the ship, the hours they could fill with passion. "I'll see you at the ship in an hour."

Locating Quentin Brown delayed their departure. Using the time, Virginia hurried to the hamlet to retrieve her special keepsakes. With the basket of remembrances on her arm, she stood in the clearing. Paths led in every direction, paths she and the others here had worn smooth, paths that led both everywhere and nowhere at once, depending on who walked them.

Logs and rocks surrounded the cold hearth and served as a meeting place for the people in the hamlet. In the beginning she'd sat on the fringe of this place. Later she'd claimed the stool-sized boulder near a sapling oak. Now the tree thrived, and she'd long since taken a position of authority near the fire.

Songs were sung here and jests played. Handmade gifts were exchanged, disputes were settled. No matter the occasion, sadness would always taint her memories of those times. She glanced down the least used path and thought of the whipping post that awaited there. Silence, save the chatter of birds and insects buzzed in her ears. She'd been spared the lash, but watching the punishment of others had left deep scars on everyone in the hamlet.

She said a silent prayer, asking God to watch over Fronie, Georgieboy, and the others. Her peace made, she went in search of Merriweather. She found him in the storehouse, a dust smock over his butler's garb, the inventory journal open on the workbench. Merriweather hated counting the stores.

She latched the door behind her. "I came to say good-bye."

He didn't look up but took great care and time

capping the ink and cleaning the quill. "Everyone else is in the fields."

Bond servants came and went. They were always held at a distance by the slaves at Poplar Knoll. Because of her age and the length of her indenture, Virginia had been accepted. Her attempt at escape had made her a prisoner. In the years that followed, the slaves had given their hearts to her; watching her leave would bring them to despair. "It's better this way. Will you—?"

"Yes, I'll tell them, and I hope you will take some fond memories with you. There have been those."

The personal satisfaction of reading a purloined newspaper. Rewards after a successful harvest. Keeping her dignity in the face of utter shame. "I shall."

"Take this also, for luck." He gave her a wooden medallion on a length of white ribbon. Carved in the smooth oak was a stately eagle.

"I don't know what to say except thank you. I'll treasure it."

"It's our symbol of liberty. Promise me you will not let some highborn Scot or Brit rob you of what you've earned here."

He was speaking again of character, of self-respect. "But I lied to Cam and my family."

He shrugged, but his keen gaze was anything but casual. "As much for them as for yourself. Worry not. The only thing your family and friends possess in abundance that you do not is guilt. Haven't they gone on with their lives?"

"Yes. That's why I told the tale."

"Kindness has ever been your way—" He pulled off the smock and bowed from the waist. "Virginia, of the ducal MacKenzies. Now you are a woman off to take the next path in her destiny. Walk it proudly."

"I will."

Folding the smock, he draped it over his arm. "What have you decided to do? Where will you go?"

She'd spent the night on Cameron's ship, but she had slept little. She and Agnes had talked themselves into exhaustion. "After we find my parents, I'll be reunited with the rest of my family in Glasgow. Horace Redding is there."

That got his attention. "Truly?"

"Yes. I plan to give him the copy of 'Reason Enough.'"

"The one you penned on that exquisite rabbit hide?"

"Yes."

"He'll be very impressed, but I imagine he'll be too busy admiring you."

She flushed. "Shall I remember you to him?"

He laughed. He'd never set eyes on Redding. "Go." He made a shooing motion with his aged hands. "Snatch up the life you were destined for."

"May I hug you?" She'd surprised him; his sudden uncertainty was proof of that. Partially for explanation but because she couldn't leave without it, she said, "My family was always open in their affection."

He tisked and shook his head. "You battled much more than any of us knew, didn't you, gal? Yet never have you looked downtrodden."

All of that was behind her. "I've won, Merriweather."

"You have. No one will ever break your spirit. Bondage certainly has not." He held out his arms.

She stepped into his embrace. He smelled of juniper berries and sad farewells.

"Don't forget," he whispered. "Your family loved the girl. They'll love the woman more."

She sighed, and her cheek grazed his wrinkled jaw. Words wouldn't come. All of her good-byes to the slaves and bond servants would be said through Merriweather. It was better that way.

In an overdone tone of authority, he said, "Don't let that dashing Cunningham sweep you off your feet before you've found them."

"He's very handsome and charming, isn't he?"

"Yes. Stand proud of yourself, gal, and think of us. We're losing a duchess. The MacKenzies and Cunningham have everything to gain."

The weight left her. "If you are ever in Scotland . . ."

"I shan't be." He stepped back and smiled. "I think I shall enjoy living under a freely elected president rather than the Hanoverian king of England."

His dignity was contagious, and pride infused her. "God bless you, Merriweather."

Tucking the medallion into her basket, she took her time walking away from Poplar Knoll. She had also said her good-bye to Mrs. Parker-Jones, who had cried and again expressed her regret. Virginia had comforted her and promised to write as soon as she arrived in Scotland.

As Virginia walked the path of herringbone bricks that led to the river, her steps grew light. She'd come here as a child. Somewhere between a bewildered ten-year-old and the woman she was today, a girl had thrived. That child had learned to tend her own wounds, both inside and out. When loneliness had threatened to smother her, she'd fought back tears by imagining herself at home in her soft bed, her mother singing a favorite lullaby.

Now she was free, but as she boarded the ship named for her and prepared to lie to those who loved her, she felt as if she were stepping into another kind of bondage.

Cameron was all smiles and charm. He'd donned his tartan plaid, a yellow shirt, and cockaded hat. The feather rippled in the breeze.

Agnes paced the deck, the heels of her shoes clicking on the boards. Quinten Brown stood at the ship's wheel. MacAdoo and two others stood ready to cast off.

"Do you have everything you need?" Cameron said, taking her arm.

Stronger legs would help, she thought, trying to still her wobbling knees.

Agnes threw up her arms. "Of course she does. But whatever she's forgotten, we'll buy in Norfolk."

Cameron closed his eyes and winced. "Save me from her, Virginia, for I swear she can drive a man to madness and bruise him with words."

He didn't look bruised. He looked confident and appealing to Virginia. She thought of the kiss they'd shared in the forest, and her stomach bobbed.

"Captain Cunningham. Wait!"

Turning, Virginia saw Mrs. Parker-Jones running down the path, a package in her hands. "You've forgotten the painting."

Painting? What painting?

Cameron yelled, "Hold the plank."

A confused Virginia watched Mrs. Parker-Jones board the ship and push a framed painting into his hands. It was the drawing from the parlor. "Why do you want that painting?" she asked.

"'Tis a gift for Mary."

"Let me see." Agnes took it from him. "I remember this. It was in the parlor. It's rather like that drawing Mary made of you and Virginia as children."

He glanced at Virginia and vowed to make her forget the name Duchess. "Aye, 'tis. Mary will appreciate the style."

Agnes grew smug. "When we return with Virginia, Mary will draw you again as a savior, but instead of redeeming Scotland's tartans, she'll give you a palm and lance and declare you Pancras, the savior of children. You'll again be the talk of the isle."

With great conviction, he said, "Nay, Mary will leave me out of her political cartoons."

Immediately alert, Agnes barked, "What secrets do you know about her?"

"Enough to save my pride. A pity you have no such weapon against Mary's wicked quill."

"You cannot hold her hostage and keep quiet about it."

They argued like Georgieboy and his sister. Virginia stepped into a familiar role. "Will the two of you bicker away the day? Or shall we leave this place?"

They both laughed. Agnes started to hand back the painting but stopped. "Mrs. Parker-Jones?" she said. "Who is this Duchess who signed the painting?"

Fidgeting, the mistress eased toward the gangway. "She was a bond servant acquired by the former owner."

Virginia hurried to say, "She left years ago for Kentucky."

Cameron took the painting from Agnes. "Well, I'm sure Mary will enjoy her work."

"I shan't detain you further. Have a safe journey. Fare you well, my lady."

At the formal address, Virginia cringed in fear. She didn't know how to be a noblewoman. Her knowledge of the gentry had ceased when she was ten years old.

Before that, she'd been forgiven slips in protocol because she was a child. She'd been indulged.

Wood scraped against wood as the plank was taken up.

Virginia marshaled her courage.

"Stand by the braces, mates," Cameron shouted. "To the sea we go."

A cheer went up, and crewmen scurried in the rigging and manned the mooring lines. Amid a slapping of canvas, the ship began to move.

The moment of freedom was at hand. Virginia's throat grew tight.

"Care to stand at the bow?" Cameron asked, his hand sliding to the small of her back. "Without Agnes?"

"Haud yer wheesht!" Agnes shouted, but her tone belied the command to silence Cameron.

Unable to speak, Virginia nodded and, on still-shaking legs, moved to the front of the ship. A MacKenzie tartan draped the bulwark and fluttered in the breeze. Everything and everyone moved too slowly. She gripped the railing and pushed as if she could speed the ship along. *Fly away from here,* she urged, and like a wagon hitched to a fine team, the *Maiden Virginia* eased into the fast-flowing current.

They stood at the bow in companionable silence. Behind them, Agnes chatted with Captain Brown. Sloops and barges passed, even a water jenny, as the tinker's boat was called. Occupants of the other conveyances waved; Cameron and Virginia returned the greeting. The farther they sailed, the more her tension eased, and when she breathed in the salty smell of the ocean, she knew a keener sense of relief.

Seemingly satisfied that Brown was not steering

them to disaster, Cameron rested against the rail. "Are you saddened at leaving?"

What could she say? What *should* she say? "A little." That was the truth; she felt miserable for the lies.

"How did you spend the holidays here?"

The truth was too bittersweet. "In church," she lied. "That's where we have the Nativity play."

He stared out at the river, his eyes narrowed against the wind. "The Parker-Joneses accompanied you to services?"

She intended to embellish the tale, then change the subject. "Yes, they have their own pew."

Glancing down at her, he said, "Tell me about the Nativity."

Around the bend in the river came another ocean vessel, its sails trimmed, a dash of colorful cloth in the rigging.

"Were you in the play?" Cameron prompted.

Merriweather had spoken of the guilt her family and Cameron carried. Virginia felt it now. "Yes. We use farm animals. When I was young, I played an angel. One year I was the wise king carrying frankincense."

"You have rare spices in Virginia?"

She smiled at that. "It was actually pieces of sugar cane . . . for the children. And how do you spend the holidays?"

"At sea most often. Had you ever considered leaving Poplar Knoll?"

She thought of the poorly made raft. That girl had swallowed defeat and learned from it. But she must be careful in her answer. She chuckled and said, "Oh, yes. Every year at spring cleaning."

He laughed too, and she reminded herself to tell him more of such stories.

"Ahoy, the *Virginia.*"

The sailing ship was almost abreast of them.

Agnes raced to the bow. Cameron clutched Virginia's arm.

"It's Papa and Juliet."

"It's your parents."

Cameron and Agnes spoke at once, but their words were unnecessary. Virginia recognized the couple at once. Papa had never cared for hats; the years hadn't changed that. He still wore his hair longer than fashion; he even sported braids at his temples in the Highland way.

Agnes waved her arms. "We've found her!"

They waved back, Mama's mouth tight with the effort to hold back tears. Papa hugged her, then cupped her face, much the same as Cameron had caressed Virginia earlier in the day. Rather than kiss Mama, Papa spoke.

She shook her head.

He spoke again.

In resigned agreement, she nodded.

Papa ripped off his jacket and climbed the ship's rail.

"Hoots!" cried Agnes. "He's going to swim over."

Virginia's breath caught, and she clung to Cameron. As she let the tears flow, she watched the best man o' the Highlands plunge into the River James to reach her.

Chapter

7

∽

"Man overboard!" Cameron yelled.

Traffic on the river slowed.

Moving behind Virginia, Cameron grasped her upper arms. "Worry not. He's an excellent swimmer."

She knew that, but it didn't lessen her shock. In stunned bewilderment, she leaned against Cameron. Crewmen on the other ship hoisted a rowboat over the side. She bit her lip to stave off a cry as her mother was lowered into the boat.

MacAdoo threw a rope ladder. Hemp squeaked beneath her father's weight. She couldn't see him, but from the movement of the rope, she could discern his progress.

Her heart clamored into her throat. Time slowed to a crawl.

As trim and as agile as a man half his age, Papa bounded over the rail and landed barefoot on the deck. He'd shrunk, she thought, but no, she'd just grown taller.

He wore a pale gray silk shirt and long breeches of dark blue wool. She stood frozen as he brushed his hair from his eyes.

In the commotion, Agnes had hurried to the bow and fetched the MacKenzie tartan. "Here, Papa."

He wiped his face, his attention fixed on Virginia. "Do you know how much I've missed you, lassie mine?"

Where would she find the strength to lie to him? And why hadn't he found her years ago?

Cameron spoke softly. "If you did remember the past, you'd run to him." A nudge at her back pushed forward. "He loves you more than spring. Go."

Her feet moved, and in the next breath, she was engulfed in her father's arms. The earliest of her memories, tucked safely beside an image of her mother brushing her hair, was this feeling of being surrounded by the strength of Lachlan MacKenzie. He radiated joy and affection.

"I love you more than spring."

He'd said that often. She wanted to tell him that he'd been in her thoughts every day, but she couldn't. The little girl in her soaked up his love. The woman squeezed her eyes shut and gritted her teeth, holding on to that love and savoring it. Dampness seeped into her dress, but she didn't care.

Drawing back, he turned with her to face the approaching rowboat. "Juliet!" With his mighty hands, he gripped Virginia. "It's our lass, our Scrapper." His voice boomed across the water. "Bless Saint Ninian, it's our lass!"

From the boat, Mama waved. "Virginia!"

"MacAdoo," Cameron shouted. "Man the ladies' chair. The duchess of Ross is coming aboard."

Virginia saw movement on the deck, saw MacAdoo hauling an odd chair to the bow, but she felt distanced from the events around her. She couldn't look away from the woman in the blue dress, the woman who looked young enough to be her sister. *Mama.*

"Virginia?"

Cameron was calling to her. He gave her a smile of encouragement, and she reached for him. Her father held her fast.

"What happened to you, lass?" Papa's voice was raw with yearning and thick with the burr of the Highlands. "Why did you not send word to us sooner?"

She girded herself and told him the first lie. "I couldn't."

"Sir!"

"Papa!"

Cameron and Agnes came to her rescue. Cameron gestured to Agnes. "You do the explaining, button maker."

Virginia didn't know why, but at the endearment, Agnes shot him a knowing look that promised retribution. "Hoots, Papa. She doesn't know who she is. 'Tis her memory. I mean to say she now knows who she is, but she didn't until—"

"You're stammering, Agnes," he interrupted, tossing her the cloth. "'Tisn't like you."

Cameron stepped between them. "What Agnes is trying to say is that Virginia has no memory of us."

"What?" he roared, his hold on her tightening.

Agnes wadded the tartan. "A horse tossed her on her head, and she lost her memory."

124

Then Papa's hands were in Virginia's hair, feeling her scalp, looking for an injury.

She found her voice. "'Twas years ago, sir."

"Sir?" His blue eyes, the same shade as hers, studied her. Awareness unfocused his gaze. Then he shook himself. "Do you recall nothing, lass? Nothing of your kin or of Scotland?"

Uncomfortable with the lie, she moved to Cameron. "Only my life at Poplar Knoll."

"They treated her kindly, Papa," said Agnes. "Never was she forced or imprisoned."

He sagged with relief and mussed his hair. "Thank the saints for that. I'd spare the beast no mercy who harmed you."

"Your grace," said Cameron with gentle reprimand. "We've overwhelmed her. She remembers nothing about us. We are strangers to her."

Her suspicions about her father's reaction had been correct. Later, when she'd settled herself within the family, she'd make amends. "I'm healthy and very happy to at last know where I belong."

Papa cupped her cheek. "No one beat you or threatened you? No man forced you?"

She'd been right to lie. If he knew about Anthony MacGowan, he'd go after that man and risk harm to himself. He'd also learn the truth. He'd know that she'd soiled her clothing aboard that ship years ago. Reeking of vomit and confinement, she'd fought like a badger while they doused her with cold water. They'd bared her chest and laughed at her immaturity. When she'd tried to run, they'd shackled her. "No."

He closed his eyes. "Thank the saints."

Perhaps she'd never tell him.

"We'll take you to Edinburgh," he said. "The best doctors are there and Sarah too."

"Hoots, Papa! The *second-best* doctors are in Edinburgh. Edward can perfectly care for her."

He seemed to notice Agnes then, really notice her, for he moved away from Virginia. "You found her," he declared. "You stubborn, trouble-finding, obstinate, half-Campbell female—"

"Papa!" The picture of offended womanhood drew herself up and stiffened her neck. With too much satisfaction, she said, "I told you she was alive. I promised to find her."

He threw back his head and laughed. "Curse me for an eel-eating Englishman, but you did." She squealed when he swung her into his arms and turned in a circle.

Cameron pulled Virginia beside him and draped an arm over her shoulder. "A thrilling moment," he said. "We've waited ten years to see them make peace."

He'd said that before, but words paled beside the joy that passed between Papa and Agnes. It was the reunion Virginia should have had.

"A pity you don't recall the past, Virginia."

Something in his voice—strangely like criticism— drew her attention.

She looked up at him. "Why?"

He gave her a bland smile. "You'd be as happy as Agnes is now."

An eerie feeling passed through Virginia, a sense of exposure, of vulnerability, as if Cameron could see through her lies.

A bundle of male clothing sailed over the railing. Quick as a snap, Agnes dashed to the left and caught it. The duke moved to the gunwale and helped his wife from the chair that had been lowered over the side. Giving her a smack of a kiss, he spoke softly to her. She started, then with eyes wide with shock, she studied Virginia.

"Oh, no."

"Take heart, Juliet. Come and see our bonnie lass, Virginia."

Again, Cameron pushed her forward. She floated into her mother's arms. Stifling a sob, she basked in her mother's love.

With the joy came anger at the fate that had robbed her of a thousand moments like this.

"Oh, my darling girl. Worry about nothing. You're safe with us. No one will ever take you away again."

She drew Agnes into the embrace. "Thank you, and God bless your brave heart, Agnes MacKenzie." Tears swimming in her eyes, Mama smoothed Virginia's hair. "You have the most wonderful sister."

"She doesn't know us."

"Is it true? You recall nothing?"

Fisting her hand, she said a silent prayer. "Only snatches." Love squeezed her chest. "But I'm so glad you found me."

Watching the pretense weakened Cameron. He had seen that kind of inner strength twice before in MacKenzie females. Mary had been the brunt of a jest staged by Robert Spencer, the earl of Wiltshire. On the night he'd seduced her, a thoroughly compromised Mary had righted her clothing and walked through a gauntlet of gloating English lords. Years earlier when Virginia's gander had died, she'd insisted on digging the grave and burying her pet herself. Cameron had held her blistered hand as she'd said a prayer for the old bird.

The earl of Wiltshire didn't deserve Mary MacKenzie. Virginia didn't deserve this torment. Her reunions should have been joyous with abandon, not restrained with prideful deception. But judging her was wrong; so he followed his instincts. Good cause was behind her behavior. It was up to him to help her.

He exchanged greetings with the other captain and told him to follow them to Norfolk. For the remainder of the voyage, Cameron watched and listened as Virginia skirted the same questions from her father and mother as she had with Agnes and him. Fixed in a smile, her mouth occasionally trembled. She often ducked her head. She always made that fist when she lied.

In port, Cameron held back as Quinten Brown ushered the MacKenzies into the Wolf and the Dove Inn. Less than a week ago, Cameron had come here searching for Brown.

Mary Bullard, Brown's partner in the enterprise, greeted them. A stout woman, her face and petite body rounded in good health, Mary limped forward, her weight braced on a cane. Over a fashionable dress of blue satin, she wore an embroidered apron. "Welcome again, Captain Cunningham."

"Have you hurt yourself?"

She waved the cane. "A twisted ankle is all."

Captain Brown grew flustered. "You've summoned the doctor?"

"Yes, Captain Brown."

Seeing the way she dealt with Brown, Cameron couldn't resist saying, " 'Tis no riddle who the 'dove' is in this partnership."

She folded her hands at her waist and turned her gaze to Captain Brown. "Coo for them, Quinten."

He flustered, but his voice was overly solicitous when he said, "Mary, me love, be of good cheer and meet the Highland rogue himself, Lord Lachlan Mac-Kenzie, and his family."

Lachlan stepped back and, with a flourish, pretended to doff the hat he wasn't wearing and sketched a courtly bow. "'Tis a delight to meet you, Mistress Bullard."

Her face flushed with embarrassment. "Ooh, ooh."

At the cooing sounds she made, Captain Brown laughed. "There's my dove."

She glared at him but spoke to Lachlan. "Sweet Betsy, when talk gets out that we've the best man o' the Highlands under our roof, we'll be deluged with grovelers and favor seekers."

Lachlan said, "Some say America is a land of ne'er-do-wells."

Her interest engaged, her gaze sharpened. "What do you say, m'lord?"

"I say you Americans should open your arms to the poor Scots who must share an island with the greedy Brits."

Cameron choked back laughter. Virginia shot him a puzzled frown. He winked and moved beside her.

In his British speech, Brown said, "I've no quarrel with your people, MacKenzie, nor does Mary."

Mary Bullard huffed. "You haven't time to quarrel with anyone. You're too busy bedeviling me, and I'll speak for myself."

He growled, jammed his coat on a peg by the door, and stormed up the stairs.

At each of his deafening footfalls on the wooden planks, Mary winced. The slamming of a door ended the noise.

Cameron had witnessed a similar row between them and thought Brown was spoiled by Mary. To her, he said, "Would you name Captain Brown a lovey dove or a mourning dove?"

As if it were a scepter and she a queen, Mary held on to the cane and smiled. "Both . . . on his good days. Well," she went on, as chipper as could be. "How many rooms will you need, your grace?"

"Papa?" said Virginia. "May I have . . . If it suits you and it isn't too much trouble—"

"What is it, lass?"

"I'd like a room to myself . . . if I may."

He took her arm to pull her away from Cameron. When she did not move, he stepped closer. His eyes twinkled with affection. "You and Lottie always do." More seriously, he said, "You'll have a palace if that's what you want, Virginia MacKenzie."

He said her name so proudly, she choked back a sob. "Thank you, Papa."

Agnes edged to his side. "Give it no thought, Virginia. He will not truly buy you a palace."

Still holding Virginia's hand, Cameron couldn't help saying, "Aye, he will. So long as it neighbors his." She looked up at him, and he added, "Don't expect him to let you out of his sight."

"She's a MacKenzie, Cunningham."

Only in reprimand did he address Cameron that way. "I know the feeling well. You fostered me."

Agnes drew off her gloves. "Ten pounds says Papa posts a guard outside Virginia's door, and it shan't be me."

Virginia shrank back.

Cameron held her fast. "Your grace, shouldn't we settle the ladies in rooms before we have the first fight over Virginia?"

The duke spoke softly, but his glare was as hard as steel. "I seem to recall saying those same words in

Edinburgh to a lad who was quick to overstep himself."

They'd traveled to Edinburgh years before. Immediately upon arrival, Virginia and Cameron tried to sneak away from their lodgings and explore the city. Lachlan had caught them before they reached the street.

But Cameron knew how to deal with the duke of Ross. "For that good lesson and hundreds more does my mother thank you. From her I learned to think first of the fairer sex." He glanced at Mary Bullard. "Rooms, Mistress Bullard, and hot baths for the ladies."

"My pleasure, sir." With a thump and a shuffle, she exited through a swinging door.

Lachlan moved closer to his wife and whispered in her ear.

She took great pleasure at his words, for her eyes closed and a secret smile curled her lips.

If love were a color, it glowed in rainbow hues around the duke and duchess of Ross. Cameron had come of age in that colorful glow. Lachlan MacKenzie knew how to love females, how to make them glow as women. Cora, Lilian, and Rowena were friendly and affectionate, but as the eldest and Juliet's first child, Virginia had received all their attention, theirs and the love of Agnes, Lottie, Sarah, and Mary. And Cameron.

Even in her mother's womb, Virginia MacKenzie had been loved and anticipated. It had not spoiled her. Rather, it made her more giving to others. Having lived amid such harmony, a solitary life was preferable to Cameron than a life without it. He'd tried to find love and happiness with others. Adrienne Cholmondeley was perhaps his greatest disappointment, if only for the number of years he'd tried. But long sea voyages left them with only lust for a bond.

"My parents are beautiful together."

What if her time in bondage had stolen her ability to share her soul and welcome him? The old pain returned but not the emptiness. Virginia was alive and free, and for those blessings, he was thankful. "Aye" was all he could say.

Lady Juliet sighed. "Much more of that from you, and I'll take a room to myself."

Lachlan grinned and challenged her. "You never would." When she did not budge, he took her hand. "I'd only break down the door."

She laughed.

Agnes laughed too. "Hoots! He's going to scold her."

Leaning close to Virginia, Cameron whispered. " 'Tis a shame you don't recall the MacKenzie way of scolding."

"It will come back to me in time."

At a time of her choosing, he was certain. "Aren't you glad we didn't sneak away from Poplar Knoll?"

Her eyes searched his. "Yes."

Both of her palms were open. Relieved that she spoke the truth, Cameron thought of the future. She still faced a private reunion with her mother. In Scotland, she would repeat the process a dozen times beginning with her sisters Sarah and Lottie, who surely awaited in Glasgow. For those occasions, he pitied Virginia.

Now he must help her. "Would you care to take a walk . . . later?" he said for her ears only. "There's a merchant's colony on Becker Street, not far from here. Would you like to see it?"

She squeezed his hand and her eyes sparkled. "A market with shops and stalls and wares to be bought?"

"Of every kind."

As children they'd had hundreds of similar exchanges. No matter the errand or mission, he could always count on Virginia wanting to go along. Until this moment, he hadn't realized how lonely he'd been.

"Cameron?"

"Come downstairs later, and I'll be waiting."

Alarm widened her eyes. "You won't be staying at the inn?"

His first reaction was to feel flattered, but the compliment was crosswise at best. Because of the lie and the emotional burdens she'd chosen to hide, she probably preferred Cameron's company. But she looked like a woman with love on her mind.

"No, I'll stay aboard my ship."

"But you'd wait here and take me to the market?"

She was much too serious, her comment much too naive, since she damned well knew he'd take her anywhere. "Not if I must carry your basket."

He remembered that smile, and with it came a vision of the happy, trusting girl she'd been.

"I haven't a basket, but I shall buy one, and thank you, Cameron, for telling me about the market."

"Words of thanks have never been needed between us." He was tempted to add that they'd always been honest with each other, but she knew that.

If her memory was intact, she also remembered the pledges they'd made. How many of those vows had she broken? How many more would she break? He didn't know, and now he faced another challenge, for her father must be told the truth.

"Come, your grace," he said, nudging her toward

her mother. "Have a dram with me while Lady Juliet builds a nest for us in this place."

The duke had been watching them, and his cool gaze moved from Cameron to his daughter, then back to Cameron. "I'd be mistaken in hearing rudeness in your tone, aye?"

It was a subtle challenge, but forceful enough to heighten the tension between them. Cameron had spent a decade under Lachlan's roof. He knew he must lighten the uncomfortable moment. Casual familiarity seemed best. Pulling a toilworn face, he said, "Your grace, have you forgotten that I've been at sea with Agnes for better than a fortnight?"

Agnes huffed. "I resent that!"

Chuckling, Lachlan tweaked her nose. "Pity any man such a fate."

She batted his hand away.

Still in the throes of the jest, he gave Cameron a smile of conspiracy. "Allowance granted, lad. My firstborn can drive a man to madness."

Agnes squared her shoulders. "Come, Mama, Virginia. Another moment in the company of these wretches, and I may resort to violence."

"Please no, dear," said Juliet.

As one, Cameron and Lachlan threw up their hands in surrender.

"Trolls."

Virginia smiled up at Cameron. Under his breath, he said, "You'll be safe here."

"She remembers all?"

Now that he'd said the dreaded words to Virginia's father, Cameron hurried to explain her actions. "Yes, she does. Time has perhaps dulled her specific recollections, but no fall from a horse stole her memory. She invented the story."

A look of disbelief smoothed the duke's features. "How can that be?"

An aproned barman set frothy mugs of ale on the freshly scrubbed table, then lit a lantern that hung on a wall sconce near the door to the kitchen. Faint yellow light illuminated the corner. Cameron had chosen the table for its unobstructed view of both the door and the stairs. The other tables were unoccupied.

He fished coins out of his sporran and paid the barman for the beverages. Pocketing the money, the man paused to stir a kettle of rabbit stew that simmered over the hearth.

Lachlan drank deeply. "Good ale."

Cameron waited until the barman returned to the kitchen. "'Tis a long story."

All contemplation, the duke stared into the mug. "On the voyage I wanted to believe that you'd found her, but as I'm a man to my soul, lad, I feared another disappointment."

Cameron had experienced the same torment. "I know. 'Twas the longest walk of my life . . . down the hall of that plantation to meet her."

Fatherly love lent a gentleness to Lachlan's rugged features. "She's bonnie, aye?"

Cameron expected Lachlan to ask what had happened to Virginia. If the duke of Ross wanted to savor the moment, Cameron could certainly oblige. "Aye, but I knew she'd be a beauty."

"Did you now?"

At the slyness in Lachlan's voice, Cameron grew defensive. "She's bonnie enough for me."

"For any man with eyes. Although her sweet Virginia speech would be a song to a blind man."

"Yes."

Lachlan's gaze, more concerned than judgmental, grew keen. "I saw the way you looked at her, but you cannot know the woman she's become, Cameron. You loved the lass, and if the past is clear to her, she remembers that she was fair smitten with you. 'Tis foolish to think that she loves you still."

Out of respect, Cameron let the insult go. No one knew Virginia as well as he. She wanted him; she just wasn't ready to admit it. "I don't expect her to ravish me right away."

Lachlan tried not to laugh and lost. When the humor passed, he said, "What happened to her?"

Cameron related the story he'd heard from Rafferty.

"You believe him?"

"Yes. She did lie about attending church, and she'd have us thinking she's been the housekeeper, but that's also a lie."

"She's afraid."

"Yes."

"Does Agnes know?"

"No."

"Pity. She believed when we did not."

A fresh bout of guilt assailed Cameron. "Yet Virginia feels safe with me."

Without malice, Lachlan grumbled, "A bolted door couldn't separate you as children."

Under the circumstances, a stretch of the truth seemed reasonable. "That has not changed, sir. Our special bond remains. She just isn't ready."

"I'm troubled by that. Have you thought of Cholmondeley? He'll not take kindly to you forsaking his Adrienne."

Cameron turned his attention to the ale, which was fresh and yeasty. Adrienne would understand or she would not. He'd signed no formal betrothal with her father, and he often thought their association was a convenience to her.

"You cannot wish away your liaison with the English girl."

Cameron almost challenged him. Lachlan MacKenzie's roguish reputation was legend. Prior to meeting Lady Juliet, he'd seduced more women than was proper, even for a newly reinstated and eligible duke. But good manners kept Cameron silent on that subject. "Virginia has a great strength about her, you know."

"'Tis my Juliet's doing."

"Aye, but she looks like you."

"She does at that." He smiled fondly. "You taught Virginia to swear."

Cameron wouldn't be baited. "'Twas Agnes who taught her that."

Lachlan put down the mug. "If you shed your honor or anything else with her before she explains herself, you'll answer to me for it."

That tone had once struck fear in Cameron. "You of all people know how I feel about Virginia."

"I remember well how a young Cameron, eager for a taste of the world, behaved around her."

"She was only ten. I respected her."

"There's the point, eh? She's a woman now, and I've seldom seen a maiden, even a decent one, prevail against your charms. I tell you, lad, we'll have this lass in our lives before we give her to a husband."

A husband? Fierce determination rose in Cameron. "She's mine. She has always been mine."

"But does she want you? Who is to say that being betrothed to you is not the reason for her deception?"

That possibility hadn't occurred to Cameron. He knew that indifference had not fueled the kisses they'd shared. Virginia wanted him. Before meeting Rafferty, Cameron had told Virginia about the betrothal. In retrospect, her reaction made sense. She had not expressed outrage or surprise. She'd asked few questions because she knew the answers.

"I say the betrothal to me has no part in her lie." He had to believe it. "Unless to strengthen her resolve to keep the past a secret."

"You've kissed her, made easy with her?"

Marshaling patience, Cameron kept a reasonable tone. "Her hands are stained with tanning potions. According to Rafferty, she lived in the slave hamlet. Pride for the way she was treated keeps her silent."

"Does pride or a guilty conscience prevent you from answering me? Have you kissed her?"

"With Agnes hovering about us?" He chuckled for effect. "Surely you jest."

Lachlan gazed at the empty stairs. "True. My apologies, Cameron. Agnes would surely break your leg—or worse."

Her foreign fighting skills would fail with Cameron, but he'd keep that knowledge to himself. Other more important matters troubled him. For honest reasons, he'd betrayed Virginia to her father. But beyond the logic lay frustration. He longed to talk openly with her about the missing years.

"What else did this Irish cooper say?"

"He swears that Anthony MacGowan brought her

here and sold her to that bastard named Moreland—
he owned Poplar Knoll at the time."

"Why did she not tell them who she was?"

"She did, and they named her Duchess for it."

"They didn't even call her by name?"

"Nay."

"Bloody hell! I cannot fathom it, nor have I the
heart to test it."

Cameron did, and when the opportunity presented
itself, he'd find out if she answered to the name
Duchess.

"Why couldn't she get word to me?" Lachlan
lamented.

Cameron's throat grew tight at the story he was
about to tell. "She tried to escape once on a raft she'd
built herself."

Lachlan winced. "Ah, the Scrapper. How she must
have suffered. As I'm a MacKenzie, I'll kill Moreland."

A greater retribution awaited the duke of Ross, and
Cameron intended to steer him there. "His wife died.
He's feebled and taken rooms in Richmond. Killing
him would be a gift. Leave him to wither in his
misery."

"Who owns the land now?"

"The Parker-Joneses. They treated her decently."

"Maybe she stays silent because she fears I would
harm them?"

"She has good cause to hate MacGowan and Moreland, but Mrs. Parker-Jones helped her."

"Where does this MacGowan make port?"

"I don't know, but I've sent MacAdoo to the
harbormaster to ask after the bastard."

Lachlan gripped Cameron's arm. "You find him,

lad, and bring him to me—alive. I'll rip his heart out."

The tricky part began now, for maneuvering the duke of Ross was no easy feat, even in trivial matters. Too much was at stake now. "She's ashamed, and we're to blame. Even you said you were relieved that she had not been enslaved. Agnes wilted in relief when Virginia said she had been well treated. Put yourself in her place, and you'll understand why she fears that we will pity her."

Lachlan considered that. Twice he started to speak. Twice he faltered. At length he said, "You always did know her mind, but Cameron, should you seduce her before she admits the truth—"

Cameron slapped his right hand over his heart and fisted his left. "On my honor as a sailor, I will not seduce her." She'd wanted intimacy between them, and he'd make sure she got it.

"See that you don't. Heed me well, lad. Intimacy with her will leave *you* vulnerable." He glanced down, then up again. "I know the pain of keeping secrets from the one you love."

Now that they were conversing civilly again, Cameron relaxed. "With four illegitimate daughters, most born of noble mothers, you had an obligation to keep secrets."

"I meant a hurtful secret, when it's kept out of mistrust." Again he glanced toward the stairs. "'Twasn't me who was dishonest."

Lady Juliet had hurt the Highland rogue? That notion baffled Cameron. Putting aside his conscience, he took advantage of the duke's vulnerability. "I think I should take Virginia to Scotland. She wants to go to Glasgow."

"Nay. She comes with me. She'll change her mind about seeking retribution. She's a MacKenzie."

Be reasonable, Cameron reminded himself. "Yet she pretends otherwise. Remember how young she was and how proud? Then think about MacGowan."

As if it were a curse, Lachlan spat the name. "MacGowan."

"You remember him? He often ported at the Black Isle."

"Aye, and he knew whose daughter she was when he took her."

"He did it to hurt you."

As if the idea were foreign, Lachlan said, "How can she accept the idea that he will never pay for his crime?"

"I believe 'tis a bargain she made with herself. She traded pride for retribution."

Lachlan pointed a finger at Cameron. "Hear this bargain. I swear he'll not get away with it."

"Nay, he'll hang from a gibbet if she speaks out. He knows that."

"But why did MacGowan do it? Why would he want to harm me a decade ago? I hardly knew the foosty scunner."

Cameron had given the matter considerable thought. "Have you forgotten? A year before Virginia disappeared, you took Brodie's side against Mac-Gowan in a dispute over the Baltic trade."

Lachlan shook his head in disbelief. "He wasn't the only disappointed captain. Four other clans wanted the trade."

"He's the only one who carried a grudge."

Nodding slowly, he narrowed his eyes. "But we questioned every captain who'd ever docked at the Black Isle."

"MacGowan took revenge, then changed ports of call, for I've not seen him in Scotland or England since."

"He must've gloated the day he took her. Stealing a child and selling her." He shook his head. "God, what a mean piece of work, Cameron. I'll kill him . . . slowly."

Surely MacGowan knew that; he'd fled to evade capture. "When he learns that she has been reunited with her family, he'll worry."

Distracted, Lachlan reached for the already empty mug. Slamming it down, he clenched his teeth. "Hanging's too good for the likes o' him."

If Cameron's suspicions were true, the duke had not considered the danger MacGowan still posed. "What if he comes after her again . . . to silence her?"

Lachlan's angry growl vibrated through the room. "He'll have to go through me, my kinsmen, and every man who names me friend."

Cameron went for the kill. "Not if you find him first."

The duke was surprised by that and confused, for he watched Cameron like a hawk after a startled mouse.

Cameron took a deep breath and prayed for luck. "I think I should take Virginia and Agnes to Glasgow. You can hire Brown's ship and go after MacGowan. Revenge should be yours, my lord."

"MacAdoo knows?"

Cameron nodded. "Aye. 'Twasn't fair to send him asking after Anthony MacGowan without knowing why."

"I'll tell Juliet."

"Will you go after him?"

"Aye."

He'd agreed quicker than Cameron expected.

"I see I've surprised you."

"Aye, you did. I thought you'd insist on taking Virginia home."

An evil glint narrowed Lachlan's eyes. "I want MacGowan. When I find him, I'll sell him to Ali Kahn. He'll rot in the hold of a Moorish galley."

Cameron's stomach roiled at the thought. "A fate worse than death in a place blacker than hell."

"'Tis decided then." He slapped the table. "I'll go after MacGowan. You're to take Virginia and Agnes to Napier, and remember this one thing. Agnes will deal with you if you misuse Virginia. I'll deal with what's left of you."

Now that he'd prevailed, Cameron could be magnanimous. "She killed three men, Agnes did."

"Men who preyed on children."

Cameron held up his hand. "I'd be mistaken in hearing rudeness in your tone, aye?"

This standoff was new.

To further his case, Cameron said, "Agnes alone will drive me to madness. Let me take Lady Juliet."

Cameron might have asked for Lachlan's ducal coronet, so incredulous was he. "Nay, you cannot have my duchess."

"All of your sons-in-law speak in one voice on that subject. They'll gladly give back your daughters in exchange for Lady Juliet."

He scoffed. "They say that to gain my favor."

Cameron laughed; it was an old story and completely false. "What favors are you passing out today?"

"As if I could give you anything you cannot buy yourself, and my daughter is unavailable."

"Virginia needs me and who better to help her?"

He pointed that accusing finger at Cameron again. "First you must help her learn to trust us, lad."

"I shall, sir, and gladly."

Lachlan MacKenzie was more protective than most men, but he'd had more practice sheltering females. With eight daughters and a protective nature, he'd become legend in the Highlands and beyond. And then, because Cameron felt vulnerable, and because Lachlan had been like a father to him, he said, " 'Tis a bloody hard thing, sir. She pretends no knowledge of me or what passed between us."

Lachlan nodded in sad understanding. " 'Twill change, lad."

Cameron extended his hand. "Good luck finding MacGowan. Promise you'll send word to us, keep us informed of your findings."

Lachlan hesitated. To encourage him, Cameron said, "You and Agnes can at last make peace."

He sighed with overdone exhaustion. A moment later he smiled with unfeigned affection and shook Cameron's hand. "Hoots! She was right, all those years when she swore Virginia was alive. Won't Kenneth crow at that?"

"Your heir will go the way all men do where Agnes MacKenzie is concerned—carefully."

"Speaking of Kenneth. When you arrive in Glasgow, send word to him and your parents. They'll want to cut short their visit in Italy."

Cameron's parents were in Venice with Cameron's sister, Sibeal, who would soon birth her first child. Both Kenneth and Cora MacKenzie fostered with Cameron's parents and had traveled with them to Italy. They'd receive word, but Cameron would not encourage them to return immediately. Virginia

144

needed time, and Cameron's parents deserved to see their first grandchild.

"We're lucky men, Cameron."

Cameron laughed. "And like to grow maudlin unless we change the subject."

"True." Lachlan called out for more ale. "Now, tell me everything that has gone between you and Virginia."

Chapter

8

∽

Upstairs at the inn, her heart racing with joy, her thoughts twisted by guilt, Virginia watched her mother command the maids.

"Bring two more pillows . . . soft and fresh ones." Turning, she smiled. "My daughter Virginia likes two pillows on her bed."

That luxury had been the easiest to lose. This battle would be the hardest to win. Mama had been a bond servant. She'd been quick to admit that her servitude had been performed with dignity. If she knew the horror Virginia had endured, her eyes would cloud with pity and she'd shoulder the blame. Virginia could not permit that.

"Thank you, Mama."

Ushering the servants out, Juliet closed the door. "We'll get you a maid of your own . . . one of the Widow Forbes's girls. Unless you'd rather a girl from that plantation?"

"No. I know of no one. I mean no one suitable for the household of a duke." Including herself, but with time that would change.

"You mustn't be afraid."

"I'm not afraid," which was the truth. "Not in a fearful sense. I am uncertain about many things . . . a stranger, you know."

"We were bereft when we lost you. I thought your father would go mad with grief, and poor Agnes was inconsolable until Cameron returned."

He had said as much to Virginia, but she still didn't understand Agnes's role. "Why was Agnes inconsolable?"

"Because she was responsible for you that day."

Now Virginia understood. On that day so long ago, she had manipulated Agnes into taking her to the docks. Under her dress, she'd worn her riding breeches. When Agnes had spotted her beau, Virginia had begged money for something to eat and made her escape. All these years Agnes had blamed herself. How would Virginia right that wrong? She didn't know.

"I'm sorry for causing her pain."

"She's happy now."

"She and Cameron looked everywhere for me. They went all the way to China."

"That they did. Now tell me. Have you questions? What do you need, love?"

"Time, I think, is all I need."

"Money. You should have money of your own."

"I have my wages."

"How much?"

Virginia hadn't asked Mrs. Parker-Jones how much a housekeeper was paid, and she couldn't tell her mother how she'd come about the money. So she told a truth. "I have one hundred pounds."

"A tidy sum."

Virginia felt a burst of pride because her mother had always valued honest work, praised those who took care of their own. Liars and laggards she disdained. Thank the saints Virginia was only one of those.

"But you'll need a bigger purse than that." Mama pulled off her gloves and untied her bonnet. Putting them on the small desk, she sat on the bed and patted the place beside her. "Your father will insist on paying your accounts."

Virginia didn't deserve such generosity, not when she lied to those who loved her. It seemed like charity or, at the least, ill-gotten gains.

The feather mattress ballooned as she sat down. "Do you also insist?"

"Insist? I chose the wrong word. You are our firstborn. Your father is a duke, and although the Hanoverian court is bothersome with its pomp and circumstance, we have a position to maintain, appearances to make. But not often. For your father's sake, will you allow him to be generous?"

Virginia despaired of ever fitting in. She repeated a pledge she'd made to her father. "I'll do my best."

In a gesture of both encouragement and understanding, Mama patted Virginia's leg. "Lachlan MacKenzie is a prideful man. Too much of it, he has, that's for certain. But you are one of the few people who can break his heart. Please do not. He asks little of us when it comes to his rank in nobility. After caring for his family, governing his people and seeing to their welfare are his foremost concerns."

Before Papa's return to Tain and his dukedom, the

people of Ross were in turmoil. With fairness and great patience, the community had prospered. Other nobles and men of authority were frequent visitors to Rosshaven Castle. Parties and large suppers were regular affairs. Knowing she'd be expected to participate, Virginia said, "Very well. I'll need some new gowns." A quick comparison of her mother's fine dress to Virginia's passed-down cotton frock pushed her to admit, "Mine are unsuitable."

Taking Virginia's chin in her hand, Mama turned her until they were face-to-face. "Never be ashamed of your circumstances. You are well loved by the finest of people." And then, as if it were a crown to wear, she said, "You are a MacKenzie."

"A MacKenzie."

"Aye. Agnes said you were the housekeeper at Poplar Knoll."

If Virginia could convince them that her memory was returning slowly, all would be well. "I may be more like you than my father."

"Papa," she said. "He insists that his children call him Papa. You look just like him."

Everyone had always said so. "Yes, I do."

"We'll visit a dressmaker tomorrow and see if they can manage a few things on short notice. Once we're home, you'll have a new wardrobe. It's colder in Scotland, and you'll need warmer clothing."

On the short voyage to Norfolk, Agnes had been a font of knowledge on everything from renovations at Rosshaven Castle to the sleeping habits of Virginia's younger siblings. "Agnes said Lottie designs dresses for everyone in the family."

"She does and receives fifty pounds for each gown."

"Fifty pounds?" Virginia had no idea how much a

dress cost, but she'd find out this afternoon at the market. Fifty pounds sounded like a fortune.

"Don't look so shocked, Virginia, and never give the money a thought."

"But—"

"But nothing. Commissioning Lottie to design a few dresses for you will do two things. First, it will allow your father his pride in seeing to your needs, and second, it will enable Lottie to repay a small portion of the debt she owes David. He's her husband."

Debt? Agnes had not mentioned that Lottie owed a debt. Surely her dowry was enough to satisfy David Smithson. Virginia remembered his name but not the man himself. "How can a wife be indebted to her husband?"

Mama sighed. "Because, upon their wedding day, Lottie foolishly proclaimed she'd bear as many children as she chose and declared that her husband had no say in it. David grew stubborn, as you would expect—if you remembered him. Lottie was so sure of herself, she wagered a million pounds on it."

"Does she have a million pounds?"

"No, and that is a constant dilemma for her because David held her to the bet and to date has given her only four children."

Virginia knew about procreation; the slaves were encouraged to be fruitful, and the women, devoid of normal propriety, spoke freely on the subject. She'd learned in odd ways the workings of her own body. Even when viewed from the distance of time, the experiences were repulsive.

"We haven't that kind of wealth, and even if we did, your father would not squander money on a wager of that nature. But Lottie is one of his own. So he commissions each of us one dress per month at fifty pounds each. David says the work keeps her out of mischief."

"Even at that, she could never repay such a debt, not in an average lifetime."

She laughed, and the sound was so familiar Virginia grew melancholy.

"You always were quick with sums."

Thanks to Mama's tutoring. The scholarly Sarah had also influenced Virginia. "I practice often, although I cannot fathom counting a million pounds."

"Neither can Lottie, yet she loves David more than herself. She designed this gown." Mama stood and untied a ribbon at the waist, which held the panniered overskirt in place. "Divine and clever, isn't it?"

The dress was beyond divine. Rather than yards of lace and furbelows, the blue gown, designed for travel, was decorated at the hem and cuffs with bands of piping in sunny yellow, which complimented Mama's fair hair. Without the formal overskirt, the gown became a practical garment of the kind Virginia remembered from her youth.

Virginia said the first thing that popped into her head. "You look too young to be my mother."

Juliet's cheeks flushed with modesty. "I used to be as slender as Agnes." She placed her hands on her waist. "Having children thickens us in the most unflattering places."

It was easy to say, "You're beautiful."

She grasped Virginia's hands. "You were ever a delightful little girl. I suspect that you are a remarkable woman."

At the sweet words, a new heartache assailed Virginia. "Cameron says I was spoiled."

"He did most of the spoiling," she chided, but

affection for him shone through. "Together, you two were as bright as God's own sunbeams. It was a rare friendship for a lad and a girl." Her voice dropped. "He suffered, Virginia. It was as if the heart had been cut from him."

Virginia knew well that pain. Too much the coward to dwell on past suffering, she broached the question that had concerned her since they'd arrived at the inn. "Papa was angry with Cameron downstairs. Why?"

"You've been told about the betrothal?"

"Yes. Cameron told me."

"Much has happened since the contract was made. You cannot know if you still want to marry him."

Oh, but Virginia did.

"And he—"

Keen to her mother's halting speech, Virginia said, "He what?"

Mama turned her attention to the piping on her sleeves. "In any event, you needn't decide now about marriage. You can't know if Cameron is the right man for you. Scotland is chocked full of eligible, young men. Lindsay has an interesting heir, and there's that exciting breaker of hearts, Cyril MacCrary. The women call him Cy." She spoke the name like a sigh. "One of Michael Elliot's friends, Michael's Sarah's husband, has a friend who is a sultan with more charm than you've ever seen."

She was avoiding the subject of the betrothal. But it was too important to let lie. "Why hasn't Cameron wed?"

"Do not ask that of me." Regret tightened her mouth. "I could sooner tell Agnes's secrets to Mary. I think you should ask him, Virginia."

"I have, with embarrassing results. Won't you please tell me?"

"You must understand. He is as a son to me. His mother, Suisan, wiped my brow and encouraged me through each of my travails. He watched you when I grew big with your sisters Lily and Rowena. When your papa ordered me to stay off my feet, Cameron visited me every day. He built me a lap loom and showed me how to weave to pass the time. I am sorry, but that must come from Cameron. Remember, both of your lives have changed."

Perhaps he'd outgrown his love for Virginia. Then why was he so protective of her, and if love did not inspire his kisses, was that enough?

"Enough about that handsome Cunningham. Agnes tells me you wish to go to Glasgow rather than come home with us to Tain. I'd like to know why."

A short time later, Juliet's and Lachlan's trunks arrived. Mama went to supervise the unpacking. Virginia donned her tartan shawl and went downstairs. She felt light-headed with joy over the simple event of going to the market. She saw Cameron and her father in a corner of the tavern, but they were too deep in conversation to notice her departure.

Outside, her feet barely touched the boardwalk. She was alone, free. She could decide for herself the smallest of things—which direction to walk in, what to purchase. She could look people in the eye. No one would question her or look on her with pity.

The late-afternoon sunshine cast long shadows on the rutted lane. A haywagon rumbled past, and the boardwalk was crowded with all kinds of people. Seamen on shore leave tipped their hats as they passed. An elderly gentleman moved aside to give her the clean edge of the lane. Well-dressed matrons maneuvered their panniered skirts through storefronts, and children crowded around a carnival hawker who walked on stilts and tossed tin pennies.

The sound of conversations buzzed in Virginia's ears and reminded her of Sunday mornings in the slave hamlet.

The first regret blindsided her. She'd never see Merriweather again. Georgieboy could be sold to the neighbor, Mr. Pendergrast. Virginia would be spared the pain of watching him, chained and dragged away from his family.

"Thank you, God," she murmured on a trembling breath. "Thank you for answering my prayers."

In the mercer's shop, she bought ribbons, soap, embroidery thread, and two plain sleeping gowns.

"Two pounds, three," said the clerk as she wrapped the items and tied the bundle with string.

Virginia counted out the coins. The clerk's eager expression made her smile and wonder. "Is the price fair?"

"Of course, my lady."

A second clerk hissed, "She's the MacKenzie they come to fetch."

"So? If that's true, she's got a long purse."

Was Virginia being cheated because of who she was? Did everyone know? She cringed at the thought of strangers gossiping about her. She also realized that quality clothes didn't matter; she might as well be dressed in book muslin again.

Regardless, she would not let it spoil her first adventure by herself.

"Her hair's too short for quality folks," the clerk said to her partner. To Virginia, she said, "Have the lice, did you?"

Virginia couldn't work in the fields with waist-length hair. The notion was laughable. Only house servants and sluggards who lived with lice had long hair, and Virginia couldn't abide filth.

Ignoring the remark seemed best. "Have you silver hair pins?"

"Got wood ones and combs too. You'll need the heavy ones."

She brought out a box with dozens of hair ornaments. Given so many choices, Virginia grew confused. She chose several, plus a brush, comb, and hand mirror. The mirror was a luxury, but she wanted it.

"Sure you won't be needin' something for the lice?"

Virginia considered what Agnes or her mother would do in the situation. Perform a kindness, surely. So, she counted out four pence and put the coins on the counter. "Here's tuppence for each of you."

The clerk withered in shame but still took the money. Her cohort stood tall. "Anyone speaks poorly of you, my lady, and they'll answer to my brother. He's a blacksmith."

"Good day to you then." Clutching the parcel, she returned to the excitement of the land.

"Virginia!"

Half a block away, she saw Cameron in a crowd, one arm raised to get her attention. Her heart fluttered at the sound of her name.

"What are you doing?" he asked.

He looked like a fire ready to spark. She wouldn't be the one to ignite it. "Following your advice. Why do you look ready to cosh someone?"

He took notice of his hands, balled into fists. Frowning, he propped them on his hips. "You shouldn't have gone out alone."

From the bottom of her heart, she said, "I'm not ten years old any more."

His expression turned possessive. "I know. If you

do not discover my honest attributes before we get home to Scotland, I'll lose you to a horde of eligible dukes."

Confused and happy at once, she responded in kind. "Who told you that?"

" 'Twas an auspicious message of sorts."

She thought of their trips to the children's circus in Tain. "A fortune teller?"

"Actually, 'twas a message I found in a bottle floating in the sea."

She could tease with him on this subject. "Which sea?"

His expression turned comical. "May as well have been the Dead Sea for all the good it did me." He held out his arm. "May I accompany you?"

Yes, yes, her heart cried. Never in her adult life had anyone asked her permission, but in a thousand maidenly dreams, Cam had. She hooked her arm in his.

"Mother thinks I should consider marrying Lindsay's heir."

"If you wish to talk about other men, I shall go back to the tavern and drink myself below the table."

"Will you carry my package?"

"I'll carry you if you tire."

She couldn't stifle a gasp.

"Or if you'd just like to be carried."

"I'd like to have a conversation with you without being outraged at every turn."

"I'm on my Sunday-best behavior. How are you feeling?"

Now was not the time for honesty; she must put her plan into action. "I'm fine, except—I don't know where I belong."

"Then I pray that is the first thing you recall."

Virginia braced herself, for the game of remembering events of the past must begin. "I'm sorry to say it was not."

"Was?" He stopped and probed her with a curious gaze. "What have you remembered?"

They'd created a jam in the foot traffic. An alcove between the milner and the jam shop offered a measure of privacy. Tugging his arm, she moved there.

"Well?"

She stared at his fancy neckcloth. "I remembered that you used to spit in my palm."

"Truly?" He sounded relieved. Chuckling, he put his hand over his heart. "I promise never to do it again."

She had expected him to hug her, to celebrate the moment. A longing for his affection had driven her to chose something about him for the first remembrance of her forgotten past.

"Must I sign a pact to convince you?"

Virginia shelved her disappointment. She hoped to return to the happy girl she'd been, but she was forced to concede that today was not the day.

Looking up at him, she squinted, even though they stood in shade. "Agnes was right about you."

"Ha! Agnes has never been correct about me."

"Even when she said you were a hero to the Scottish people?"

"My mother did the work. I only presented the request to Parliament."

From Agnes she'd learned that the text of his speech had been sent to the king, who had considered knighting Cameron. "A man so modest would never spit in a girl's palm."

He glanced up and followed the flight of a pigeon.

Narrowing his eyes, he smiled. "What would you like for supper?"

"A companion who does not divert the conversation."

His expression warmed. "Diversions can be pleasant."

He said one thing and meant something else. A French term described it, but the words, taught by Sarah, had faded from Virginia's vocabulary. Not much use for the old tongue at Poplar Knoll. Bothered by the loss, she asked him for the words.

"Double entendre?"

"That's it." She soaked up the knowledge.

His hand found her wrist. Her fingers reached for his. When they were joined, he said, "What else have you remembered, other than pranks I played?"

"That my father is the best man o' the Highlands."

He nodded in greeting to an elderly couple and smugly said, "You heard Captain Brown say that."

She clung to the simple joy she felt at acknowledging strangers out of respect. "Careful or I'll think you don't want me to remember."

"You'll think I—?" He shook himself and his mood grew chilly. "Now would that be a Christian deed."

His sarcasm puzzled her, and she grew defensive. "You're meaning is . . . ?"

"I thought the past would return to you in a snap of the fingers."

An interesting answer, but it asked more questions. "No, the past comes back to me in bits and snatches."

"What compels it? A sound or a color or a feeling?"

"What do you mean?"

"When I kissed you, did it summon a memory?"

He spoke casually; yet his attention was firmly fixed

on her. "Yes, kissing you reminded me that I should know better."

"Why? I'm the man you promised to marry. I'm the man who shared your every heartache, toothache, and bellyache."

Maintaining the facade exhausted her. "Please, you must think of me as a stranger."

"I could sooner hack off my right hand and toss it into the sea."

The sheer honesty shamed her; at the touch of his lips on hers, she had seen a glimpse of the girl she'd been. Had she embraced the image too vigorously? "I don't know what to say, Cameron."

"Cam," he insisted. "You always called me Cam."

A clever conversational nudge, she had to admit. "I'm certain the past will come back to me, Cam."

"How can I help?"

"You already have, and Agnes has promised to aid me."

"Believing her is a mistake."

He'd said that before. Agnes proclaimed them as close as brother and sister. The search for Virginia had forged their friendship. "Even when she told me you asked to be named godfather to her new daughter?"

As if he were asking after the fit of her shoes, he said, "Care to share the duties with me?"

She almost tripped on her own feet; it was customary for husband and wife to fill the roles. "You're bold."

"I was hoping for a yes rather than a character judgment."

The hot edge to his tone sparked her defiance. "I'd *care* to consider it."

He stopped at a fruit stand. "Then you haven't recalled the truly important things about us?" That poignancy spoken, he innocently said, "Apple? Or something else? Have whatever you like."

He wouldn't get away with that. "Agnes was correct. Troll perfectly suits you."

He winked and eyed the apples.

Leaving him to his deviltry, she let her gaze wander over the exotic bounty before her. Early melons, coconuts, oranges, and three shades of berries overflowed their baskets. Ordinary plums were considered a delicacy at Poplar Knoll. She eyed the candied figs. Her mouth watered, and she tried to remember how long since she'd been given a choice at mealtime. Had she ever tasted a coconut? She couldn't remember, yet she knew the word and recognized the nut. It was a true memory loss and annoying. Not only would she have to work at feigning knowledge of the past, she had to work to remember other things.

"Are you ignoring me? I've bored you."

So befuddled was she by his easy charm, she lost the gist of the conversation. "What were we discussing?"

He laughed. "Our appetites."

"Are you mocking me?"

As innocent as a spring lamb, he said, "By asking if you've made up your mind what to eat?" He indicated the baskets of fruit.

The vendor thumped an apple, then began polishing it on his apron. Cameron held up his hand, and the man tossed the fruit.

The sound of him biting into the crisp fruit made her stomach growl. But she couldn't make up her mind.

Cameron nudged her. He held the apple in his teeth and with his hands, picked up three coconuts. Leaning down, the apple in his mouth, he spoke to her with his eyes. "Take the apple," he said without words.

She reached for it with her hand. He backed away. "Coward."

Emboldened, she moved to him and sank her teeth into the unblemished side of the apple. A teasing light gleamed in his eyes. Or was it something serious?

After the trouble she'd had with a simple term like *double entendre,* how could she be expected to discern anything as complex as his thoughts?

He winked and let go of the apple. For an instant in time she felt adrift, felt herself waver. Inside she teetered on the edge of the very emotion she wanted from him: love. But without trust and honesty, affection had no foundation on which to grow.

"A coconut for your thoughts." That said, he began to juggle the nuts.

She recalled the May Fair where he'd learned to juggle. He'd paid a gypsy to teach him.

"Come, Virginia, what are you thinking?"

"I had it in mind to ask if you were flirting with me."

His hands faltered. The wickedness of their youth made her say, "You're bungling the juggle."

The silliness of the exchange captured them both, and they giggled as they had a thousand times. It was the kind of spontaneous laughter that had drawn reprimands from their parents and jealousy from their siblings. He caught wayward coconuts, kept one, and asked the vendor for a knife. He pitched the nut into the air and with a downward slash of the machete, whacked the fruit in two. Milk splattered to the ground.

Waving half of the coconut under her nose, he grinned. "Are you thoroughly captivated?"

Her mind silly with the joy of the moment, what could she say but the truth? "Yes."

"Then I *was* flirting with you."

"What if I had said no?"

"I would have admitted to no more than conversational prying."

Which was exactly what she was doing. Cloaked in a playful mood the repartee seemed harmless, but that was deceptive and dangerous. Much more of his charm and she'd give herself away.

From his money pouch, Cameron paid the vendor. "Send the coconuts, apples, and . . ." He paused, soliciting her preference.

Her mouth watered. "The melons."

"And the melons—all of them—to my ship, the *Maiden Virginia.*" Pausing, he glanced down at her. "So named for this fair flower of Scotland."

Virginia blushed to her toes. How much sweeter could this man get, and how could she keep up the facade in the face of so much male charm? An answer escaped her.

The commerce concluded, Cameron accompanied her to the bookstore, the chandler, and the smithy, where she purchased her own flint and steel.

At the fishmonger's stall, a commotion broke out. A child wailed, a young boy shouted in alarm. The fishmonger stood over the children, his eyes blazing, a terrified kitten clutched in his beefy hand. With a flex of his fingers, he could crush the little cat.

"Off with you ruffians," he yelled at the children. "Your mousers ate yesterday's profit. And this one"— he shook the kitten—"this one still bears a cut on its nose from the pinch of one of my crabs. Reckon I could use this one for bait."

"Oh, no, please," the lad begged. "She's the only one left from the litter." He opened his hand. "See? We got a penny each for the others."

The frightened cat began to wail too. The monger shook the poor thing again. "More fool he who pays good coin for nonsense. It ain't worth a penny alive."

Virginia dashed forward. "I'll give you a penny if you will not hurt that cat."

He slung the cat. Virginia gasped. Limbs sprawled, eyes bulging, claws bared, the poor thing flew through the air toward her. Even before she caught it, Virginia winced. But when the needlelike claws sunk into her breast, she yelped.

Cameron cursed and reached for the cat.

"Wait." In a soft voice, she tried to comfort the kitten. In response, the terrified bundle of fur crawled up her chest and clung to her shoulder.

Cameron snatched up a herring and shoved it under the kitten's nose. Hunger won out over fear, and the cat latched onto the fish. Cameron put both down. The tiny kitten tried to drag its catch away, but the fish was twice its size.

The lad soothed his sibling until the little girl quieted. In dirty, chubby fingers she held an empty basket.

"You've bought yourself a kitten, Virginia."

"Oh, no." She had only wanted to prevent a cruelty to the animal. Pets were unthinkable. In the spring of her thirteenth year, she'd gotten attached to a crippled duckling. The overseer had killed it for his Christmas dinner. This kitten she could save.

Cameron was frowning. To the lad, he said, "She comes from mouser stock?"

"The best in the tidewater, sir."

"I just so happen to be in need of a ship's cat."

"She'll make a fine one, sir. Girls make the best mousers."

His sister giggled.

Cameron handed the boy a half crown. At the sight of the coin, the lad's mouth dropped open.

Pushing the money into the boy's hand, Cameron said, "I'll need the basket as well."

"For that much, you can have my sister too."

The girl screwed up her face and yelled.

"I didn't mean it, Hixup."

To bear out her name, the girl was suddenly beset with hiccoughs.

Stunned, Virginia watched the exchange of money for goods. Then Cameron pried the kitten from the fish and, dodging bared claws, shoved it into the basket. Over what could only be called caterwauling, he fastened the bone latch on the basket's flap to keep the animal inside. "Would you care to trade?"

He had said he wouldn't carry her basket. The troll. "How thoroughly male and generous of you."

"Why, thank you."

Smug troll. Parcels switched, they headed back the way they'd come.

"Why didn't you want the cat?"

What could she say? The truth begged to be spoken, and because that wasn't an option, she managed a part of it. "I couldn't be sure that I could keep it at Agnes's home."

"You could stay with me in Glasgow."

It was scandalous the way he baited her. "Does Agnes like cats?"

His sly grin told her he was aware of her switch in conversation. "If the cat were yours, she would tolerate it, but I bought the creature—"

"Creature?" She reached for the basket. "I'll buy it back from you."

He held it up, out of her reach. "A trade suits me better."

Oh, Lord. What would he ask for? She didn't know enough about the workings of polite society to carry on the jesting game with an adult Cameron. Fortunately, she could tell the truth about that. "I will not go down a path of intimacy with you."

"Then name the path you will travel with me."

"Friendship."

She might have told him she'd inherited the British Isles so broadly did he smile. "Splendid." He slipped the handle of the basket over her arm and took the parcel containing her personal items of clothing and violet-scented soap. He looked at ease, as if he often carried the intimate clothing of ladies. But that was unfair. For a promise of cordiality from her, he'd given her a kitten, and she was too excited about having a pet of her own to argue.

The sound of her father's voice calling her name stopped her. She looked at Cameron, and his expression turned stormy. She followed the line of his vision and saw Papa coming toward them, his strides long and angry. Beside him, MacAdoo hurried to keep pace.

"Why is he angry, Cameron?"

"Because he's overprotective. He's the chieftain of his clan. He's a duke to the English." He shook his head and expelled a breath. "Shall I go on?"

Not even when she'd used his best sporran to gather bugs for her pet lizard had her father shown such anger.

"He'll not be angry with you. I should have told him that I was taking you shopping."

No. Cameron had always borne the brunt of Papa's lectures, no matter if Virginia had played a part, which was often the case. She'd been too young and selfish to stand up for herself. Not any more.

Before he could unleash his fury on Cameron, Virginia stepped between them. Smiling brightly, she held up the basket. "Look, Papa, Cameron bought me a kitten. What should I name her?"

Only slightly distracted, he didn't answer but glared at Cameron, who was almost a head taller.

"Papa, you cannot be angry because Cameron took me shopping. He offered to carry my purchases . . . even the ladies things."

The bundle fell to the grass. Handing Cameron the basket, she scooped up the parcel and took her father's hand. "Very generous of him, wouldn't you say?" Her father said nothing. Glancing back at Cameron, she gave him a wink. "Oh, goodness, Papa. I've embarrassed him."

Cameron chuckled as she led her father away, but the sound held as much humor as her father's expression.

"Doubtless you've embarrassed him, lassie," her father said with overdone sarcasm. "Everyone knows Cunningham's a stranger to a lady's toilette."

Feeling out of her depth, she chided herself for broaching the subject in mixed company. "Where are we going?"

"Back to the inn, where you'll stay unless a family member accompanies you."

But Cameron was "family" to her; he had always been. "We're friends, Papa."

"'Twill go no farther than that, I assure you, until we're home."

Part of her thrived on his attention, but she'd been

on her own for too long. For ten years she'd sought permission for the most basic of life's needs. With freedom came volition, and she intended to exercise her own. Yet she owed her father an explanation.

"Papa, I have never been to Norfolk. I hadn't the means to—"

"Bloody hell!" He faltered, and when he looked at her, his eyes gleamed regret. But not pity, thank heavens. "I'd forgotten, lassie. I did not think about that. Still, you cannot traipse about with Cunningham."

Loyalty, ingrained and practiced in her youth, urged her on. "Because you are a duke, I cannot have a friend?"

"Because he is a rogue."

She couldn't help but laugh. "Everyone says the same about you."

" 'Tis different."

He didn't squirm well, but the exchange was so welcome she couldn't let the subject die. "How is it different?"

"I'm not bound to answer you."

"But you will."

As if the words were pulled from him, he said, " 'Tis different because you are my daughter."

"You gave Agnes to Edward Napier without a fight."

"Agnes knows what she wants."

"How do you know that I don't?"

"There's the root of it, isn't it, lassie?" He bore down on her, and she had the distinct impression that he was angry at her for more than not telling him she'd gone off with Cameron. But that was ridiculous; Papa couldn't know that her memory was intact. Almost intact.

Placating him seemed wise. "Forgive me. I shan't go out again without telling you."

"Good, because I'm trusting Cunningham to take you to Glasgow. Agnes will accompany you—"

"You're not coming with us?"

"No." He stopped at the tanner's stall and made a show of examining the hides on display. "Napier and I own a factory in Boston."

His gruffness surprised her. Did he feel guilty about seeing to his own affairs? He'd come a long way to find her, and he'd never been one to shirk his responsibilities. The disappointment tasted bitter, but she'd shouldered worse. She had years to enjoy his company now that she'd been given back her life. Struggling to sound chipper, she said, "Everyone in America knows of Edward Napier. His sliding fan motor revolutionized the tobacco industry."

Again, he paused. "You sound like Sarah."

This gentle tone was the one she remembered. Soon Virginia would see the sister who had taught her to count and hold her own with Lottie, Agnes, and Mary. The prospect brought tears to her eyes.

"What's amiss, lass? Would you rather come to Boston?"

"No. Yes. I don't know." She had assumed they'd all return to Scotland together.

"You sail with Cameron and Agnes. Your mother and I will be there before you can put names to all of the new faces."

Uncertain of how to proceed, she shifted the bundle. "When do you sail?"

"On the morning tide. Same as you."

"Cameron said nothing about leaving tomorrow."

"Oh, well, it must have slipped his mind. Have you more errands?"

She didn't believe him, and now he'd changed the subject. Or perhaps Cameron followed her father's orders. No, she couldn't picture that.

"I've arranged for a private dining room. Your mother's meeting with the cook."

"Does Mama know we're leaving tomorrow?" She hadn't mentioned it earlier.

"Aye, that's why we want you there."

All she could think to say was, "I'll miss you."

He draped an arm over her shoulder. "By harvest next, you'll be calling me overbearing."

It will come a little at a time. She took that pledge to heart. By harvesttime, she'd have told him the truth and begged his forgiveness. They'd be on even footing, as they had in her childhood. Now she must hold back and play the role of stranger.

"I hope I shan't give you reason to bear down on me. I hope to make you proud."

"You will, lass, when the time is right."

She had the oddest notion that he knew the truth. She changed her mind during the evening meal.

169

Chapter

9

⁓

Over a feast of cloved ham and cabbages, steamed crab and creamy oyster stew, the family laughed and shared each other's follies. Nestled around a plank oak table in a private dining room, the table set with ironed linens and Irish crystal, Virginia sat beside Cameron and listened to story after story.

Agnes revealed that Cameron had gotten so drunk in Canton he'd boarded a ship bound for San Francisco. With the Emperor's guard for escort, she had rescued Cameron before the anchor was weighed.

After losing a year-long battle with the collegians in Edinburgh, Sarah was sponsoring an orphaned lad at Glasgow University.

Against great opposition, Lottie managed to get a Hanoverian to visit Tain.

In London, Mary had marked the occasion of Cameron's father's first day in the House of Commons. In cartoon she pictured Sir Myles Cunningham dressed in an elegant suit of black velvet. He stood in the hallowed chamber surrounded by Englishmen wearing kilts and sporrans. The absurdity of English nobility honoring the tartans of Scotland brought new scandal to Mary. The telling of the story kept Virginia and her family laughing through dessert.

Surrounded by the warmth of family, Virginia felt a measure of redemption for the lonely nights she'd spent huddled on a prickly pallet. That girl and the events that had shaped her life seemed a far cry from the happy woman included in this cozy gathering. The goblet felt heavy in her hand. The hashes melted on her tongue. Cameron had complimented her more than once: Her dress was his favorite shade of pink, and she smelled of the prettiest of flowers. He'd laughed charmingly at her recollection of General Arnold and the ill-fated poplars of Poplar Knoll.

Before making a third toast to Virginia's recovery, her father called for more wine. When the glasses were again full, he cheered Quinten Brown. "To the pilot who steered us to Virginia."

Cameron cleared his throat in a sound—a signal—that Virginia remembered from their youth. She looked up. Their eyes met. He winked and, behind his napkin, murmured, "Next he'll toast the carpenter who crafted the ship's wheel."

Virginia struggled to hold back her laughter.

"Cunningham," her father called out. "Are you expected in London, lad?"

Cameron tensed, a crab claw in his hand. Agnes and Mama shared a meaningful glance, then watched him. Virginia grew puzzled.

Cameron took his time chewing. More time passed as he put down the pincher and wiped his hands and mouth. Finally, he said, "I won't know that until I arrive in Glasgow. I hope your trip to Boston is enlightening."

Papa shrugged, but the careless gesture seemed inappropriate, considering Cameron's reaction. "Feel free to go on to London after you've gotten Virginia and Agnes to Napier. Surely your affairs there need attention."

With only a trace of jollity, Cameron said, "You cannot think I'll leave Glasgow without hearing what you encounter in Boston? 'Tis a grand town."

Into the tense moment, Mama said, "I'm told they have a theatrical company that performs an Indian play. I should like to see it."

Although Cameron said nothing, Virginia knew he fought to compose himself. Why? Was it Papa's authoritative tone or his possessiveness toward her? She didn't know, but then she didn't know what events had transpired between them during her absence. In her last year in Scotland, Papa had often separated Cameron and Virginia.

"Would you care for more pie?" Cameron asked her.

At the simple request, a polite grouping of words she hadn't heard in years, Virginia's heart took flight. She'd come through these difficult days, and very soon she'd reclaim her place in Cameron's life. They'd share a jolly laugh over her faked memory loss. "No. I couldn't eat another bite and still be able to breathe in this corset."

Agnes froze, a fork laden with sorrel hash halfway to her mouth. Mama's hand tensed on her goblet. Papa stared at the stuffed pheasants that hung from the ceiling.

Virginia despaired at her conversational error, even

as she wished the words back. How could she be so careless as to discuss her undergarments at table? She knew better. She'd gotten too comfortable with them. Too much laughing, too many tales told in good spirit, too much of the rich, fruity wine.

Only Cameron was unmoved by her mad manners. Putting down his glass, he whispered, "You'll need help getting out of those laces." His gaze darted to her breasts.

He might have said, "That's a nice dress," so casual was his tone. Certainly nothing in the cadence or pitch of his voice suggested anything vulgar. She burst out laughing.

Papa cleared his throat. Cameron grew distant.

Had she hurt his feelings? Surely not, for the bold remark warranted a slap to his handsome face. Unless she, by speaking so frankly, had encouraged him. Was that the case here? She didn't know. "A shilling for your thoughts," she asked him.

He lifted the wineglass to his lips. A dimple appeared in his cheek, and his eyes danced with mischief. "What I'm thinking is worth more than a shilling."

She wanted to know, but another intimacy with him with her family looking on was more than she dared. Later, when she'd stopped wrecking conversations and bringing shame on them all, she'd trade quips and clever rejoinders. Now she used the truth and shielded it in a double entendre. "Perhaps a shilling's worth is all I can afford just now."

He knew what she was saying, for his eyes narrowed. "As an inducement, I'd be prepared to give you three guesses for free."

He'd always been tenacious when he wanted something. Being the object of his determination flattered and frightened her. For both reasons, she chose caution. "And if I don't guess on the third try?"

"I'll have to start charging you."

Virginia strove for composure when she wanted to toss the contents of her glass in his face. He wouldn't look so smug with red wine dripping down his chin and staining his perfectly tied silk neck cloth.

"He's a martinet," Mama said, but she was chuckling.

Agnes tried to engage Papa in a discussion about Napier's new engine, but he only half listened.

"Oh, very well. I'll give you a hint." Cameron leaned close and said, "I *wasn't* thinking about spitting in your hand."

When she was completely aghast, Cameron congratulated himself and said to the table, "I was thinking that the Irish MacKenzies in Boston are in for a surprise."

Virginia relaxed beside him. Agnes gave up her attempt to distract Lachlan, who laughed and said, "The MacKenzies of Boston are Irish and will do as they may."

"Of course they will, my love," said his duchess, "so long as you're buying them whiskey."

His thrifty nature came to the fore. "I'll not beggar us with coin spent in taverns."

"I know." She patted his arm, but devilment glimmered in her eyes. "Where did your kin go wrong, my lord? Why did some of them move to Ireland?"

He smiled affably. "My ancestors scared them off."

Agnes shook her head in mock pity. "There's something to be said for being half Campbell."

Her father pointed a finger at her. "Nothing a full belly can stomach."

Cameron congratulated himself. Theirs was a family suited to gaiety, but he'd noticed a reserve tonight in the duke and duchess and not because of anything that had occurred between Cameron and Virginia. Her parents were hesitant because they knew of Virginia's pretense.

Virginia. Back with them again. With Cameron. Joy spiraled through him, and for the tenth time he wondered if he were dreaming that she was here.

Sitting beside her, he caught an occasional whiff of violets. She'd washed her hair and donned a dress he hadn't seen before. Of pink satin, with bows at the shoulders and lace at the neck, the gown was well cared for, but years out of fashion. He'd like to see her in a rich green velvet with a daring décolletage. He imagined the dress trimmed in creamy lace to compliment her lovely complexion. To accent her shiny auburn hair, he pictured a golden belt draping her narrow waist. A golden sporran, of filigree, studded with emeralds and complete with tiny tassels, should hang from a chain, drawing his attention to her femininity.

At times during the evening he could think of little else save having her. She must have sensed him watching her; she lifted her chin and tipped her head in a way that drew his eye to her elegant profile, and when she rested her hand on his arm, a lightness filled his soul. Feminine to the tiny auburn curls at her temples, she'd always had her mother's grace and her father's command of attention. The best qualities of both of them, Lachlan liked to say. Cameron had to agree.

Turning a little more, she gave him a shy smile. Looking into her eyes, he felt as if he were peering through a keyhole in a door of her own locking. The

Virginia he knew lay behind that door, the Virginia who made no pretense and told no lies. Would she be as he remembered, or had the years hardened her? Had life robbed them of their destiny or merely postponed it?

The latter, he hoped.

"Have I cobwebs in my hair?" she asked. "Or are you looking for new ways to bedevil me?"

At her spunky questions, her family laughed. "That's my scrapping lassie," boasted her father.

Cameron shined up his charm. "In answer to both of your queries, definitely not. You look lovely."

She thought of a stinging retort, her eyes told him so, but she demurred and thanked him.

Lady Juliet said, "Virginia plans to make the acquaintance of Horace Redding when she gets to Glasgow."

"Redding?" Lachlan looked from his wife to Virginia.

"The revolutionary scholar," Cameron supplied, anticipating a battle even as he said it.

Her father slammed down his glass. "Troublemaker. He lost his last audience when the colonies prevailed. So he brought his angry pride to Scotland. Heed me well. Sheriff Jenkins will deal with him."

Agnes scoffed. "With more success than the good sheriff has had in the past, one can hope. Jenkins couldn't keep order in a monk's colony."

Lachlan pointed at Virginia. "You stay away from Horace Redding."

Cameron hoped she'd protest, same as Lachlan's other daughters would have balked. But Virginia looked puzzled. She turned to Cameron. "Scotland has forsaken self-rule?"

A very interesting question from a woman who

could not remember her heritage. But she had mentioned reading the newspaper. "Nay."

As if they'd forgotten something basic, she said, "That is Redding's philosophy, self-rule."

"True, but it matters not, for your father has made somewhat of an enemy of Redding."

"Oh." She took a long sip of wine. "I'm sorry to hear that. I thought—"

"Don't be getting your temper up over it, lass." Her father's placating tone took the sting out of the words. Or was Virginia so encumbered by the facade that she wouldn't stand up for herself?

Cameron detected no anger in her. Following a lifelong compulsion to help her, he addressed her father. "Your grace, shouldn't we hear what Virginia has to say? You interrupted her."

Lachlan scowled, a reaction he would have condemned in others, but his heart and his pride were engaged.

"Cameron's right," Juliet said, giving Virginia a smile of encouragement. "Finish what you were going to say, dear."

Virginia pressed her napkin to her lips and spent a long time folding the cloth. "I'm not angry. I'm just disappointed."

That honesty captured her father's attention. "Why, lass?"

"For two reasons, Papa." She faced him squarely. "First, because I didn't expect to disobey you so soon. Second, because I had hoped you'd understand my side of it." To everyone at the table, she said, "I haven't lived in Scotland in ten years, and most of the time I'm not sure I lived there at all."

Cameron held his breath. Lachlan knew she was lying, and he was angry over her patronage of

Redding. Combined, those things might be enough to make Lachlan forget himself and challenge her. Hopefully not, for they had years to learn the why behind Virginia's lies.

Lachlan picked up the goblet and waved it to the table at large. In his legendary, good-natured way, he said, "That Warwickshire poet would have us believe that the pen is mightier than the sword." He rested an elbow on the table, and as if revealing a confidence, his voice dropped. "But not in any battle that I know of."

Agnes laughed, and her humor acted as a spark for the others, except Lady Juliet, who tried to hide a yawn.

"Find our bed, love," Lachlan said. "I'll just have a wee stroll with Cameron and then join you."

She kissed his cheek. "Come, Agnes and Virginia."

The women moved to rise. Cameron got to his feet and pulled out Virginia's chair. "Shall I have a maid awaken you?"

"No, I'm an early riser."

As she followed her mother and Agnes down the hall, Cameron remembered what Lachlan had said about not having the courage to find out if Virginia answered to another name. To test it, he called out, "Duchess."

Both Virginia and Juliet turned.

"Yes?" said the duchess of Ross.

Virginia bowed her head and examined her hands.

Behind Cameron, the duke spat a curse and whispered, "Bless the saints, they robbed her of her name."

With heartfelt regret, Cameron knew the cooper hadn't lied.

"Did you want something?" the titled duchess asked.

"Just to say good night, your grace," Cameron said. "And have a safe journey to Boston."

"Thank you, lad. Take good care of our Virginia."

He willed Virginia to look up. To his relief, she did, and when their eyes met, he said, "I shall." Tonight he intended to set the tone for the voyage home. Once she arrived in Glasgow and the MacKenzies descended on her, she'd need Cameron; she just didn't know it yet. But he wouldn't be a pawn; he'd be her lover. He wouldn't hold her hand, not without her heart and her soul.

As soon as he'd conferred with her father, Cameron intended to delve deeper into Virginia MacKenzie, but he'd have to visit the kitchen first.

Virginia dabbed witch hazel on the scratches the kitten had inflicted earlier in the day. Mama always traveled with a chest of medicinals. When the time presented itself, Virginia would acquire her own. She'd have a fine chest made. She'd purchase Fanny Ludstrom's book as a guide to growing and concocting her own medicinals. One day she'd pass the chest to her own daughter.

Alone in the confines of her room at the inn, Virginia dropped the facade. No lies here. Just her, free and happier than anyone had a right to be, especially a child torn from those she loved.

She thought of Saffronia again, the woman who had given Virginia her first wad of rags for her woman's time. In anticipation of her next menses, she'd acquired new cloths today. Picking up her brush, she couldn't resist grooming her hair again. The fine bristles tickled her scalp and brought a shine to her hair.

Her brush. Her dresses. Her comb and mirror. Worldly possessions, but they were hers and stood as tangible proof that she could get her life back. Her heart grew light, and she thought she might fly around the room, touching every item she possessed.

Instead, she buttoned her nightgown, gave the kitten a good-night pat, and went to the window. Her room faced a darkened alley, but if she laid her cheek against the glass, she could see activity on the next street over. Freeing the latch, she opened the window and leaned outside. The air smelled of the sea and the city, and she could hear the voices of drunken men and sultry women.

A weight pressed in on her, and she slumped beneath it, her hands clutching the edges of the window frame. She knew what troubled her. She had foolishly thought that her problems would end once she left the plantation, but with sad acceptance, she understood that she hadn't come alone to Norfolk; loneliness had traveled with her.

Tears filled her eyes, and she had to bite her lip to hold back a sob. She'd been a strong child. When last her family had seen her, she'd been decisive. Because of her lie, she must keep herself apart from them.

Closing the window, she climbed into bed. She had just fluffed her pillow for the tenth time when a knock sounded at the door. She grabbed her tartan shawl, lit the candle on the desk by the door, and went to see who was there.

Cameron stood on the threshold, a pail and saucer in one hand and two tankards in the other. His expression sharpened. "You've been crying."

"I couldn't sleep," was the best excuse she could think of. "What have you there?"

His mood brightened, and he clicked his heels together in military fashion. "Lemonade for us and milk for Hixup."

He'd exchanged his formal evening clothes for his tartan kilt. He wore the same shirt and silk neckcloth; the latter was still perfectly tied. Dressed casually, he looked different and yet the same. One thing was certain; he didn't look the least bit sleepy.

All she could think to say was, "Hixup?"

"The kitten. 'Tis a better name for a ship's cat than Mermaid or Balthezar."

"Ship's cat? I thought you gave her to me."

"Then we should discuss it. May I come in?"

Again she was captured by the sound of good manners. Before she remembered propriety, he shoved the mugs into her hands and walked straight to the basket where the kitten slept.

As if he were talking to an old friend, he chatted to the little cat, picked her up, and held her nose over the pail. The mewling kitten tried to dive into the milk.

"Whoa!" He separated the two. "I'll need some help here, Virginia." He pressed the cat to his chest. The wiry, hungry animal scurried up his shoulder and down his arm to get back to the milk. With no hint that he'd been hurt by those needlelike claws, he said, "Close the door, so we don't lose her."

Virginia did as he asked, then took the pail and saucer from him.

He sat on the floor. She sat beside him and poured the milk. The instant Cameron put the cat down, it raced to the saucer and began to drink.

"You bathed the cat."

"She stank of fish. I couldn't keep her here smelling like that."

She'd always taken responsibility for her pets.

"Have you news for me?" she asked.

"I thought you might be worried or frightened about the voyage."

Any reservations she had about returning to Scotland paled beside the knowledge that she'd welcomed him into her bedroom. But it was too late for regrets. She'd let him stay for a few minutes, then she'd ask him to leave. "What should I be worried about?" The fear she'd keep to herself, for it mingled with the loneliness.

He handed her a mug and drank deeply from his own. "We'll be at sea for weeks, and there's little privacy."

Life in bondage had prepared her for that. "I'll be fine."

"Unlike your sister Mary, you've never suffered from seasickness. In case you were wondering."

A woman with little memory should have considered the aspects of a long voyage. "I hadn't thought of that." To cover the mistake, she drank the sweetened juice.

"No?" He scratched the kitten behind the ears. "What have you been thinking of?"

Of how dear he is to me, she wanted to say. Of how precious was every moment spent in his company. Hope for the future kept her silent about her feelings for him, but she couldn't resist scooting closer. "I was wondering what you and Papa talked about—on your walk?"

As if he were merely tossing out words, he said, "The voyages, the port of Boston . . . the mundane."

Following his lead, she kept her tone light. "He was certainly insistent about you going on to London. Were you bothered by that?"

"Was I bothered?" He shook his head. "Nay."

Niceties forgotten, she huffed and sent him a look rife with tried patience. "Liar."

Light from the single candle illuminated only half of his face, but his gaze was steady, probing. "Because he wants to keep you away from me. He wants to rule your life."

Now they were getting somewhere. "Then why is he going to Boston and sending me to Glasgow with you?"

The vulnerability of the words clashed with the intimacy glowing in his eyes. His interested gaze wandered over her hair, which was only a little longer than his.

Her pulse raced and her thoughts drifted to the romantic.

They were both beset with a passion neither could hope to deny.

He couldn't resist touching her; she couldn't deny him.

The cat meowed, breaking the spell. Virginia added more milk to the saucer. "We were discussing my father."

Cameron reached for her. "Let's not."

She leaned back. "Let's do."

He dropped his hand. A slight hesitation preceded a shrug. The end of his tartan, a rectangle of cloth wrapped and belted at his waist, slipped from his shoulder. "You said you wanted to go to Glasgow rather than to Tain."

He danced around the question, but she was determined to have an answer. "If he's so determined to rule my life, why give in to my wishes?"

"He's no ogre, and if you recall, he told me to go straight to London."

"Do you have important business matters there?"

"Didn't I mention that my father sits in the Commons?"

If he could be obtuse, she could be coy. "Oh? Have they changed the session dates?"

"How would you know if they had?"

She prayed for patience. "Remember the *Virginia Gazette?*"

"Of course." On a self-deprecating laugh, he patted her hand. "Forgive me."

His winning ways had probably gained him absolution for much greater blunders. She'd drop the matter of his business interests in London for now, but a long voyage awaited, and she'd have plenty of time to question him. She chose a more immediate subject. "I wondered how I should dress aboard ship."

Quietly, his attention on the kitten, he said, "Did you?"

He sounded so very interested, and it pleased her greatly. She could wait and ask Agnes in the morning, but Cameron was here and he obviously wanted to chat. She touched his tartan-covered knee. "Yes. Will I be comfortable in my fancy dresses?"

His gaze slid to her hand. "You have always been at ease with me, no matter the circumstances." Her palm grew damp and her hand trembled, but she could not take it away. "But to answer your question about what to wear, you will be more comfortable in modest clothing, or if you're game, you could wear seaman's breeches."

She'd shamed Agnes and her family at the table with bad behavior; Virginia had no intention of doing it again. "What will Agnes wear?"

"Lottie created a feminine version of seaman's pants." He wiggled his brows. "Very revolutionary."

"Sounds perfect for me. I know all about revolutions."

He chuckled. "Aye, you do."

Like a new bridge spanning a river of time, the companionable moment soothed and inspired her to say, "But Agnes is much smaller than I am. I shan't be able to wear her revolutionary wardrobe."

"I'll find you something comfortable."

Her recently acquired independence asserted itself. "I have money."

He looked up and gave her a bland smile. "Money from your mother?"

She moved her hand. "From my wages."

"You won't need to spend it on seaman's breeches. I keep an assortment of garments in the purser's closet. You'll need your sewing kit."

He went back to stroking the kitten. As she had on many occasions since his arrival, Virginia watched him but felt detached from the scene, as if she were dreaming that she and Cameron Cunningham sat crosslegged on the floor discussing everyday things.

Again, he looked up. "That's an interesting smile."

She flushed, feeling like a window peeper who'd been discovered.

"Give me your hands." When she did, he curled his fingers into hers. "Promise me something, Virginia."

At the gentleness in his tone, she grew wary. "I don't think we should—"

"Just hear me out." He squeezed her hands and

185

haltingly said, "If you are ever afraid, swear that you'll call out for me."

Her throat grew thick with love for him, and words wouldn't come.

"I'll be there to help you." Leaning close, he pressed his cheek to hers. His breath was warm against her ear, and he smelled of an exotic spice she couldn't name. "If bad memories or frightening times from your past come back to you, promise you'll tell me. We'll face them together."

A sob broke through. He embraced her, lifted her, and set her on his lap. Without the cumbersome corset and heavy dress, she felt the heat and strength of him through the cotton nightgown.

"You don't yet realize," he went on, "how completely you can trust me. Sharing all things . . . pain, joy, pride at a job well done, was ever our way."

This man was her Cam, and nothing would do but to feel his lips on hers again. At the first touch of his mouth on hers, her head spun and she grew breathless. Yet she couldn't get enough of him, couldn't get close enough, couldn't quench the thirst of a decade spent without him.

She couldn't tell him the truth, not in words, but her body couldn't lie. Comfort came with that understanding, and she deepened the kiss, the way he'd taught her, the way they had always planned. Hadn't he said that she talked too much? Yes, and if she could not say what was in her heart, she could show him.

Her decision pleased him, for he growled low in his belly, and the sound vibrated against her, setting off a hollow ache deep inside. Her hands shaped his head, then brushed his ears and his cheeks. The slight stubble she found there tickled her palms. Inspired, she threaded her fingers through his hair. The ribbon tie at his nape slipped free, sending his hair cascading to his shoulders.

With an insistence and power that promised an end to her yearning, he brought her to the edge of a swoon. He trailed kisses over her cheek, down her neck and lower. How had her gown become unbuttoned? When his warm breath touched her breast and his lips closed over her nipple, she didn't care how he'd gotten there; she only prayed that he would not stop. At his gentle suckling, she couldn't hold back a moan.

He moved to her other breast and lavished it, suckling, licking, and priming her for what she did not know.

Contentment settled like a blanket over her, but with the happiness came a new need, a yearning to crawl inside his heart and curl up for a lifetime. She felt real desire, not the breathless, romantic urgings of her youth, but the deep, sensual longing of a woman for her man.

The drag of his palm against her inner thigh felt heavenly, and her knees trembled, but when he touched her intimately, she froze. Old horrors rose to meet her. She squeezed her legs together to force him out. "No. Don't touch me there."

He withdrew his hand, and his mouth left her breast. Tenderly, he cradled her against his chest and rocked her. "I'm sorry, Virginia."

He'd gotten it wrong. The fault lay with her and the degradation she'd endured. If unburdening herself would better their circumstances, she'd trip on the words to tell him. Only Merriweather had known the extent of Virginia's suffering, and it had taken almost two years for the pity to leave his eyes. But no civil man, least of all a lover, could countenance the perversions of her life at Poplar Knoll.

Still, she owed him some gentling words. "I'm to blame, not you."

"Has someone hurt you? A man?"

He thought the greatest harm to a woman must come from the male of the species. He was wrong. Women could be heartless to their own kind; Virginia had learned that lesson firsthand. At a time when men ruled the world, women should help each other; they should be mentoring sisters, doting aunts, and loving mothers, not twisted villains eager to mete out the cruelest blows. Shared vulnerability of the weaker sex should be a catalyst for trust and honor, not a license to hurt and betray. But there it was.

"Don't be afraid, Virginia. Tell me about it."

"It's vague. I'm not sure." Nor did she want to think about past betrayals.

"You probably don't recall this, but years ago, while we were riding, my horse pitched me into a bramble patch. You pulled thorns from my bottom for hours. I never once worried that you'd tell anyone how often I yelped in pain."

She had cried along with him that day. He'd stripped off his breeches, giving her her first look at a naked male. Her youth and the crisis they faced had given great innocence to the event. But there was nothing innocent about the way his hands roamed over her.

"You were always my true heart," he whispered.

At the betrothal ceremony, as he'd slipped the ring onto her finger, he'd teasingly said, "No more swooning over other beaus. You are my true heart, and I'm the man for you. The only man."

Not until his arrival in Virginia had she received her first kiss, for the peck on the cheek he'd given her years ago hardly counted. She hadn't imagined passion, certainly not the churning ache that spread to her loins and melted her resolve.

"What pleasantry occupies you?" he asked.

"I was thinking that resolve is much overrated, no?"

His eyes gleamed with happiness. "Especially 'tween you and I. And that frown on your brow must go." He kissed her there, then studied his handiwork. "That's better."

In the next kiss, he made chaste work of what had gone before. She felt caught up, drawn out, by his loving. The strength of his embrace and the absolute serenity he inspired made her want to shout out loud, but other more physical needs beckoned.

Following his lead, she let her hands roam his chest and arms, and when her fingers again slipped into his hair, he eased her back onto the hearth rug. With a slight jerk, he untied his neckcloth. The ends of the silk trailed over her. "Unbutton my shirt."

Captured by his dreamy gaze, she lifted her arms and slipped the pearl buttons free.

"Touch me."

A mat of downy hair fanned his chest and cushioned the pads of her fingers. But beneath the softness lay muscles taut from the strain of holding himself above her.

"Come here," she heard herself say.

He lay full upon her, their loins nestled. Against her leg, she felt his desire, insistent and boldly male. As she lay beneath him, a decade of failed hopes and tarnished dreams vanished like the stars at dawn.

A volley of sensations exploded in her mind, and when her hands circled his neck and discovered the drumbeat of his pulse, the rhythmic pounding found an echo in her woman's core. He tilted his head to the side, opened his mouth on hers, and sought entry. She let him in, and the gentle stabbing of his tongue matched perfectly the thrusting motion of his hips.

Desire rang in her ears and thrummed in her belly. Her hands curled into fists.

"Ouch!"

She'd pulled the hair on his chest. At the dreamy look in his eyes, she said, "Have I hurt you?"

His smile was shy, knowing, and he lifted his brows. "Yes, and I know just the treatment. Come with me."

He got to his feet and held out his hand. She let him pull her up.

"Close your eyes."

She did. Then he was kissing her again, only his lips touching her. He seemed so restrained, so in control, while she teetered on the edge of something fine. Eager to discover it, she slid her tongue against his and kissed a groan from him.

She heard the rustle of clothing, the slip-slide of his leather belt, and as his tongue twined with hers in a daring, sensual dance, she swayed. Seeking balance, she reached for him, and her hands met warm, naked skin. Rather than shock, the discovery inspired her, and she traced the breadth of his shoulders and the strength of his arms. Cool air touched her knees, her thighs, and he broke the kiss long enough to pull off her gown. Then he enveloped her, their bodies touching from lips to toes and a hundred more interesting places in between.

The hair on his chest tantalized her nipples, and the length of his desire rested hot and heavy on her belly. She felt damp and empty for him, but he knew that, for he sent his hands roaming her back and lower, cupping her bottom and pulling her closer. When he undulated against her, she went languid inside.

He scooped her up and with an ease that contrasted sharply with her own sense of urgency, he strolled to the bed.

"Turn back the covers."

Lowering her, he waited until she'd moved the blanket, then he laid her down and followed, his loins finding hers. "Spread your legs."

Images of the doctor and the cold marble table came to mind. She cringed and said the word she'd been forbidden to utter at Poplar Knoll. "No."

"No? I thought you wanted me."

The burr in his voice had a soothing effect, but the memories were too much a part of her. "I won't be forced."

"Forced? It's me, Cameron."

He kissed her again and murmured lovers' phrases in Scottish. Hearing the romantic endearments in the language of her youth banished all thoughts except those of him.

"Open for me."

Had he asked, she would have stood on her head, so desperate was she to have him. Then he was pushing inside her, pressing her into the feather mattress, and she wanted to cry for the sheer joy of it. But he was moving too slowly, so she lifted her hips to hurry their joining.

A searing pain stopped her.

He pulled back. "Easy, love."

Virginia held her breath, and the pain ebbed. "What's wrong?"

"'Tis your maidenhead."

She'd been so caught up in the passion, so desperate for his loving, she'd forgotten about her innocence. That in itself should have been the first step toward healing old wounds. Hoping it was so, she whispered,

"Please don't stop, Cam. I want to be rid of it." Truer words had never passed her lips.

"Very well." Clutching her hips to hold her still, he pushed forward, and before she could draw breath, he broke through that barrier. Even muffled against his shoulder, her groan of discomfort sounded very loud.

"'Twill pass, love, and never come again. I swear it on my soul."

Filled with him, she held on tight and waited. In the interim, he kissed her deeply, rekindling her desire until she was again breathless with yearning. He moved again, and from that moment on, he took her on a blissful ride to a destination so glorious she went weak with the joy of it. An instant later, her passion burst in a series of tiny explosions.

In the aftermath, she learned the true meaning of euphoria, a satisfaction that permeated even the darkest corners of her soul. But when Cameron tensed above her, then joined them fully one last time, she felt his release, felt him touch her womb, heard him moan in pleasure. Or was it exhaustion? His chest heaved and his breath rasped against her ear.

"Are you all right?"

She'd never be the same, and for that gift, she turned and kissed his cheek. "Yes, I'm—divine."

He chuckled, rolled to his back, and drew her to his chest. Still breathing raggedly, he hugged her tight. "Good, for I almost botched it."

"Why would you say that?"

He didn't want to answer; she could feel his hesitation, but now was not the time for lies. "The truth, Cam. Tell me the truth."

As if the words were dragged from him, he said, "You said you wouldn't be forced. I thought you had been raped. I was wrong."

A reasonable deduction from a man who'd thought she'd been raped but then breached her maidenhead. "No." Comparing what had been done to her to the passion they'd just shared was like matching pigs to patriots.

"Curse me," he hissed. "I should have known better."

Completely puzzled, she strained to look up at him. "Known better than what?"

With a self-mocking laugh, he pulled her back. "To discuss rape at a moment like this."

"My hunch is you were glad I wasn't taken against my will."

"That would be foolish, for you *were taken* against your will. Never would you have run away from Scotland or me."

Like a cold wind, guilt swept through her. But she must think of him, of his pride. "I'm back now, and that's all that matters."

"What of justice for those who wronged you?"

She knew of whom he spoke, but there was plenty of blame to pass around, beginning with a cocky ten-year-old girl.

"Virginia?"

Caught off guard by the yearning in his voice, she said, "Who is to say he is still alive?"

"He?"

She'd erred, but the circumstances didn't lend itself to cleverness. "Or they."

"More than one person abducted you?"

Like standing too close to a fire, she felt the burn of shame. The coward in her urged her to pretend sleep, but a yawn was all of the deceit she could manage. The moment was slipping away, and she fought to hold on to the intimacy a little longer.

A light rapping sounded at the door. The latch clicked. Her mother stepped inside, an artist's tablet in her hands, a blank look of surprise on her face.

Virginia struggled between embarrassment and self-condemnation. Mama was dressed as she had always been when she came to tell Virginia good night. Wearing a belted night robe, her braided hair draping her shoulder, she held the door open and leaned into the room. "I'll just put Mary's sketches of the family here." As she slid the tablet onto the desk, she sent Cameron a look rife with disappointment. Virginia, she did not look at.

Then she was gone, and with her, she took the remnants of joy. Next came a lengthy pause filled with only the sound of breaths exhaled in relief and hearts pounding in surprise.

Tormented, Virginia shrank away from Cameron.

"Nay." He pulled her back. "You mustn't be ashamed of what has gone between us. We've done nothing wrong."

But she had. With only a little imagination, she pictured what her mother had seen: a once-favored daughter lolling wantonly, naked, in the arms of a man she wasn't supposed to remember. What better behavior could be expected from someone who spoke vulgarities at table and lied at every turn? From a girl who'd cleaned the privy to earn a sliver of precious soap? Where would she go from here? The consequences deluged her, but she had to ask, "What if she tells Papa?"

"She will not, because she knows he'll forego Boston and blame me."

"It wasn't your fault. I wanted you."

"I'll tell him so when his business is done and he returns to Glasgow."

She needed to think, to be alone. "You should go."

He turned her to face him. His hair was mussed, and in his eyes a trace of shared passion lingered. "I should stay."

Clutching the remnants of her pride, she managed a smile and foraged for a warm reply. "What if Papa comes in the morning to bid me farewell?"

He gaze turned hard, probing. "I'm not fooled, Virginia."

He was too serious and she was too uncertain. "But you will go lest I ravish you again."

With little humor in the sound, he chuckled. "You can bet your dowry that we'll revisit that issue often in the days to come. You're mine, true heart. You have always been."

Chapter

10

～

On the first day out of Norfolk, just as the sun made a dash for the horizon, and Cameron took his watch at the wheel, he began his quest for a truth from Virginia.

"Cameron's right," Agnes said from her perch on the hammock. She lounged crosswise on her stomach, and with her foot, she kept the string bed in motion. "Since the day we fetched you from that plantation, we've told you stories about our lives. You know everything about us."

Virginia, sitting on one of the six freshwater barrels that were lashed to the mast, paused in her needlework—embellishing the plain nightgown he'd stripped off her last night. She was embroidering thistles around the hem. "I hardly know everything."

She hadn't forgotten that the thistle was the natural symbol of Scotland. Cameron had questioned her about that; she'd cited the embellishments on one of

Agnes's dresses as the source. But she'd become an expert at talking her way out of verbal traps. Not tonight.

He'd trade his flagship for an hour's worth of honesty from her. He couldn't stop thinking about her, couldn't forget the taste and feel of her, the perfection with which she fit against him, the grace with which she'd yielded her innocence. He couldn't put to rest the feel of her naked beneath him, wanting her again.

But she didn't want him, nor did she remember their passion. If her demeanor were a sign, she hadn't shared the greatest of intimacies with him last night.

Patience dwindling, passion running high, he pressed her. "Tell us about the friendships you made at Poplar Knoll."

"You know Merriweather. We shared the newspaper and discussed events of the day. After his wife died, he left England and became a reader of the news. He . . ."

Cameron stopped listening. She wasn't sharing events of her life; she chronicled the adventures of a butler. Agnes didn't see through the ploy; she was too enthralled at having Virginia back.

"Tell me about your butler," Virginia said to her sister.

Agnes took the bait.

Cameron ground his teeth and turned his attention to the ship and the sea. A strong southeasterly breeze carried them briskly across the Atlantic. If the winds prevailed, they'd reach Glasgow before the stores grew moldy.

On the deck, the yellow and white kitten batted a ball of twine. Steam from a caldron of fresh turtle soup perfumed the ocean air. The day crew had gone below deck; the night watch went quietly about their duties.

All was well on the *Maiden Virginia* except the maiden herself.

How could she act as if nothing had happened last night? Like a loose topsail, flapping at predictable intervals, the annoying question kept coming back to annoy Cameron.

When Agnes began a story about her children's dancing master, Cameron's patience snapped. "Oh, please," he said, "can we get to the stable boy's sleeping habits and be done with it."

Virginia knotted her fists, but she didn't look up.

Agnes shot him a withering stare. "My, my, aren't we testy today?"

"She's done it again—led you on a conversational goose chase." Because she refused to look at him, Cameron added, "All we know about her is what we discovered last night."

That got her attention. She tried to glower at him, but fresh embarrassment spoiled the effect. "Last night I made a glutton of myself on Mary Bullard's trifle. The excitement of the evening dwindled from there."

She could bite, he decided, but so could he. "So you enjoyed the trifle. Was it your first?"

The instant she grasped the double meaning, her mouth tightened. "And my last until I find one that sits better with me the next day."

His pride stinging, Cameron retaliated. "What about the painter? The woman who moved to Kentucky."

She pricked her finger. "You mean Duchess, the bond servant?"

The hammock stilled. "Cameron, I doubt she made friends with a bond servant."

Unwittingly Agnes had again driven Virginia to retreat. Cameron would have none of it. "Put that way, Agnes, I doubt she'll admit it." With remarks like that for incentive, Virginia would keep her secrets.

Agnes worried her bottom lip. "Right again, Cameron."

Virginia put away her sewing. "Duchess and I were friends. Her father was the overseer."

Agnes spat an expletive. "A man indentured his own daughter? He should be skinned with a dull, salty knife."

As if she were explaining the difference between cotton and wool, Virginia said, "Not all men are honorable, certainly not that overseer."

Had the overseer been cruel to Virginia, or was he too a figure of her imagination? For a certainty, some man had hurt her. "Was he unkind to you?"

Reaching up, she extinguished the lantern. "I did not know him."

Not an answer, but her tone held no loathing, and she smiled, further confusing Cameron. "Yet you befriended his daughter."

Agnes fairly preened. "The MacKenzies are always hospitable and charitable."

Virginia's smile was as sunny as the day had been. "At the time, I did not know that I was a MacKenzie. Charity did not enter our friendship. We were the same age; it was natural that we become friends."

A gust of wind from the north sent the sails flapping. Cameron adjusted his course. Virginia turned her face to the breeze and watched the crewmen trim the sail.

Determined to delve deeper, Cameron said, "You never suffered a cruelty at Poplar Knoll?"

"Oh, yes." She rolled her eyes. "Every time the chimneys were swept. We had to dust and scrub for days afterward."

He decided she could make light work of a revolution. She would not belittle or ignore their intimacy. "What happened to Duchess?" he asked.

Virginia dangled the gown over the kitten; it sprang on spindly legs and latched onto the cloth. "She was fortunate. She caught the eye of a visiting glazier, a freeman. He came back for her when her indenture ended. They were wed at Poplar Knoll and moved to Pennsylvania."

Aha! She'd mispoken. If she talked about herself using the guise of another person, she could at least tell the truth. "Pennsylvania?" he asked. "I'm certain you said they went to Kentucky."

She watched him so closely he wondered if she could read his mind. "By way of Philadelphia, where he had yet to complete a commissioned work. Then they moved to Kentucky, where there's no taxes and plenty of land, but only for those with hearty spirits."

If that was meant as an insult to Cameron, it fell short of the mark. "Phrased so romantically, I'm tempted to go there myself."

"I'm sure they will welcome you."

And she did not, that much was clear. He had news for her. "I'd resolve to repay them in kind, but as I recall, you would not. In your mind, resolve is much overrated."

If a look could cut, he'd be sliced to ribbons. Virginia turned to her sister. "Would you go there, Agnes?"

200

"To avoid taxes? I'd be tempted."

Virginia embraced the topic. "The colonists revolted over taxes."

She did not include herself but spoke of the Americans as other people.

Sounding like the last great scholar, Agnes said, "All wars are fought over money or wealth or the rule of it."

"Precisely," Virginia replied, rescuing the gown from the kitten's sharp claws and completely ignoring Cameron. "Better the money stays here than go to England."

In a smooth move that did not upend the hammock, Agnes got to her feet. "English expansion allowed Cameron to trade in China."

He wouldn't be baited by Agnes MacKenzie Napier; he intended to get rid of her. "A willingness to lose all to pirates and foul weather allows me to trade with other lands."

Agnes grinned and snatched up the kitten. "With a prince's wealth for prize, which you quickly spent on the purchase of that mansion in Glasgow."

That made him chuckle; Napier House was grand by the standards of royalty. "Me, own a mansion?"

Virginia eased off the barrel and edged toward the bow. Cameron cursed himself for once again allowing her to steer the conversation away from herself. He called her back. "You'll be glad to know that one of Agnes's finest qualities is her sense of knowing when she's gone far enough to regret it. Good night, Agnes."

"Now you just wait a minute." Agnes marched up to him. "I won't be sent off to bed by you." In a quieter voice, she said, "Sweeten your disposition or I could make a slip of the tongue that you will regret."

She meant his affair with Adrienne Cholmondeley. He could make Virginia understand; she wasn't naive. She was also moving back to her spot near the barrels.

If Agnes persisted, he'd threaten to tell the world that he caught her disheveled and deflowered the morning after with a naked earl of Cathcart. "Let's speak of happier times, Agnes. Like the first time I saw you in Napier's laboratory."

Through narrowed eyes, she glared at him. "You're a wretch."

She could curse him in any tongue, so long as the words prefaced her exit. To that end, he feigned confusion. "I doubt Mary would even be interested."

Real anger flashed in her brown eyes. "A man might think twice."

Into the heated moment, Virginia said, "Please don't quarrel."

Ignoring the protest, Agnes scowled. "Pardon me while I launder my small silks." She smiled at Virginia, then moved to the hatch.

Cameron couldn't help himself; she was leaving them alone, and quarreling with Agnes MacKenzie had been a way of life for too many years. Besides, Virginia remained with him. "Agnes . . ." When she turned, he said, "My tartans could use a wee bit of freshening."

She went still in surprise. In an expression reminiscent of her father, she cocked a warning brow and pointed a finger at him. "Clever repartee does not excuse you of poor manners, but . . ."

He had a plan to busy Agnes, and as captain of this ship, he could expect cooperation from the crew. "But?"

"But it makes you a passing fair traveling companion." She glanced at Virginia, then glared at

202

Cameron. "If you forget yourself with my sister, Papa will want to deal with you."

"There's no chance of that," he said, loud enough for Virginia to hear.

"Stop." Virginia pounded the barrel. "I am not a child anymore, and I resent you—both of you—speaking as if I'm not here. I've lost my memory, Cam, not my pride or my ability to feel."

She'd lost her innocence, and that should be the most precious memory of all. He'd make certain she didn't forget it again. "Agnes and I always bicker," he said. "Were you not here, we'd argue over the color of the sky."

"Cam?" said Agnes, suddenly excited. "Virginia, you called him Cam, not Cameron. Have you remembered something else?"

Time alone with Virginia was ticking away. Cameron cursed his luck; Agnes would not leave them now.

"Yes." Virginia looked up at him. "I've remembered the difference between good and poor behavior."

She was referring to lust and the regret in her eyes was clear. He'd change that. "You remembered good manners at the same moment you recalled my name? How flattering. Tell me every detail. Did my name come to you in a breathy whisper, or did you cry out in the night?"

Agnes spoiled the moment by touching Virginia's cheek. "Be gentle with her, Cameron. She's working very hard to remember, and she needs her rest. You're so pretty. Every eligible nobleman in Europe will want to meet you."

Virginia took the kitten from Agnes, then moved to the companionway. "I'm not a walkabout girl, too naive to resist a charming stranger, titled or not. He might engage my affections for an evening but only that."

He snatched up the challenge before the insult slapped him in the face. If she thought she could ignore him, she was in for the fifth great revelation.

The next day he began an all out campaign to prove her wrong. Getting her alone posed the biggest obstacle. He cornered her in the galley, trapped her near the laundry barrels, and surprised her in the necessary. What did he get for all his careful maneuvering? A knife and a mountain of turnips to pare, shriveled hands and an aching back, and a slap to his face that made him wince when he thought of it.

His frustration grew to dangerous levels.

On the evening of the fourth day out of Norfolk, after Agnes had gone to bed, Virginia decided that the situation with Cameron couldn't go on as it was. She dragged herself up the companionway steps. She must talk to him. They couldn't continue to snap at each other; the insults had begun to hurt.

She'd been overconfident and naive in spite of her earlier declaration to the contrary. She'd forgotten propriety. In a scandalously short time, Cameron had had her naked on her back, crying out his name. She knew better, but she'd confused the young man he'd been with the skilled seducer he'd become. They'd only been acquainted for a few days. The shame of it chipped away at her pride and threatened her confidence, but avoiding him was making the situation worse.

As fair winds carried them across the ocean swells,

and a half-moon bathed the sky in a pearly light, she joined him at the wheel. From below decks came the skirl of the bagpipes as MacAdoo performed his evening concert.

Neither Cameron nor Virginia spoke.

At length, he chuckled.

"What amuses you?" she asked.

"Watching you embroider. As a lass, you swore that patching sails was the closest you'd ever get to stitchery."

Grasping the cordiality, she settled herself on a sea chest. "How did we pass the time aboard this ship, besides patching sails?"

"You haven't remembered that?"

"No, not that, but many things. Events. Moments. I remembered being on board and drawing a map but only that. Not how I came to be on the ship or where we were bound. You were still a boy."

"What passed between us in your recollection?"

"Pleasantries for the most part."

"Once you didn't talk to me for a week."

"I know you better now."

"You know me intimately in case that has also slipped your mind."

She deserved his anger, but he must see her side of it. "You don't understand. Mama saw us." Even as she said it, she cringed inside.

"Did you never interrupt your parents during a delicate moment?"

What did that matter? Having no answer, she fell back on the facade. "I don't know."

"Of course you don't. You only remember in bits and snatches. Be sure to let me know when you remember the bits about our betrothal and the snatches that involve our future. Taken together with your recently yielded maidenhead, 'tis enough to send us scrambling for a church.''

Outraged, she slapped her hand on the wheel and waited for him to look at her. When he did, she said, "If that is a proposal of marriage, I must decline."

She stomped off and spent the next few days embroidering every garment she could find. A triple row of thistles at the hem and neck of her sleeping gowns. Odd-shaped leaves on her bed linens.

Cameron's anger ebbed, and in its place, confusion ruled. But loneliness was also a part of him. He missed her. He had vowed to help her, but pride got in the way. That must end.

As was her habit, she came on deck after the watch change, when Cameron was busy at the wheel. To pursue her, he must abandon his post. If he wanted to talk to her, he must call out to her and risk a rejection. Well, he'd never been overprideful for long, not where she was concerned.

"Virginia! Join me. We'll call a truce."

She turned, and in the next instant, her indifference melted to a smile of affection. He watched her stroll toward him, her head high, her long legs a definite allure in seaman's breeches. She wore a kerchief to contain her thick hair, and her MacKenzie tartan draped her shoulders.

"I meant what I said about a truce between us."

"Then tell me what we did on the ship as children."

Patience, he reminded himself. "You drew maps and I helped."

She stepped onto the sea chest and stared at the ocean swells. To the unknowing, she seemed at peace. Cameron knew better. She was simply gearing up for a battle of words.

"You sharpened my pencils?" she said.

"I thought you used ink and quill."

"Did I?"

Her expression was too guileless to hide a lie, or did he simply want to believe her? Either way, they were talking civilly and that was a step. "Yes. Your sister Sarah gifted you with the supplies on your sixth birthday."

"I'd like to see those maps."

"You will. Have you remembered anything else?"

"Yes. I remembered that you owe me twenty pounds."

What an interesting occasion to recall; it had been a merry time and one of the last they'd shared. "Then you remember the wager?"

"Yes."

She'd been nine, he seventeen. She had declared that she could gain entry into a gaming club he had just joined. She'd been reckless with jealousy over it; he'd been outraged as only a cocky youth could be.

"You knew I would dress as a boy and try to get in."

Leaning back, he checked the stars and made a minor correction at the helm. "I didn't think you'd enlist MacAdoo's help and come as the prince of . . . I cannot remember the place."

She trailed her hand over the railing, a fond smile curling her lips. "Valtavia."

"An invented place."

"The doorman believed me, and the patrons bought me brandy."

"Moncrief offered you his mistress."

"That's when I took my leave . . . without your twenty pound forfeit."

"A pleasant recollection, nay?"

"Most assuredly."

He took one hand off the wheel and stepped back. "Do you remember piloting the ship?"

As a girl, she'd stood on a box before him. He'd taught her the names of constellations and the phases of the moon. No longer that lanky lad, he stood at the helm of his ship like a king ruling all he surveyed.

Determined to have a cordial exchange, she stepped in front of him and grasped the wheel.

He tapped the compass, which he used only in poor weather. "Keep her north by northeast."

"I will."

"We shared a pallet on this very deck. Have you remembered that?"

Getting this close to him was a mistake. "Cameron, we are strangers."

"Your memories of us together are fond?"

"Yes, of course."

"Then I think we should make a new memory."

He spun her around and, with a hand around her waist, pulled her against his chest. Before she could draw breath, he kissed her. They swayed in perfect harmony to the movement of the deck. She should break the kiss, stop the seduction, but she'd spent too many lonely nights reliving his embrace and remembering the absolute peace she felt in his arms.

To her surprise, he broke the kiss. "We'll consider that our first kiss."

She didn't know whether to laugh or scoff.

"Are you mocking me?" he demanded.

"Are you expecting me to go along with that ridiculous farce?"

"By all means."

He'd use those means, any means, and although she wanted his love more than she could say, she would not yield to him again. She told him the truth. "You have me at the disadvantage."

Against her cheek, he said, "Having you at all was once a dream to me."

If she didn't keep her wits, he'd steal her last independent thought.

"Before you disappeared, I took you for granted, tragically so."

"We parted badly?"

"I was rude and callous."

She'd been demanding and selfish. Peevish and wilting. Why, then, did he shoulder the blame when she had been at fault? Because he recalled their lovemaking without guilt.

"Nothing will ever hurt you again, Virginia."

He couldn't know that she'd suffered a hundred heartbreaks before reaching Poplar Knoll. Once there, when the cruelties began, she'd begged for the very protection he freely offered. She curled her arms around him. Muscles rippled beneath her fingers as they swayed in rhythm with the movement of the deck.

"You'll be old and haughty before danger again finds you."

Much more of his tender persuasion, and she'd forget her last scruple and fall into his arms. "Haughty?"

"Phrased in nobler terms, I'm sure."

The honesty intimacy in the exchange was new. In her experience people didn't show so much of themselves, but those in bondage had little, save their private thoughts, to call their own. It was another advantage of being free, and she grasped it. "By then, you'll be a master at verbal persuasion."

"I'll have to be, now won't I?"

He might have patted her head, so coddled did she feel. She leaned back and looked up at him. The ocean breeze rippled against her back, but the warmth of the man infused her. Tall and strong, he loomed before her, obliterating visions of the youth he'd been and recalling memories of their loving. His eyes were closed; yet he held the wheel steady and steered into the wind. His lazy grin did dangerous things to her resolve.

To break the spell, she said, "Are we on course?"

He gave her a broad smile and moved closer. "Perfectly."

No artifice there, only outright seduction. She laughed.

He sniffed the air, and his smile faded. "Hold on." With both hands, he gripped the wheel. His legs stiffened. "Haul out the main." Although he spoke softly, the command in his voice was unmistakable.

Holding tightly to him, she glanced over her shoulder. A pair of shadows skittered up the mast. Amid a flapping of canvas, the ship lurched to port. The instant the sails caught the wind, the ship seemed to take flight.

"What is it?"

"Slavers off the starboard bow."

She saw them then, three lumbering shapes illuminated by green lanterns. From the healer, Saffronia, she'd heard the stories of the "death lights" as the lanterns were called. The poor souls, on their way to the living hell of captivity.

"Take the wheel, Virginia."

Eyes misting with sorrowful tears, she said a prayer for the prisoners on board and did as he asked. The wood was warm from his touch. The added sail gave the ship great power, and it took all of her strength and concentration to hold the course. Cameron's arms enveloped her, holding her as if he'd never let go.

"Will you trade that twenty-pound debt for a trip to France? I did promise to take you there."

France. Oh, how she'd wanted to see that place. "Shall we go now?"

"With Agnes for companion? Nay, she hates the French, and they were overjoyed to see the last of her."

To the crewmen, he yelled, "Trim the main." To Virginia, he said, "What makes you smile?"

Surely he couldn't read her thoughts. "Something popped into my head."

"What?"

"Hamish, Margaret, and Catherine." Names they had picked out for the children they would eventually have.

"Hum." Leaning close, he whispered in her ear. "Hamish sounds rather old-fashioned today."

The crewmen hauled in the sails, and the wind died down. The ship slowed. She adjusted their course and gave herself poor marks as a sailor; her instincts were correct, but her technique was sloppy. "We were fanciful children. Much has happened since then. I'm not that girl."

"Oh, aye, you are. You show it everyday."

"How?"

"The expression in your eyes when you look at me. The way you look . . . your appearance."

"I don't at all look the same."

"I would have known you in a crowd of beautiful strangers."

"Tobacco feathers," she scoffed.

" 'Tis true. I also remember your bad habits."

"Name one."

"Turn around."

She did, and when she looked into his eyes, he said, "You talk too much."

He kissed her again, and the commanding tone of the kiss shocked her to her soul. Finding herself yielding to it surprised her more. She should shun his embrace for now, but she couldn't force her heart to slow or her body to still. He compelled her desire, called to the woman and taunted her with the need to be his.

"Now, isn't that more enjoyable than talking?"

"It's an unfair question. If I say yes, you could take it to mean that talking to you is boring."

"Never would I think you meant that."

"You're very sure of yourself."

"If you answer no, how shall I see it? As a lie?"

"No, as clever repartee."

Against her breast, she felt laughter rumble through him. "Agnes put words into your mouth," he grumbled good-naturedly. "I think I should toss her over the side."

"Her husband might take offense at that."

"For my part, I take offense at discussing Agnes at a time like this."

"What shall we talk about?"

"I'd rather kiss you than talk."

Virginia's routine changed the next morning. Only rain and exhaustion drove her below deck. As Cameron looked on, she cleverly questioned her sister about events of the last ten years.

She glided over the deck and tramped up and down the companionway stairs like a frisky doe in a field of clover. She squealed with delight when a school of dolphins frolicked around the ship for the better part of the morning. She was disappointed the next day when they weren't there.

She sat entranced as MacAdoo played the bagpipes. She even sang along when he played the tune "Loch Lomond."

At times Cameron almost forgot that she'd spent a decade in servitude; inexperience more than naîveté fueled her enjoyment of the smallest thing: a passing fleet of Dutch merchantmen, a swift pinnace flying the pennons of the duke of Orleans. Giving credit to Agnes and the stories she told, Virginia pretended to remember events of the past.

Not until they were three days out of Scotland did he succeed in getting her alone.

Chapter

11

∽

At the meridian, his regular time to arise, Cameron emerged from the companionway. Shirtless, he wore a leather vest and seaman's breeches. His hair was damp, his face freshly shaven, and he looked rested in spite of getting to sleep at dawn. As he walked toward her, Virginia noticed a contradiction about him. He swung his arms and hummed a tune, seemingly carefree. But the expression, the set of his jaw, and the dead serious look in his eyes bespoke determination. A man on a mission, she thought. A barefoot man.

"Did you forget your shoes?" she asked.

He stopped, turned out his feet, and wiggled his toes. "I won't need them."

Waving to MacAdoo, who piloted the ship during the day, Cameron said, "Wallace is at his tubs. He'll be bringing the laundry up to dry it."

MacAdoo called up to the lookout in the crow's nest. "Laundry coming up."

The man tucked his spyglass into his belt, slung his boots over his shoulder, and, like a squirrel in an oak, scurried down the main mast.

Beside Virginia, Agnes murmured, "Our captain is certainly decisive today."

Cameron moved about the deck, giving orders and examining every sail and spar. Virginia said, "Must have been his bath."

Agnes whistled. "He's wickedly handsome in this mood."

Cameron and Agnes had spent months together on this ship. Both were openly proud of their friendship. Virginia couldn't resist saying, "More handsome than Edward Napier?"

Love transformed her features. "Edward is . . ."

"Is what?"

She sighed like a lovestruck girl. "Edward is . . . perfect for me. I look at him and my stomach turns to porridge."

Virginia knew the feeling well; she felt it every time she thought about Cameron. When he approached, Agnes nudged Virginia, and in unison, they saluted.

He returned it. "Smartly done, ladies." He glanced at Agnes, then quickly back. "What have you done to your hair?"

She shook her head. "I cut it."

"Why? What will Napier say?"

She rolled her eyes. "I grew tired of envying Virginia her shorter hair, and Napier will say I look lovely."

Cameron mussed her hair, then moved to the water barrels to check the level inside. "Of course Napier will."

The gesture was typical of Agnes's kind nature. No one would look askance at Virginia's unconventional style without insulting Agnes. Once, when Lottie had twisted her ankle and limped, Agnes had hobbled right along with her. But Virginia had not suffered an accident. Shorter hair had been a necessity in her life, for both cleanliness and comfort in the fields. Perhaps now she'd grow it very long, as it had been before bondage.

Cameron clapped his hands and announced. "Cook says we must eat the rest of the chickens tonight." Looking from Agnes to Virginia, he asked. "Who volunteers to pluck?"

Virginia glanced at Agnes, who fidgeted with indecision. "We've also had a bath this morning," she grumbled. "So you do it, Cameron."

He chuckled. "I claim captain's privilege."

Agnes sighed. "Must one of us pluck those poor creatures? And don't say 'tis woman's work. You've never had a woman among your crew, and I haven't dressed out a fowl in years."

Bored from the morning's inaction, Virginia said, "I'll do it."

Cameron stretched. The leather vest rode high, exposing his naked stomach above the ordinary seaman's pants he wore. But the garment was anything but ordinary on him. He must have had them tailored to suit his long frame, for they fit just shy of snugly from the drawstring waist, over his lean hips, to his knees. There they flared to the hem, same as Virginia's and those of the other crew.

Agnes groaned. "Will you stop preening, Cameron."

"What's amiss, Agnes? Do you pine for Napier?"

"I *lament* over vainglorious rogues."

Virginia was drawn into the friendly banter. "Tell all, Cam. Are you a rogue?"

He glanced over his shoulder, where the purser pitched dripping laundry to a man in the rigging, who hung the sheets out to dry.

In anticipation of his answer, Agnes folded her arms in taskmaster fashion.

Affability hung in the air around him. "In MacKenzie terms, I am a rank amateur."

"Hoots!" Agnes laughed, and Virginia did too.

Lachlan MacKenzie's reputation was legend. As a girl, she hadn't grasped the meaning of the implications except to know that women liked her father. As an adult, she understood that before his marriage to her mother, her father had attracted the attention of many women. His rugged good looks and easy charm were only part of his appeal. He loved his children, and all women loved him for that.

Agnes bumped shoulders with Virginia. "Did I not speak the truth about Cameron?"

Since leaving Norfolk, this casual banter was part of their day. Virginia easily joined in. "Was he never the gallant?"

"Oh, aye," she said, "He once rescued me from a disreputable establishment."

Love for both of them swelled inside Virginia. "Where?"

They told her a story more entertaining than any fireside tale. An opium den masquerading as a cutler's shop. A surly clerk who took liberties. An outlawed border Scot turned pirate who ruled an island of colorful rejects and pulled off a daring rescue. A ransom Cameron had yet been called upon to pay.

"After her training in China," Cameron said, "only fools or better fighters put themselves against Agnes MacKenzie."

"You must make him take you there someday. No matter what happens—" As if she'd said more than she should, Agnes halted and looked at Cameron, her expression apologetic.

What had she said and regretted? *No matter what happens.* No matter what happens when? No matter what? Suspicious, Virginia met his gaze and looked for answers. To her dismay, objectivity fled, and she saw a man more dear than her father: Cam, the valiant knight who rescued her from bondage.

"Forget me." Agnes flapped her arms. "I'm not a part of this traveling party."

Cameron closed the distance between them, his legs limber, his gait easy. "As I recall, we chatted at length just before dawn."

Virginia surmised that whatever had gone between them, Agnes had come out the loser. But how? Then Virginia figured out why. "Cameron knows something about you—a scandal—and he's holding it over your head, isn't he?"

Agnes's silence was a small answer.

"Tell me, Cam," Virginia insisted. "What mischief has Agnes done?"

He squatted before them, his confident gaze rested on Agnes. "Shall I tell her?"

The real Agnes surfaced. Her complexion flushed red with anger. "You can tell the king, just don't tell Mary."

As sisters, they'd taught Virginia to prank and bedevil, to forgive and forget. Agnes had always been the leader, but Mary could connive the best.

"You must tell me. I'm completely trustworthy."

"Agnes anticipated her wedding vows."

"No." Virginia thought of the man behind the

machines that modernized the world, the man who put happiness in Agnes's heart. "Edward Napier seduced you."

A completely disgruntled Agnes shot to her feet.

Cameron howled with laughter.

As she passed him, Agnes shoved his shoulder, sending him for a tumble. Quick and agile, he sprang to his feet, crouched low, his palms open, his hands held stiffly in a defensive position. "Care to try that again, countess?"

Tried patience glittered in Agnes's eyes. "You'll be sorry, Cameron."

"Will I?"

She sighed and took up the challenge, giving Virginia her first glimpse of weaponless fighting. They squared off, circling like poorly matched adversaries, for Cameron dwarfed Agnes.

Then she spun on one leg, the other snapping like a whip to kick him in the chest. In a blur of motion, he grasped her foot and flipped her over his shoulder. Blond hair flying, she came to rest on her back, Cameron's knee bracing her body, his elbow poised above her neck.

Thinking he'd hurt her, Virginia jumped up. "Let her go, Cam."

Agnes's eyes bulged in surprise, and she grasped his arm. "Where did you learn that?"

"From Auntie Loo's cousin." Cameron sprang to his feet and extended his arm.

Agnes took his hand and stood. Righting her clothing, she said, "I don't think I like that. Nay, I don't like it a wee bit, but—"

"There's more where that came from." As cocky as a rooster with a new hen, he towered over her.

She marched off, wearing her pride like a mantle.

"Agnes," he called after her, "we'll finish it properly."

Halting, she turned. Grudgingly, she placed her hands on her knees and bowed to him.

He returned the gesture, then waved her off. "Now go and pluck the chickens."

Cameron came back to Virginia. "We'll make port any day now. Would you like to climb to the crow's nest?"

She'd roamed the ship from stem to stern, but she had yet to climb the mast. In her youth, the crow's nest had been her favorite place aboard ship, but she wasn't supposed to know that. "How can you tell how close we are to port?" She waved her arms in a circle. "It all looks the same to me."

He pondered the question. "I suppose instinct best describes it. And there are currents. They run like rivers in the ocean."

She recalled a conversation between him and Quinten Brown during the journey from Poplar Knoll to Norfolk. "Like the Hampton Roads, which aren't roads at all but water?"

His gaze captured her. "Bright lass. In the tidewaters, the currents are smooth and steady. Here, they are swift and powerful."

"Can you see them?"

"Sometimes." He held out his hand. "Climb up with me, and we'll look for one."

He pulled her up with ease, then called for the spyglass. Tucking it into the waist of his breeches, he led her to midship. She preceded him up the mast. They passed crewmen, who were too busy with the laundry to spare a glance. Work in the fields kept her body strong and nimble, and she wasn't even winded when she reached the top.

The crow's nest, larger than a water barrel, seemed smaller than she remembered, but she'd been a child the last time she'd stood up here.

Cameron stepped in beside her. "There." He pointed to a spot off starboard.

In the midst of the ocean swells, she noticed a slight difference in the pattern of the waves. It did look like a river. "Where does it lead?"

"Eventually to the continent of Australia—New Holland 'tis sometimes called."

The penal colony. England's current dumping ground for criminals, seditionists, and those accused of treason. Virginia's stomach soured at the throught. "What's that current's name? Is it famous?"

His arm brushed hers. "You name it."

She considered every nautical term she'd heard during the voyage. "Neptune's Trickle."

He scuffed her head, which was covered by a kerchief. "Well done. Now 'tis famous."

She almost laughed at his gallantry. What had come over him this morning? "Save your charm."

"For who?" He turned, his hip grazing hers. "My betrothed?"

In the narrow space, their bodies constantly touched, but it seemed to Virginia that his elbows brushed her breasts too often and lingered overlong. "As if you've spent the decade chaste."

From below, MacAdoo yelled, "Laundry's afloat."

A ghost of a smile lifted Cameron's lips. "Shall we debate man's primal need for a faithful mate?"

He looked ready to debate Thomas Paine and win; Virginia retreated. "No. It's very selfish and unfair."

" 'Tis a manly thing." He rubbed the edge of her kerchief between his thumb and forefinger.

The fresh scent of his bathing soap mingled with the tangy salt air. Virginia's mouth watered. "How many women have you had?"

"If you wish to know how many women have engaged my affections, I can truthfully say one."

Even in the face of that compliment, she refused to demur. "If I ask you to name the others?"

His smile turned rueful. "I will decline to answer."

Martinet perfectly described him. "I didn't really expect one."

"You brought it up to make trouble between us, because you are confused by your feelings for me."

Meaning the opposite, she said, "You know me so well."

If a look could speak, his expression said, *Better than you think.*

He wouldn't get away with that. "Better trouble between us than ruin."

"That's vague, Virginia. Say what's on your mind."

For weeks, she'd thought about that evening. Awake in her bunk, she'd relived those glorious moments of loving. But the imagining always ended the same. "I can still see Mama's face. I shamed her."

"Nay." A peculiar rumble deepened his voice and his knee brushed hers. "She loves you well."

"I was naked in your arms."

He sighed and lifted his gaze to the sky. "I remember it well."

Flattered and embarrassed at once, Virginia looked out to sea.

"Juliet was your father's lover before they married."

222

According to Papa, Mama was the most honorable woman in Scotland. Virginia huffed. "No."

"Aye." Cameron pulled out the spyglass, and his arm touched her breast. "Ask them. Now that you're older they will tell you. I assure you, your mother wasn't shamed at what she saw. She was sad because she doesn't want to lose you so quickly to me."

A likely view of the situation for him. "Then why not take me to Boston with them?"

He braced his feet apart, bringing his leg in contact with hers, and raised the glass to his eye. "Perhaps she thought you were *engaged* by choice."

Engaged? A benign term for the passion that had passed between then. "You *did* come to my room intending to seduce me. Don't you dare deny it. I just made it easy for you."

In a smooth motion, he scanned the horizon, his chest rubbing against her. "I'm very glad you wanted me, but I have one, small complaint . . ."

"Complaint?" Aghast, her pride reeling, she squared her shoulders, hitting his arm and almost making him drop the spyglass.

"Yes." He leaned into her, tipping her back over the rim of the nest. "You've been keeping secrets from me."

Virginia grew apprehensive. "I have?" What did he know?

He pressed his thighs and his hips against hers. He didn't bother to hide his desire, rather he lifted his brows, pointedly drawing her attention to his arousal. "You didn't think I would see the truth, did you?"

Perched high enough in the air to make an ordinary fellow dizzy, she felt completely secure. And absolutely free. Joy filled her, and she gave up the fight to resist him. "Please don't tell Agnes."

"Why not?" He undulated against her. "She'll understand."

Under the circumstances, only honesty would do. "I'm not ready, Cam. They aren't either. They should get to know me before judging me a wanton."

"They are fair people, and they love you."

She wouldn't be swayed. "I need more time with them."

He turned on the full force of his charm. "And with me?"

Yearning filled her. "I do not recall being dragged up the mast."

His gaze roamed over her face, her neck, and her breasts. "You came willingly with me."

"Oh, very well, yes, I did, but I have one complaint."

Her declaration pleased him. "Complaint?"

"And a bargain. You're too charming by half. If you'll belay some of it, I'll admit to being susceptible to some of it."

He pressed closer. "Only that?"

Her boldness had limits. She grew defensive. "I didn't sail the Atlantic looking for you."

"But you would have come to me"—he leaned full against her until her back arched over the edge of the nest, and he touched his lips to hers—"the moment your memory returned."

Conscious thought fled. He'd brought her to the top of the world. Now he wanted to take her to heaven. She couldn't summon a protest.

He was so close she could count his eyelashes. "Someone will see us."

He tipped his head and glanced over the side. "No. Look at the deck."

She peered over the side and relaxed. The laundry

had been cleverly hung out to dry in such a way that blocked the view of the next from the deck.

"Now look at me."

She did, and the affection glittering in his eyes robbed her of the strength to resist him. But she wouldn't go meekly into his arms. "It does not give you leave to rule my life."

He threw back his head and spread his arms wide in surrender. "Then I give you leave to rule mine."

"For how long?"

Watching her, he opened his mouth to say something serious but changed his mind. Grinning, he said, "An hour or so, I should imagine."

Flushed with embarrassment at both his bold words and what they were about to do, she couldn't resist tickling him.

"Nay, nay." He struggled as he always had.

"You wiggle like a hooked worm."

He grasped her wrists to stop the torment. "You remembered one of our finer moments."

That earned her a languid kiss more sweet than seductive. Just when her thoughts turned to dreamy imaginings, he knelt at her feet and trapped her legs between his. Looking up at her, he slipped his hands under her shirt and splayed his hands over her breasts.

She sucked in a breath. He closed his eyes and smiled as he caressed her.

"Take off that kerchief," he said. "Let the wind have your hair."

She did, holding the scarf into the breeze and watching it flutter. One thought rose in her mind: here they were, she and Cameron and the horizon in every direction.

When his lips touched her belly, the thought fled and she almost lost her grip on the cloth. His palms still kneading her breasts, he used his teeth to untie the drawstring at her waist. His warm breath teased her navel, and she shuddered with anticipation of what was to come.

Abandoning her breasts, he began to ease her breeches over her hips. With each tug on the garment, his lips moved farther down. By the time her thighs were revealed, he was kissing her in a way that set her knees to trembling. She grew dizzy and grasped his head for balance.

"Nay," he said against her most private place. "I've got you." To prove it, he squeezed her waist. "Now fly, Virginia." That said, he devoured her so thoroughly, so erotically, so scandalously, she thought it surely must be a sin.

Beyond protestations, she flung out her arms, and as she let go of the kerchief, she cast every reservation to the wind.

She felt cleansed, so much so, that had he asked her to name the man who'd brought her to Virginia, she would have shouted Anthony MacGowan's name to the heavens. But it was Cameron's name that she called out over and over. She was still saying it when he spread her legs, rose, and, in one smooth motion, filled her.

He hadn't lied when he said she'd feel pain only that first time, for as he began to thrust and withdraw, she begged him for more.

"You're so eager," he said between gasps for air.

In her mind, she fell out of the sky and plunged into ecstacy. On a groan of frustration, he quickened the pace of his thrusts and, heartbeats later, followed her.

Flush with perspiration and the remains of their passion, she felt the wind cool her heated skin.

"Now our betrothal is doubly sealed."

Now who was eager? He couldn't love her yet. He didn't truly know her. His feelings must stem from guilt or obligation. In time, he might love her for herself but not now, not until she told him the truth.

She cleared her throat. "Cameron, it's too quick to reinstate the betrothal. I need time, and don't ask me to choose between you and what I must have." When her parents returned to Glasgow, she'd gather the entire family and explain to them why she lied. But first, she'd find a private place and tell Cameron the truth.

To her surprise and delight, he took the news in good spirit. "You're in luck, then, for I just happen to have an abundance of time where you are concerned. Patience is what I lack."

"Perhaps a trip to London to distract you?"

He smacked his lips. "One delicious distraction is enough, thank you very much."

A trip to London to explain the situation to Adrienne Cholmondeley proved unnecessary for Cameron.

Her carriage awaited them at Glasgow Harbor.

Standing at the rail, Virginia stared at the quay. She thought that short of a prince, the empty carriage must belong to Edward Napier. When asked, a workman on the wharf said the carriage had come to the dock every day at high tide for the last week.

As big as a room, lacquered in black with a golden shield on the doors, and drawn by eight magnificent grays, the carriage was the grandest she'd ever seen.

But then everything here was grand. The ships, the commerce, the constant comings and goings of free people. No slavers made port in Glasgow; Cameron had assured her that was so.

Cameron. Her heart fluttered when she thought of the times they'd shared during the last three days. Just yesterday he'd cornered her near the upended ship's boat. He'd kissed her breathless, and when MacAdoo said a very loud hello to Agnes, Cameron had pulled Virginia beneath the boat. With her sister only steps away, Virginia had mounted Cameron and made love to him. He'd been wild, relentless; she'd felt wickedly wanton, and at the moment of his climax, she had covered his mouth with her own lest Agnes hear them.

The experience had changed Virginia, given her confidence, made her brave. Now her life would change again. Glasgow and her family awaited. Sarah, Mary, and Lottie and their families. Her younger sisters, Lily and Cora, and her brother, Kenneth. Rowena was away in Vienna. From the drawings in Mary's sketch book, Virginia had become familiar with all of their faces. She'd even come to know some of her nieces and nephews.

Agnes, garbed in a glorious red gown and plumed hat, joined her at the rail. Virginia wore her best gown, the modest pink that Cameron favored. Even so, standing beside Agnes, she felt like a wren in the shadow of an exotic bird. No melancholy accompanied the comparison, for one day soon, Virginia would make peace with herself and find her place in Scotland among the MacKenzies.

She nudged Agnes. "Is that your carriage or Lord Napier's?"

"No."

"Then to whom does it belong?"

Agnes turned and let out an ear-piercing whistle, followed by a yelled, "Cameron!"

The ship went silent. Gulls squawked overhead and activity on the other vessels went on as normal, but the *Maiden Virginia* was as still as a tomb.

Below a door slammed, then the hollow stomping of boots sounded on the companionway steps. The hatch doors flew open, and Cameron burst onto the deck. Alarmed, his sleeves rolled up, a pistol in each hand, he paused and followed the line of Agnes's arm.

He uttered a curse, handed the pistols to MacAdoo, and bounded down the gangway. The driver spied him and climbed down. He gave Cameron a letter, which he stuffed into the sash of his tartan. They conversed briefly—Cameron calmly, the driver obviously confused. Hands on his hips, Cameron began a series of instructions, for the driver nodded, listened, then nodded again. That done, Cameron retraced his steps. The driver called out. Cameron stopped and waited while the man reached into the carriage and pulled out a basket overflowing with fruit. Cameron took it, waved the man off, and returned to the ship.

MacAdoo awaited him. Cameron handed off the basket and approached Virginia and Agnes.

Rolling his sleeves down, he said to Agnes, "I asked the driver to stop at Napier House and tell Edward that we have docked."

Virginia knew that Glasgow proper was fourteen miles away. "We should have taken that carriage," she said, "since the driver was going to Agnes's home anyway. We could have saved Lord Edward a trip."

Agnes smoothed the fit of her black leather gloves. "That carriage is already taken."

Spoken without inflection, the words and their meaning confused Virginia. "By whom?"

"Come, my ladies." Cameron fastened the horn buttons at the cuffs of his sleeves. "I've paid the crew. Let us thank them with a toast."

The smell of roses drifted to Virginia. Sniffing for direction, she discovered that the perfume was coming from Cameron. The corner of the letter peeked from beneath his tartan. A scented letter. A carriage that was taken. A basket of fruit.

A woman. But who and what place did she occupy in Cameron's life? From the crest on the carriage door, which Virginia couldn't make out, she knew the woman was of noble birth, not a mistress in the ordinary sense.

If you wish to know how many women have engaged my affections, I can truthfully say one.

He had meant Virginia, she was certain of that. Or had he? She looked up and found Agnes staring at her. So was MacAdoo, but the instant Virginia's eyes met his, he glanced to Cameron. Scanning the others on deck, she found them all watching their captain.

Among the crew, Virginia had made a few friends. Most of the seamen were shy; none of them were sallow faced, as MacGowan's crew had been. To a man, this crew would not have countenanced what had been done to Virginia. These men were husbands, fathers, brothers . . . gentleman all.

And they watched Cameron with what could only be anticipation. For what?

Virginia didn't know, and before she could ponder it longer, Cameron led them below and commenced toasting the voyage. During the casual ceremony, Agnes stayed very close to Virginia. But the moment word came that the Napier carriage approached, Agnes put down her glass and raced to the deck.

Virginia followed but stopped in her tracks at what she saw.

Chapter

12

～

Carriagelike only in that it rolled on very large wheels
and was drawn by horses, be they only two, the round
conveyance moved swiftly through the traffic in the
crowded lane adjacent to the docks. Passersby
gawked. Virginia marveled. The carriage didn't
bounce or sway, teeter or lurch, but whipped around
wagons and drays like a swift pinnace among lumbering battleships.

Perched on the driver's box that wasn't a box at all,
but rather a cushioned shelf, were two boys. As they
came closer, she recognized the younger from Mary's
sketch book. He was Napier's son, thirteen-year-old
Christopher.

The other lad, who was older and unfamiliar to
Virginia, hauled back on the reins. The carriage rolled
to a stop. A pair of doors on the side opened, and a
man stepped out. His hair was pale auburn, and he
wore a blacksmith's apron. He was Edward Napier;

Virginia would have known him anywhere, even without Agnes jumping up and down beside her.

Raising an arm, he waved and called out, "Ho, the *Maiden Virginia* and Agnes."

"Edward!" Agnes yelled back.

As he walked in a brisk, yet careful pace, he held his other hand over a bulge in the bib of his apron.

Agnes hugged Virginia, then took off down the gangway, her plumed hat fluttering as she ran. Agnes was faster, and she reached him before he made it to the quay. He looked down at her with such joy and love Virginia grew weepy. Holding Agnes at his side, he pulled back the bib on his leather apron to reveal a baby. Virginia's heart lurched; Agnes had left her newborn behind. Until now, she hadn't understood or truly appreciated the extent of Agnes's loyalty and unselfishness.

Loyalty and unselfishness, two qualities Virginia had once possessed.

Make amends, her conscience urged.

Once more, she vowed that she would. When her new life didn't seem like a garden maze fraught with thorns and dead-end paths, she'd clean the slate.

Agnes reached for the child, and to Virginia's surprise, Edward held her back and motioned toward the ship. Watching him, a nobleman respected by everyone in America, cradling his child with the ease and confidence of a midwife, Virginia thought Edward Napier the third best man in world.

A hand touched her arm. "That carriage is Napier's latest invention," Cameron said. " 'Tis twice as fast as the Edinburgh mail coach and uses only one-fourth as many horses."

Her feelings were still in turmoil over that rose-scented letter. Moments ago, during the celebration with the crew in Cameron's quarters, she had seen him slip the letter from his tartan and put it in his sea chest. He'd been discreet, but she'd been watching him.

Thinking of that, she tried to summon civility. She managed to say, "Who is the lad with Christopher?"

"You recognized Napier's elder son?"

"Yes, from Mary's drawings."

"The other lad is one of Sarah's orphans. His name is Oliver Wallace, but we call him Notch."

From Agnes, Virginia had heard of Notch; Sarah was sponsoring him at Glasgow University.

Cameron tightened his grip on her arm. "Shall we join them?"

Knowing full well that she shouldn't, that rummaging through another's possessions was wrong, Virginia couldn't help herself. Her heart was involved. She'd given herself to Cameron Cunningham, and she had to know if she'd blundered.

She smiled up at him and pulled her arm from his grasp. "There's something I've forgotten. I'll be right back."

He frowned, and fearing he'd follow, she shook a finger at him. "If you leave without me, I'll never forgive you."

Cameron relaxed as he watched Virginia go below; she hadn't noticed the letter from Adrienne; he'd hidden it in his tartan, and Agnes had avoided Virginia's question about the owner of the carriage. With a careful maneuvering, he'd get Adrienne out of Glasgow and his life quickly—before Virginia became the wiser. Odd that he'd changed his mind about that. At first, he'd planned to tell Virginia about his mistress, because he believed she'd understand.

But considering their shared passion during the last three days, he'd reconsidered. Better that he avoid the subject or, at the least, broach it after the fact.

He'd go with Virginia to Napier House, get her settled in. Then he'd go home and deal with Adrienne.

"Cunningham!" Napier called out. "Permission to come aboard?"

"Permission granted." Cameron glanced at the hatch and wondered what was keeping Virginia. He considered going after her but thought better about it. Or did guilt hold him back? Before he could ponder it longer, she returned to the deck, her MacKenzie tartan draped over her arm, the cat's basket in her hand. Why she'd gone back for those things in particular he did not know, but one thing was certain. Having them gave her confidence, for she held her head high and her steps were smooth and sure.

Thinking that she'd need help until she found her land legs, he hurried to her side. "Be careful walking as you leave the ship."

"Why?"

Her smile was friendly, but a new aloofness glittered in her eyes. What had put it there? Probably the prospect of meeting Napier, a man she admittedly held in high regard.

Cameron took the basket from her. "Because you're still wearing your sea legs." When her expression turned bland, he decided she was much too serious. "Your very beautiful sea legs."

She gasped and flushed, but the sound was soft and the blush subtle.

"Virginia!" Agnes called out as she stepped on deck. "Come meet Edward."

Still confused at Virginia's behavior, Cameron let her pull the basket away from him. Without a word, she went to meet Edward Napier.

Cameron followed.

A beaming, teary-eyed Agnes said, "Darling, meet Virginia."

Reaching out, Edward grasped both of Virginia's hands in his. "Welcome home, Sister. We prayed for your safe return to the family."

Cameron didn't particularly like the way she smiled at Napier or the length of time they held hands. Then he laughed at his own jealousy. It was just because he faced a separation from Virginia. But they wouldn't be apart for long; he'd make certain of that.

"I'm grateful that Agnes found me."

Agnes? Cameron's temper flared. How dare Virginia give the credit to Agnes? Fate had led him to Glasgow at the right moment, else Agnes would have been the one to discover the damned kegs.

"Agnes said you suffered a trauma to your cranium," said Edward, his physician's demeanor in place.

Virginia frowned and Cameron knew why, so he said, "Your head."

She nodded in understanding but omitted any expression of gratitude toward Cameron. "Yes, my lord. A fall from a horse when I was young."

"How young?"

"I cannot be sure, but of late, my memories are returning."

Agnes beamed. "In bits and pieces. She recalled that Cameron used to spit in her hand."

Napier looked askance at Cameron. "Rather an ungallant lad, weren't you?"

Bits and pieces, ha! She remembered at planned

intervals and used her conversations with Agnes during the voyage as an excuse.

All he could think to say was, "My sordid past is behind me."

Edward turned her hands over and examined her palms, which she tried to withdraw. "Have you experienced any odd memories?" he inquired. "Remembrances that do not fit?"

"Yes." She took back her hands and glanced at Cameron. "I keep having visions of Cameron as a gentleman."

Napier and Agnes laughed, but Cameron was slow to grasp the humor. Something in Virginia's demeanor troubled him, not to mention her testy dispostion. What had come over her?

"Cameron, 'twas meant to be funny," Napier cajoled. "Be a good sport and laugh along."

Excellent advice. Smiling, he shook Napier's hand. "After weeks at sea with your wife?" For effect, he rolled his eyes. "Now there is a jest."

"Hoots! Cameron. You're a troll with scales and barnacles."

"Shush, Agnes," said Napier, patting the baby's head. "You'll wake Juliet. She had a fretful night."

Wide-eyed with alarm, Agnes peered at her downy-haired child. "She's ill?"

"Only from too many cousins feeding her too much clotted cream. The lads can't abide her closing her eyes for more than half an hour. The wee thing's exhausted. I've kept her in the laboratory with me today."

Agnes relaxed. "Whose lads?"

"Lottie's." He sent Cameron a pained glance. "She arrived a fortnight ago."

Cameron chuckled; Lottie had spent three months at his house while decorating it. After a week, he'd moved to Napier House. "My condolences, Napier. I'd say we're fellows evenly tormented by MacKenzie women."

Putting her palm against her husband's cheek, Agnes murmured, "Poor, dear man. A fortnight with Lottie. Tisk, tisk. You must feel like Job on his last forbearance."

In his typical, gentlemanly fashion, Napier shrugged. "I should like to boast that I had reformed her bossy ways, alas . . . I failed. But 'tis better with Sarah there. She arrived yesterday."

Virginia stepped forward. "Oh, Agnes. You said they'd be here. I cannot wait to see them."

Cameron felt left out. How dare she ignore him completely, family reunion or no family reunion. He moved closer and took her arm. "Shall we go meet them?"

"Yes, but I'll carry my own basket."

She didn't look at him, so he couldn't see the expression that accompanied that ambiguity. She wasn't referring to any courteous gesture on his part, and she wasn't joking. What had come over her? Did she worry that he intended to keep the kitten? Was that why she'd gone below just moments ago? Come to think of it, he hadn't actually told her the kitten was hers to keep, not in so many words. He'd been too busy thinking of ways to get her alone.

He gave himself high marks for his efforts in that respect. The last three days and nights had been heaven.

"Shall we?" Napier said, holding out an arm toward the smoothest-riding and fastest carriage on earth.

As she exited the ship, Virginia said, "Carriages have certainly changed since I left Scotland."

Cameron pounced on that. "Do you remember leaving? The name of the ship that took you?"

She kept walking toward the carriage but closed herself off. "No, I haven't remembered that."

Nor would she ever, he was beginning to suspect. That troubled him, for if she did not unburden herself before word of her father's return reached them, Cameron would have to tell her all he knew. Lachlan would take his revenge whether she approved or not. Cameron did not relish her reaction. But he had time to deal with that later. Now he must learn why she sat stiffly beside him in the carriage and spoke not one word to him during the ride to Glasgow.

It couldn't be that she knew about Adrienne; Agnes had sworn herself to silence on the subject, and Agnes MacKenzie never went back on her word. Could it be that Virginia was having second thoughts about him? No, not after her eagerness to evade Agnes and share intimacies with him. Virginia could be apprehensive about meeting Lottie and Sarah.

He was still pondering the subject when the carriage entered the gates of Napier House.

Edward pounded on the roof, and the carriage stopped short of the residence. Taking Agnes's hand, he stepped out of the carriage. "Give our regrets to Lottie and Sarah."

"Aye," said his wife. "We are indisposed."

Napier pulled a laughing Agnes from the carriage. "Notch," he called up to the driver.

"Aye, sir."

"You and the carriage are at Lady Virginia's disposal."

"Anytime, my lord."

Cameron remembered Mary. "Edward, wait. Mary's child. What did she have?"

"A girl."

Her husband had wanted, demanded a son. "Poor Mary," Cameron said.

"Nay," Edward called back. "Through Sarah's husband, Michael, Mary placed a bet at White's that her child would be a girl."

"How much did she wager?"

He laughed. "A million pounds, and guess who matched the bet?"

"Robert Spencer?"

"Aye, Mary's own husband."

Mary had gotten the idea of betting a million pounds from Lottie. "Does Lottie know?"

He nodded. "She was inconsolable for days."

A laughing Agnes said, "Lottie's always inconsolable but especially when someone mentions that wager she lost to her husband."

Arm in arm they strolled across the greensward and disappeared behind the new greenhouse.

Virginia eyed the empty seat. If she moved, he'd take her back to his ship right now and sail to France. With all his might, he willed her to shift that pretty bottom to the facing seat.

"You were right about this carriage."

How could Virginia witness the obvious affection between her sister and Napier and not be moved by it?

She glanced up at him, started, then looked away. He had every right to scowl.

"It's a wonderful home. Look, Cameron. There's an old round tower in the back."

Small talk didn't suit her.

"What is wrong with you?" he blurted.

The carriage began moving again. She checked the position of the cat's basket when it was obviously unnecessary.

"Nothing is wrong with me."

Oh, he knew that female trick. He just hadn't expected it from Virginia. Since learning of her deception, he'd helped her at every turn. When she grew too comfortable with Agnes and almost let the truth slip, Cameron had come to her rescue.

"Yes, something is. Tell me now, or I'll tell Notch to take us back to the ship."

"What about Lottie and Sarah?"

She wasn't supposed to ask about her sisters. She was supposed to talk to him. But if she couldn't be honest about her feelings now, she could face her sisters alone. "You're distant to me, and I demand to know why."

Her expression grew chilly, and she lifted one brow. In that imperialistic MacKenzie way, she said, "You demand?"

He'd earned the right. She loved him. She was just too distracted by her own lies to admit it. "Aye, and with good cause."

"Remember what I said. You will not rule my life because we . . ."

"Because we made love standing at the ship's wheel 'neath a full moon?"

A blush started at her breasts, which were displayed a little too lavishly to suit him. "Or were you thinking about the bath we shared on the night before last?"

Her neck flushed pink.

"No? Perhaps you were remembering our lengthy inventory of the purser's closet? You were ever so helpful, you know."

Color blossomed on her cheeks.

"Not that either? Then you must have been thinking about the luncheon we shared in the crow's nest."

"Haud yer wheesht!"

What an interesting time for her to remember Scottish. That she told him to shut up seemed particularly clever. Now he must recognize it and encourage her or give himself away.

He followed his conscience. "You've remembered how to speak Scottish."

She gave him a coy smile.

He couldn't help saying, "Although your choice of words is questionable."

The carriage stopped. She picked up her basket. "Obviously your understanding of the language is poor"—she opened the door—"for you are still talking."

Virginia left him sitting in the luxurious carriage, his mouth agape, his pride sizzling with offense.

The deceitful troll.

Later, she'd find out where he lived, and she'd go there. She had to see for herself if what she'd read in Adrienne's letters were true. Letters. A dozen or more tucked neatly in Cameron's sea chest. No wonder he hadn't taken her to his cabin during the voyage, the room was a veritable shrine to Adrienne Cholmondeley. Well, that was an exaggeration. But the knowing saddened Virginia. Were it not for her own deception, she might have thought twice about spying on him and certainly regretted it later. And why hadn't he opened the last message the woman had sent?

He stepped out of the carriage, and she fought the urge to stomp on his toe and kick him in his manly parts. Parts he'd spent the last few years sharing with Adrienne Cholmondeley.

"You can be sure we'll visit the subject again, Virginia." He looked beyond her, at something over her shoulder. Indecision clouded his features, as if he were grappling with something that bothered his conscience.

"What issue?"

Notch and Christopher climbed down from the box. Cameron held up his hand. They kept their distance. "The issue of why you refuse to carry on a conversation with me. What has happened to you?"

Struggling for nonchalance, she shrugged. "Nothing. Nothing at all. Everything is fine. Neither of us has reason to doubt the other."

Looking completely baffled, he said, "What, in the kingdom of Neptune, is that supposed to mean?"

"Please, Cameron." She stared at her hands, which were clutching the basket in a death grip. "Don't you see that I'm—I'm apprehensive about meeting Lottie. To hear you, Agnes, and Edward speak of her, she must be a terror."

He relented. "All right, I confess. In her own way, Lottie is a treasure but only when taken a bit at a time. You'll like her." The front doors of Napier House opened. "Here she is now."

Determined to bear up and hide the hurt his lie caused her, Virginia gave him the only smile she could manage, then turned to face Lottie.

Like Virginia, Charlotte Antoinette MacKenzie had their father's blue eyes and auburn hair. But more than her features, Lottie's graceful carriage and queenly demeanor were unmistakable. Thinner than was common for a woman who'd borne four children, Lottie didn't look her age. She wore a stunning gown of lavender blue velvet trimmed in panels of heavy lace that had been tatted to form tulips.

"Cholmondeley's driver said they'd found you—Oh!" Slapping a hand over her mouth, she glanced at Cameron. Then she covered the slip brilliantly by chuckling and saying, "What am I saying? He could have been Lucifer's driver and I wouldn't have uttered a protest so long as his news was true." She hugged Virginia. "You haven't changed at all except to grow more beautiful. Bless God and all the saints twice."

A familiar tightness squeezed Virginia's chest. Lottie, who made the beautiful dresses. Lottie, who wagered a million pounds because she loved children.

"Oh, Virginia. What happened to you? Where have you been?"

Lottie didn't know about the loss of memory story; how could she? At least Virginia's show of recalling the past slowly was working. But why didn't Cameron step in and explain as he usually did? Oh, bother him and his noble mistress.

"I had an accident a long time ago. I lost all memory of who I was or where I came from."

"Then you don't remember us?"

"It's coming back to me a little at a time. Cameron and Agnes told me all about you. I have remembered that you tried in vain to teach me to sew, and after seeing some of your gowns, I wish I had been a better student."

"Oh, fither that. One dressmaker in the family is plenty, and I haven't enough work to keep me busy as it is. I'll design a new wardrobe for you. You'll need a dozen ball gowns, something unforgettable for when Papa presents you to the queen. The king is a dry patch, they say."

"The queen of England? Virginia quaked inside. "No, you mustn't—"

"Speak not another word of protest, Virginia. 'Tis my duty to ensure that we are the best-dressed women in Scotland, England—" She fluttered her hand. "Everywhere we go."

Why did Cameron remain silent?

Suddenly serious, Lottie said, "Where is Papa? Where's Juliet? Has something happened to them?"

Virginia hesitated, certain Cameron would explain. She hadn't seen Papa since their farewell dinner at the inn in Norfolk. Her last sight of Mama, standing on the threshold of Virginia's room, was a moment she'd as soon forget.

When Cameron said nothing, Virginia thought him the grandest troll of all. That decided, she answered Lottie.

"Boston? Whatever for?"

"To inspect a mill."

Cameron cleared his throat. Turning, Virginia saw him glance pointedly toward the house. She looked over Lottie's shoulder and spied Sarah, standing in the entryway, an identical boy on either side of her, tears streaming down her cheeks.

"Is that really you, Virginia?" she said on a sob.

Lottie released her, took the basket, and gave her a nudge. As she hurried to Sarah, she heard Lottie say, "Virginia has lost her memory, Sarah. That's why we couldn't find her. But she's remembering more every day."

"Oh, Virginia." Sarah held out her arms. "Praise God for leading Cameron to you. We thought you were—we just did not know what to think."

Virginia knew. They thought her dead and why not? They weren't soothsayers, able to conjure up spirits and see into time. They were a family who had grieved over her loss. But now they were blessed, which is exactly how Virginia felt as she stepped into Sarah's embrace.

Sarah, the scholar. Sarah, with a heart of gold. Sarah, who towered over everyone in the family except Papa and Cameron. Sarah, who upon her wedding day, asked her husband to pledge her dowry for a boarding house to aid the poor.

"Where have you been all this time?" she asked. "What has happened to you?"

Again, Virginia expected Cameron to come to her aid, but he did not. He chatted with Lottie about what colors and fabrics would flatter Virginia's complexion and height.

"It's a long story. I'm back now, and that's all that matters."

"Who took you?"

Cameron's continued silence unnerved Virginia more than the masquerade. He had no reason to be unhappy with her; she hadn't lied about having a lover. She had every right to scorn him.

"Were you hurt or ill-treated?"

"No, not at all, and Agnes has told me everything that's happened in the family since I've been away."

"She never lost hope, bless her heart." She touched Virginia's cheek. "You're the image of Grandma MacKenzie."

"Mama?" said one of the boys. "Who is she?"

"Sarah," Lottie said, shooing the twins into the hands of a nanny. "We do not ask embarrassing questions while standing in the entryway or compare anyone to the dead."

Sarah gave Virginia a quick hug, then stepped back. "How remiss of me to forget rules number 3 and 26 in Countess Lottie's book of etiquette." She winked at

Virginia. "We are only allowed to ask embarrassing questions while in the parlor."

Like water rolling off a mallard's back, the insult didn't faze Lottie. "In the case of Virginia's resemblance to our grandmama, I temporarily suspend rule number 26—but only until after dinner."

Sarah templed her hands and bowed. "Oh, thank you, my lady. You are ever wise and generous."

"I'll leave you ladies to your reunion," Cameron said. "Notch will take me home."

Virginia almost called him back. But if she were honest with herself, she couldn't decide if she wanted him to stay for her benefit or just to keep him from another woman.

Let him go, her pride said.

Beg him to come back, her heart pleaded.

"What's gotten into Cameron?" Sarah asked.

Her sisters couldn't know that Virginia had always loved Cameron, let alone lain with him. Jealousy and the need for confirmation of his affair made Virginia say, "I suppose he's in a hurry to visit the Cholmondeleys."

Sarah chuckled. "He always breaks rule number 6."

Lottie gasped in outrage. "But he is betrothed to Virginia."

In her typical scholarly fashion, Sarah said, "If she has no memory of him, then the point is moot, and because Virginia obviously doesn't give a bent twig about it, why should we?"

"Have you quarreled with him?" Lottie asked.

"Lottie!" Sarah admonished. " 'Tis none of your business, rules of etiquette aside."

Because she could, Virginia said, "He has a reputation, I suppose."

Lottie sniffed in indifference. "We shan't go into that, except to say that he is popular in certain circles, which you'd be advised to avoid."

Any satisfaction Virginia gained was short-lived. Women liked him; the feeling was mutual. Bully for him.

The kitten began to fuss and claw at the basket. Lottie peered inside. "Yours?"

Virginia grasped the change in topic. "Yes, am I allowed to keep a pet here?"

Lottie passed the basket to Sarah. To Virginia, she said, "You could keep an elephant and no one would mount a protest. But let's let Mrs. Johnson care for the kitten until you're settled. Now come inside. I'll show you Agnes's home."

In the portrait gallery, Lottie paused at every canvas and gave a tidbit of gossip about each of Edward Napier's ancestors. The last three paintings were recently done and unmistakably the work of Mary Margaret MacKenzie. The first captured Christopher and Jamie sitting atop the round carriage. In the foreground, Hannah played with a stack of blocks. The next two paintings were stately portraits of Agnes and Edward in their role of earl and countess of Cathcart.

Agnes had posed in a striking gown of black and white. "Did you make that dress?" she asked Lottie.

"Aye."

Sarah said, "Our sister Lily wore that same gown, only in purple and white, for her wedding."

Lottie said, "Purple will never do for you, Virginia. I think pink and a dark shade of murray will better suit your complexion. No stripes, though. I learned that mistake with Sarah." Her prim composure slipped. "My, you two are tall."

New dresses would bolster Virginia's confidence, but even a closet full of Lottie's creations couldn't make her forget that Cameron had a highborn mistress and was with her now. What were they doing?

A respite came when she was swept into the nursery to meet her nieces and nephews.

From Lottie, Virginia gained information on the where abouts of their other siblings and the date when each would arrive. Virginia passed on regrets from Agnes and Edward.

Lottie thrust her chin in the air. "You needn't pretty it up, Virginia. Carnal pleasures is what they're after. They've locked themselves in the old tower. I doubt we'll see them before the morrow."

Sarah tapped Virginia's shoulder. "Lottie is an expert on carnal pleasures."

"Sarah Suisan!" Lottie hissed.

"Oh, goodness me." Sarah pressed a hand to the bodice of her gown. "I've broken rule number 4."

The years of separation rolled away, and Virginia laughed.

Lottie laughed too, but the sound held little humor. "Are you mocking me?"

Sarah grinned and feigned innocence. "Me, mock you, the countess of Tain?"

With a pointed look at Sarah, Lottie walked over to the twins and said, "Hamish, Charles."

Like children after sweets, the boys scrambled to their feet.

She patted their heads. "Did you know that your mother is going to buy you each a pony?"

"She is?" they said in unison.

"Yes. Pretty golden ponies with fancy saddles."

Over the cheers and shouts of her sons, Sarah groaned. "Why do I even try to outwit her?"

Lottie preened. " 'Tis a mystery to me."

Joyous that she was fitting in so well, Virginia told Sarah about their parents' trip to Boston.

"Why ever would they go there?"

"To visit a mill that Papa and Edward own."

"That's odd." Reaching down, Sarah pulled a hairpin out of the hand of Henry, Lottie's three-year-old son. "Michael inspected it only months ago."

Virginia half-listened, thinking about Cameron and his reunion with his mistress. The more she dwelled on it, the angrier she got. What if the liaison continued? Surely not. With that uncertainty, she knew what she must do: find a way to turn the conversation to Cameron and learn the location of his house.

Two hours later she succeeded.

Two hours after that, she borrowed a black cloak from Sarah and made her getaway.

Even in the fading light of sunset, she spotted the house from two blocks away. The closer she walked, the more nervous she became. But she pushed on, determined to learn the truth no matter how painful it would be.

A coach rumbled past. Virginia darted behind a hedge. Crouched there, she trembled in fear. But fear of what? She intended to confront Cameron. Why then was she cowering in the bushes?

The truth dawned.

She didn't fear discovery from Cameron; she grew frightened out of habit. As a bond servant, her whereabouts were always known. She couldn't have excused herself for a leisurely stroll before dinner.

But all that was in the past.

She was a MacKenzie, the daughter of the duke of Ross. She didn't have to ask anyone's permission to

250

walk down the lane. She had a right to find out if Cameron loved someone else; all she needed was gumption, and a MacKenzie had courage to spare.

The residence was too fine, and too few lights shone in the house and none upstairs, where Cameron's bedroom would be. She wouldn't confront them there; she didn't need to see him in Adrienne Cholmondeley's arms to learn the extent of his feelings. She'd read it in his eyes.

But first she had to get inside the house.

Three stories tall, with six marble columns across the front, each as big as a century oak, the mansion occupied the better part of a city block. Abutting a finely manicured parkland, complete with pond, gazebo, and dovecote, Cunningham Gardens, as the plaque on the gatepost named the residence, belittled its larger neighbors. No wonder Lottie had been wild to decorate the place; in elegance and style, it took Virginia's breath away.

She chose a path that skirted the pond and led to the carriage house. A peek through the windows would tell her if the crested coach were here.

"Evenin', miss."

Gasping, she whirled and saw a man coming out of the carriage house. He wore livery, and although she couldn't see his face, she suspected that he was the driver who'd come to the dock today.

"No need to be afraid. The streets here are safe."

"I wasn't afraid."

"Having a walk in the park, are you?"

She had every right to be here. "Yes. It's a pleasant evening."

"You ain't Scottish."

She didn't feel Scottish either. "No, I'm from . . . Philadelphia."

"Come here with that Redding chap, eh?"

"Why would you say that?"

He folded his arms and eyed her up and down. "'Cause folks *leave* Scotland for America. Not the other way 'round."

Agnes had told Virginia that during the voyage. But this man spoke of Horace Redding. Virginia had been too caught up in loving Cameron Cunningham to think about Redding. What had Cameron said? That Redding traveled with an entourage. She grasped the safe subject.

"I had hoped to make the acquaintance of Mr. Redding."

"You'll find him at the Carlton Inn."

Could she go to an inn by herself? She wasn't sure. But if this man knew about Redding, others would also. She'd find him, and that certainty pleased her.

"Good evening to you, sir."

He pretended to tip the hat he wasn't wearing and went back into the carriage house. Virginia turned back to the main house.

A door banged open.

"MacAdoo!"

It was Cameron's voice. He sounded angry.

Carefully, so as not to draw attention to herself, Virginia moved to the path that led to the park. Behind the concealing hedgerow, she paused.

"Nay. I will not do it," MacAdoo said.

"Of course you'll do it."

They stood not twenty feet away. Virginia held her breath.

"Fifty pounds says you'll fail."

Cameron chuckled. "We've a wager then. Now come inside and eat . . . unless you've lost your taste for fresh beef."

Virginia squatted down and found a thin spot in the hedge. A coatless Cameron had his arm around a reluctant MacAdoo, and they walked back toward the still-open door. From what little she could see, the room they entered was lined with bookshelves. Cameron's study, she supposed.

As the door closed after them, Virginia got to her feet. Cameron Cunningham occupied too much of her life and left her too little. But not loneliness. The part of her that yielded to loneliness was forever filled.

The urgency that had driven her to Cunningham Gardens faded, and with it came the beginnings of a new plan. By the time she returned to Napier House, she knew exactly what she would do.

Chapter

13

Situated between the baker's hall and a mercantile, the Carlton Inn, according to the lad Notch, boasted the freshest ale and the finest family accommodations in Glasgow. If the number of children playing out front could be credited, Notch had spoken the truth. Virginia, however, had lied to him. She'd told him she wanted to buy toys for her sisters' children and asked him to take her in the Napier carriage. Reminding her that both he and the carriage were at her disposal, he left her at the toy store and promised to fetch her and her purchases in an hour. The moment the carriage was out of sight, Virginia walked the two blocks to the Carlton Inn.

She couldn't help looking over her shoulder. Were she discovered, she had an excuse ready, but she still felt hesitant about entering the hotel.

As a precaution, she went into the retail store next

door and pretended interest in a table stacked with bonnets and white gloves near the front windows.

She'd spent a sleepless night, alternately loathing and longing for Cameron. When he'd arrived this morning, looking chipper and well rested, to take her on a tour of the city, she'd managed to decline with civility.

Lottie, bless her, had rescued Virginia from the uncomfortable moment by insisting that they postpone the outing for at least a week, so that Virginia would have a proper gown to wear.

Cameron's parting words still echoed in Virginia's ears.

Nothing too daring, and I prefer her in green.

That he'd spoken to Lottie rather than Virginia only irritated her more. That Lottie had been impressed by his "masterful" tone, as she'd called it, didn't bear consideration. At least she hadn't protested later in the day when Virginia announced that she was going out to purchase necessities.

Still irritated and determined to proceed with her plan, Virginia left the mercantile and went in search of Horace Redding. Although she'd never seen his likeness, she imagined him as a dignified man, a man of President Washington's stature, of Jefferson's vision. She thought of Merriweather and vowed to write to him and relate every detail of her visit with Redding.

She paused, struck by the irony. Here she was, standing in Scotland, thinking about her life in Virginia. For ten years she labored there, imagining herself home in Scotland. But she didn't feel at home. She had expected to find peace here. But how could her soul find contentment when her heart was full of lies?

"Going in, miss?" said a liveried doorman, his gloved hand holding the door open.

Shaking off the confusion, she went inside.

No clerk manned the desk that stood just inside the door. Near the stairs, a group of women conversed quietly. Across the room, an elderly gentleman sat in a wing-back chair, a book in his lap. Servants came and went: maids hauling coal buckets; a bootboy carrying polished shoes to the guests.

Unsure of herself, Virginia examined the paintings on the wall. Had she expected Redding to station himself in the receiving room? Yes, she admitted, because she hadn't thought the matter through. She'd been befuddled by Cameron Cunningham and heartbroken. But never again.

That decided, she moved freely through the room. A table containing reading materials caught her eye. Relief spread through her when she picked up a notice bearing Redding's name, but no mention was made of *Reason Enough,* his essay on the American Revolution. Most exciting was an announcement at the bottom of the page, inviting the ladies and gentlemen of Glasgow to a reception in Redding's honor on Friday evening at the cordiner's hall.

She'd have a new dress by then, a proper one. But she couldn't go alone even though ladies were invited. Or could she? Asking any of her sisters to accompany her was not an option; Papa disapproved of Redding, and it would be unfair of Virginia to ask Agnes, Sarah, or Lottie to openly defy him. For her part, Virginia didn't see it as defiance; Redding's words had given her courage during the bleak years and had inspired her to think about the time when her indenture would end. In the simple act of thanking him, she would take another step toward putting the past behind her and begin a new life.

Mission accomplished, Virginia tucked the paper into the purse her mother had given her and returned to the toy store. She had just paid the clerk and turned to leave when Cameron strolled in.

Over a jaunty striped waistcoat, he wore a tailored jacket and knee breeches of dark brown velvet. Plain white hose accentuated his muscular legs, and a simply tied neckcloth enhanced his strong neck and handsome jaw.

At the sight of him, the clerk, a fresh-faced girl of about Virginia's age, tittered with excitement. On the third attempt, the girl managed to say, "Good day, Captain Cunningham."

"The same to you, Betsy." He turned that winning smile on Virginia. "My lady."

Did he also have designs on the shop girl? Obviously a mistress and his betrothed weren't enough women for him. Hating him, Virginia picked up the box of toys and headed for the door. "Fancy seeing you here."

He held out his hands. "Let me take that for you."

"Thank you, but Notch is waiting."

"No, he isn't."

"What happened to him?"

"I'll take you home." Softly, he added, "Unless you'd care to make a scene?"

A scene. The novelty of it struck her as funny. She hadn't heard that term or faced that dilemma in a very long time. She wasn't quite sure she knew how to make a scene. Smart bond servants didn't cause trouble. They toiled all day and prayed for good health.

"The notion humors you? Odd, for I doubt it would be laughable to Betsy or to Lottie, should your sister get wind of it."

Virginia hadn't thought about Lottie. She'd spent too many years looking out for herself and trying to forget her queenly sister; it was the only way she could survive, alone and an ocean away. Now she must remember and consider the effect of her actions on others. But she wouldn't forgo paying her respects to Horace Redding; Papa would just have to live with that.

"My coach is outside."

If Cameron had come in that fancy black carriage, she'd make him regret it. And probably create her first scene.

Giving him the box, she left the shop. He followed, indicating a plain but elegant carriage. She breathed a sigh of relief and hated the weakness of it.

The driver jumped down and helped her up. Cameron sat beside her.

"Must you?" she challenged, eyeing his closeness.

"Me? You took the wrong seat."

"What are you talking about?"

He tapped the roof, and the carriage began to move. "Carriage etiquette."

"Don't expect me to believe that nonsense."

His grin was indulgent and too cocky. "The gentleman always takes the backward-facing seat."

"Fine." She moved to rise.

He flattened his hand on her skirt, trapping her there. If she persisted, she'd tear her dress.

She plopped down. "What do you want?"

"Long life. A dozen sons."

She laughed at the absurdity and turned her attention to the traffic in the lane. Sailors, inland from the port, strolled the lane, tipping their hats to the ladies they passed. Nannies herded children along, and servants walked several paces behind their masters.

"Perhaps you meant to ask what I want from you."

Thoughts of him and his mistress fouled her mood. "Perhaps I needn't speak at all, since you know my mind so well."

"Not so well as I know your body, but there's time aplenty, which also, I think, answers your original question." His voice dropped. "I want you."

"How gallant that you have the time."

"What is that supposed to mean?"

A whip cracked. The carriage slowed. A dray, loaded with barrels, rumbled across the road, the oxen bellowing loudly.

When the noise abated, Virginia summoned courage. "Adrienne Cholmondeley."

Cameron winced and scratched his jaw.

Virginia reveled in his discomfort. "Don't bother insulting me by denying the affair. I saw the shrine to her in your cabin."

"My what?"

She had him on the run. Bully for her. "In your cabin."

"You spied on me?"

She wasn't proud of the fact, but what was she supposed to do? Stand by and let him make a fool of her? "Do you deny that she's your mistress?"

"I hardly call one miniature and a few letters a shrine."

"I *hardly* trust your opinion."

He stared out the window, but he wasn't looking at the rows of boardinghouses or the churches they passed. He focused inward but on what thoughts she could not imagine.

Because he didn't seem inclined to respond, she sought distraction in the scenery. As they left the city, the odors of rubbish and commerce faded. The subtle smell of his bathing soap teased her senses and reminded her of their private moments during the voyage.

She'd lain with him. In his arms she'd voiced intimacies about their loving that seemed scandalous to her now. She'd loved him all of her life. Losing him once had scarred her deeply, but she'd been a child then, and fate had torn them apart. Losing him again to the woman who'd taken her place disappointed her to her soul. Cameron Cunningham was no knight in shining armor, but he had rescued her, and for that she'd always be grateful.

At length, he said, "You've been gone a very long time, Virginia. A man has needs. You now know mine."

Did he expect her to fall into his arms? "You could have told me. I thought we were friends."

"There are things you could have told me."

He sounded cold and distant, and for a reason she could not name, she grew alarmed. "Such as?"

"If I knew, I wouldn't have to ask, now would I? But I don't think you've been completely honest with me."

The carriage rounded a corner, jostling her against him. He steadied her, but his hand did not linger.

Confused anew, she grew defensive. "Then we are well matched, for you wouldn't know honesty if it crawled into your shoe."

He stretched out his legs and folded his arms over his chest. "Even as children, we never lied to each other."

How dare he bring that up? Because she'd led him to it. But no, she refused to take the blame for his indiscretion.

She grasped what she hoped was a benign topic. "How did you find me?"

"This time?"

Fuming, she snapped, "Yes, and get off my skirt."

He raised up, a lifting of his hips that brought to mind carnal images of him naked, beneath her, urging her in lusty phrases to ride him to glory.

Heat flamed her cheeks, but she couldn't help torturing herself with thoughts of him giving his love to another woman. In a strange way, she felt a greater humiliation now than she ever had at Poplar Knoll. At least there, she'd come to know what to expect. Rules were put down, those who chose to break them paid the consequences. Slaves faced beatings. Bond servants saw their indentures lengthened.

Needing something to do with her hands, she toyed with her purse, which had been caught between them.

"I found you because Napier's carriage is hard to miss."

A convenient answer, but he'd have to do better. "Lottie or Sarah could have taken it."

"Nay. Edward would have offered Lottie a conventional coach, and Sarah brought her own from Edinburgh."

"Why did you send Notch away?"

Only his eyes moved as he looked at her. "You should have an escort."

She scoffed at that. "To visit a toy store?"

"You might have had other errands."

Did he know about the Carlton Inn? So what, her pride said. For reasons he could never understand, for heartfelt gratitude and admiration, she must come face-to-face with Horace Redding. "I'm perfectly capable of managing a shopping excursion."

"Appearances are important. Your father is a duke. Your siblings are well respected."

"Which requires me to have a lying, deceitful womanizer carry my packages?"

"No." Putting his feet down, he turned slightly toward her. The calm in his voice belied the anger in his eyes. "Our betrothal gives me the right to escort you—among other privileges."

The gates of Napier House came into view. Boldness captured her. "Including the right to keep a mistress."

With the same hand that had caressed her in private places, he touched her purse. Paper rustled. "A letter to a beau?"

She ignored him.

"Confess to it, Virginia. You're jealous."

Probably, but that didn't excuse him for being a rogue. Aboard ship, the blighter had asked her to come home with him. All the while, he had a mistress waiting for him there. That deceit tasted bitter. "You could have told me. You should have told me."

"What purpose would it have served?"

Without thinking, she blurted, "It would have kept me out of your bed."

The smile he gave her sent shivers down her spine. "Nothing could do that, and to be precise, 'twas your bed we first used."

She felt used. Used and cheated by the man who should have been her avenging knight, her life's partner. Obviously he'd forgotten the promises he'd made years ago. "Oh, do shut up."

"So, we're back to that."

Drat her prideful tongue.

To her relief, the carriage stopped. "And we're back home. Thank you for the ride."

He chuckled. "You may ride me again any time you like."

"Cam!"

He shrugged, and his self-effacing grin reminded her of the boy she'd known. "At least you've stopped calling me Cameron."

"Rest assured, a dozen ways to address you come to mind, but Lottie's rule number 9 prevents me from using them."

"Do you know rule number 7?"

"No."

"A pity, for it certainly applies."

She wasn't sure she wanted to know, but he'd probably think her a coward if she didn't ask. "Tell me."

"I'd rather show you."

In the circular drive at Napier House, where anyone within or without the house could see, he pressed her into the corner of the coach. The velvet cloth of his jacket felt baby soft against her skin. Staring at her mouth, he smiled and licked his lips.

An absurd thought popped into her mind. Would he taste of someone else? The fighter in her—the child who'd tended her own blisters and sang herself to sleep—couldn't abide his kissing another woman.

When he touched his mouth to hers, she decided to give him something to remember. Finding pleasure in his embrace was easy. Convincing herself that this was the last intimacy she'd enjoy with him proved more difficult. But she could not, would not, share him. Let him have his English mistress. Let him remember Virginia MacKenzie and the passion and friendship they'd shared.

Her plan worked, for when he drew back, his eyes gleamed with awareness and a familiar desire. "Behold rule number 7," he said in a husky murmur. "Lovers always part with a kiss."

Disappointment plagued her. He wanted to master and keep his mistress too. The unfairness of it drained Virginia of strength, but she had her pride.

Because she could think of nothing else, she said, "Are you going somewhere?"

"Aye, to Edinburgh. I've business with Michael Elliot, and he misses Sarah. He'll come back with me."

Was he taking his mistress along? Her frustration must have shown, for his smile turned crooked, endearing.

"Stay out of trouble until I return."

Hating her own weakness and vowing to better conceal it in the future, she strove for lightness. "How can I get into trouble with Lottie running the household?"

"Agnes will take care of that—after she's taken care of Napier."

Virginia fought a blush and lost. "The things you say—they're scandalous, and you do it to discomfit me."

"Oh, I'd like very much to discomfit you—for days and nights without end."

Uttered in a breathy whisper, the words and the seduction they bespoke robbed her of a witty reply.

"Hold that thought. We'll explore it when I return on Saturday."

She wouldn't wish him a pleasant journey. But

because he was leaving and because she knew first-hand how capricious fate could be, she spoke from the heart. "Be safe, Cam."

That night, as she drifted to sleep, her last conscious thought was of Cameron and Adrienne Cholmondeley. It was also the first topic of conversation at the breakfast table.

Lottie slapped the newspaper on the table. "There. Read it for yourself. Adrienne Cholmondeley has taken rooms at Carlton House. Cameron's turned her out."

Her heart racing, Virginia wanted to snatch up the paper, devour every word, then wave it around the room. Instead, she feigned indifference and casually scanned the column.

According to the *Glasgow Courant,* Miss Cholmondeley, the daughter of the distinguished minister of trade, had taken rooms befitting her station at Carlton House, the elegant quarters owned by the same family as the Carlton Inn.

Curiosity, tempered by the security of family, made Virginia say, "Is she beautiful?"

Lottie paused, a scone in one hand, a knife laden with butter in the other. "Not so pretty as to draw notice."

"Lottie?" Sarah chastened, a lift in her voice. "Virginia deserves the truth."

"You weren't here to see Cameron dictating to me the style of dresses and the choice of fabrics Virginia should have. I tell you, Sister, the man is smitten."

"And I tell you, Sister, be honest with Virginia."

Lottie slathered butter on the scone, her mouth pursed in stubbornness. "The truth does not always serve."

"It does if you happened upon a good view of the drive yesterday afternoon and witnessed Virginia and Cameron and their adherence to rule number 7."

Lottie put down the knife. "You kissed Cameron good-bye in public?"

Papa used to say that in good and faithful company, old habits returned. Virginia knew it was true. "He said he was going away. What if harm befell him?"

Keen-eyed Lottie said, "No softer reason guides you?"

Virginia had lied enough to these women who loved her. "I thought he'd take her with him. I was frightfully jealous."

"With more than enough cause," Lottie proclaimed as she nibbled on the scone. "I shudder to think what Agnes would have done in the circumstances."

"Forget Agnes." Sarah put down her teacup. "That's not like Cameron. With Virginia back, I knew he'd do the proper thing."

"That's because you are naive."

Sliding Virginia a pained look, Sarah tisked and shook her head. "If I am naive, Lottie, you are obtuse."

"You're just miffed because I got the best of you yesterday when I told the boys you'd buy them ponies."

"I take back obtuse," Sarah said to Virginia. "Lottie is mean to the core."

With Adrienne Cholmondeley out of the way, Virginia relaxed and basked in her sisters' battle of words.

"I'm not mean, not truly. I'm just beset with bad humors."

Sarah howled with laughter. "You're always beset with bad humors."

"Oh?" As if gearing up for another verbal assault, Lottie narrowed her eyes and took aim. "Look who's talking." She glanced at Virginia to enlist her support. "But then, Sarah's chamber pot never stinks, does it?"

Virginia choked on her tea.

Sarah blushed carnation red and threw up her hands. "Once more, I am forced to yield to your vulgar tongue."

"You yield because you are outwitted."

"I *withdraw* temporarily because Virginia has forgotten the past, and *I shudder* to think of the impression she must have of us."

"We're family. She loves us."

"In spite of the fact that our conversation has run to the selfish."

"Run? Run where?" Lottie stammered.

"Since you are obviously outwitted, Lottie dear, I will remind you that we have done nothing but talk about ourselves."

"Nonsense. We discussed Cameron and his turning out of his mistress."

"A truly delightful topic on which to begin the day."

"'Tis true, I tell you," Lottie insisted. "Just look at her and you'll see."

To Virginia, Sarah smiled. "Now that we have exhausted Lottie's limited supply of civility, what would you like to do today?"

"She's going to sit for fittings."

"Since when does that preclude her from answering a question?"

"I was just trying to be helpful."

Her patience gone, Sarah snapped, "Will you please let her answer for herself!"

With a self-deprecating grin, Lottie acknowledged

the truth of that statement. "Are there other things you'd like to do today?"

"Nothing in particular, but there is some place I'd like to go on Friday night."

"Of course." Lottie fluttered her fingers. "At least two of the gowns will be ready."

"It's a reception."

"Wonderful! We'll all go. Sarah, you wear the red gown. I'll wear black, and Virginia will dazzle them in the pink."

Sarah's brow furrowed in confusion. "Who are we going to dazzle and where?"

"It's a reception at the cordiner's hall in honor of Horace Redding."

Sarah winced. "Oh, my."

Lottie gaped. "What ever will we do? Redding despises the MacKenzies, thanks to Papa."

"I'm so sorry, Virginia."

She wouldn't take no for an answer. "I'll go alone, and I won't stay for long. It's very important to me to meet Redding."

Agnes solved the dilemma the next day. "'Tis simple. Edward will escort you."

Lottie wasn't convinced. "But what will your Mr. Redding say when you tell him that your father is Lachlan MacKenzie?"

As it turned out, Redding was more impressed with Edward Napier, but Virginia hadn't had the opportunity to say more than how do you do. Later, after the men had exhausted their discussion on the merits of the Napier carriage, she planned to approach Redding again.

"It's an odd-shaped contraption, to be sure,"

said the constable of Glasgow. "Why is that, Lord Edward?"

Dressed in the bold black and white tartan of the Napiers, with a black velvet jacket and pure white shirt, Edward towered over the constable. "'Tis dynamics, Jenkins," he said. "The principle by which objects move through the air."

"Nonsense." The constable laughed. "A carriage moves at the whim of horses. Next you'll tell us with gulls at the harnesses, the carriage will fly."

As polite as Agnes was bold, Edward smiled and generously said, "Rumor has it you've a yearling that shows promise at six furlongs."

As their conversation moved to sporting subjects, Virginia eased away, content to simply observe Horace Redding.

He could have had no hair at all under his lightly powdered short wig and her opinion of him would not have changed. Slightly portly, with large blue eyes and a small, thin mouth, he stood shoulder to shoulder with the distinguished and elegant Edward Napier. Comparing them was unfair, for Redding was old enough to be Napier's father. A native of Glasgow, Redding admitted to tracing his ancestors back to the Viking invasions. Yet he was an American. His opinions were uninhibited by traditions, save those favorable to the common and free man. But what captured her most about Redding was the tone and cadence of his voice. He had a way of capturing attention; even Napier listened avidly, although he was far from spellbound by Redding, unlike so many others in the room.

One of those disciples of democracy, as Redding dubbed his followers, broached the subject of English expansion. Virginia visited the refreshment table, then moved to the edge of the room, where a large standing screen marked the entrance to the ladies' necessary. A row of potted palms denoted facilities for the men.

Her petticoats rustled as she walked, and she felt another burst of pride for Lottie's newest creation. Others in the room noticed, too, and she committed every compliment to memory so she could pass them on to her sister. Of pink velvet, the bodice and split overskirt complimented the yards and yards of white silk that formed the underskirt. A border of embroidered green leaves trimmed the lace at her cuffs and the neckline. Down to her matching slippers, Virginia felt like a princess.

"An' who's surprised those MacKenzie women dress so well?" said a harpish voice from behind the screen. "They've the Napier mills at their beck 'n' call."

Virginia couldn't see the woman or her companion, who chirped, "They've more money than the church."

A couple walked by, the man dapper in a black suit and white waistcoat. The woman smiled at Virginia, moved away from her companion, and disappeared behind the screen.

"Won't his grace of Ross toss a caber when he learns his daughter came out tonight. He hates that Redding fellow. Blackened his eye when last their paths crossed."

"Which daughter is she?" said the harpy. "Or is she one of those uppity bastards of his?"

Her companion laughed. "Who's to know where she fits in the MacKenzie litter?"

Virginia went cold inside, and the fruity punch she'd drunk turned bitter on her tongue.

"Someone from the *Courant* should find out what that new MacKenzie girl is doing in Glasgow."

"Why don't you ask her instead of hovering like fat mice after dirty crumbs of cheese."

Twin gasps sounded.

Without doubt, Virginia knew the plaintive voice belonged to the woman who'd smiled at her moments before.

"Well, I never," spat the harpy.

"No, I don't imagine you've ever had the courage to speak openly," the good-hearted woman continued. "But then, who would be interested in anything you have to say?"

Blustering, the harpy said, "Have we met?"

"Fortunately for me, no."

Fabric rustled. A moment later, the harpy said, "Who was that woman?"

Her friend lowered her voice. "She's Adrienne Cholmondeley. We read about her in the paper today."

The bottom dropped out of Virginia's stomach. She hadn't expected kindness from Cameron's mistress. Former mistress. How could she thank her? Did propriety allow it? She didn't know, so she made her way back to Edward Napier, and when the opportunity for privacy presented itself, she asked him.

"You could send her a note and a gift. Perhaps a silk scarf." Grinning, he added, "I know where a few lengths of cloth can be found."

Virginia laughed. According to Lottie, the Napier family mill had prospered since medieval times. "I do feel like a bumpkin."

He pulled a funny face reminiscent of the expression his son Jamie wore when Agnes sent the lad to bed. "Bumpkin? Nay."

"I *am* out of my depth."

"Me too."

"You?"

"Aye. Try explaining dynamics to a man who thinks the moon is purgatory because the face of it resembles his first wife's."

Gaiety filled her. "Do you know what Americans say about the image on the moon?"

"Tell me. I'm certain it's revolutionary."

Completely charmed, she said, "I can see why Agnes loves you."

A hint of color stained his cheeks. Reverently, he said, "She is a gift I never thought to receive, but you of all people know that. Now finish what you were going to say about the moon."

"May I join you?" Horace Redding said.

"Oh, please." Virginia stepped closer to Napier. "In fact, Lord Edward and I were just comparing tales. Perhaps you'd convey to him the American opinion of whose face is on the moon."

"Delighted." In his orator's voice, he said, "Some Americans believe that the pocked face of the moon is the burial ground for the corrupt souls of English kings."

Jovial and serious at once, Napier said, "How nice that you've excluded the Stewart monarchs."

Seeing his blunder, Redding swallowed hard. "Well, I . . ."

"Seem to be out of punch?" Edward glanced at Redding's full glass.

"Gone flat it has, as flat as the constable of Glasgow's good humor."

"Then allow me." Edward also took Virginia's glass. "I'm certain the two of you have pleasantries to exchange."

Virginia watched him walk away. "The father of invention."

"He is that and your brother-in-law too, I'm told."

Virginia nodded. "Yes, he married my sister Agnes. I'm staying with them."

"He said you spent some years in the tidewater."

With absolute certainty, Virginia knew that her family had not elaborated on her time in America. They were too loyal to reveal secrets. Once again, she was glad she'd kept the truth from them. "Yes, that's where I first read *Reason Enough*. It's a remarkable work and best describes the state of mind prevalent in American both before and during the war."

He demurred with "Some say Burke put it better than I ever could."

She remembered Cameron's words, spoken what seemed like years ago in Virginia. "Burke disdains any progress beyond a snail's pace."

"Well said."

Since learning of tonight's event, she'd rehearsed what she wanted to say next. "I was wondering if you would accept a gift from me. It isn't much, but I made it myself."

He frowned. "A gift? But we've only just met."

"I know that, but . . ." She took the rolled document from her purse. "I wanted to give you a copy of *Reason Enough*. I scripted it myself from the *Virginia Gazette*." On a rabbit hide that she'd tanned herself and with ink she'd distilled from lampblack and her own urine, Virginia had labored over the work. But she wouldn't tell him that.

He took the scroll. "I'm . . . I must confess, I'm at a

loss for words. A happy turn of events some would say."

"Your words inspired me at a time in my life when I'd given up hope."

"A duke's daughter without hope? Sounds contradictory."

Unwilling to divulge the bad turn her life had taken, she made light of the subject. "It no longer matters, but I wanted to say thank you and wish you well."

He didn't unfurl the document but tucked it into his coat. "I shall treasure it, Virginia MacKenzie."

"Treasure what?" said Edward. "Not Virginia, I hope. Cameron Cunningham will have something to say about that. They are betrothed."

To her surprise and small disappointment, Redding said nothing to Edward about the gift. In fake gruffness, he asked, "Where is this Cunningham? I hope not with the duke of Ross. That man could teach stubbornness to King George."

Both Edward and Virginia laughed. She said, "Cameron's in Edinburgh, but he'll be home on Saturday."

Unfortunately Cameron's return was overshadowed by the arrival of the *Glasgow Courant*. In boldface type, the newspaper reported that Horace Redding had been arrested and charged with possession of treasonous material.

The evidence?

A tanned rabbit hide bearing the outlawed text of *Reason Enough*.

Chapter

14

~

"What will happen to him?" Virginia collapsed into a chair but couldn't sit still. Getting to her feet, she paced the length of the spacious dining room and stopped.

Cameron, Lottie, Sarah, and Edward sat at the table. Michael Elliot, Sarah's husband, stood in the doorway.

"Please sit down, Virginia." Lottie sniffed into her napkin. "You'll make yourself sick with fretting."

"Leave her be, Lottie." Across the room, Agnes paced too, the baby, Juliet, clutched to her shoulder.

Cameron helped himself to another oatcake. "Sarah knows what will happen to him."

"I'm not a barrister," Sarah said.

But she knew, Virginia was certain of that. Facing them, her stomach sour with worry, she repeated a familiar phrase from her childhood. "Sarah knows. Sarah knows everything."

She signed in resignation and pushed away her untouched meal. "That pamphlet is considered treasonous material. If he's found guilty, he'll be hanged or transported."

Virginia rolled the newspaper and whacked the back of Cameron's chair. "Transported to where?"

"Australia."

Cameron rose, took the paper from her, and held her hands. " 'Twill be all right. Father knows people."

Misery weighted Virginia, misery and anger at her own ignorance. "It's all my fault."

"Nay." Cameron pulled her against him and, murmuring "shush," rubbed her back. "Trust me."

She basked in his comfort, but the blame was hers. "I tell you, I'm responsible."

A chorus of objections filled the room.

Virginia squeezed her eyes shut. They were her family and bound by loyalty to support her. Years ago when Mary had drawn her first satirical cartoon and sent it to the mayor of Tain, the family had rallied around her. They'd stood by her even as she apologized a week later.

Sarah's husband, Michael, who'd arrived earlier in the day with Cameron, poured Virginia a glass of water. "How can Horace Redding's problems be your fault?"

Sarah said, "Redding brought it on himself. He's a troublemaker."

"Of course he is," Agnes declared. "He knew better than to bring that essay with him."

Lottie blurted, "Others have gone to the gallows for possessing that essay."

That's why he hadn't unrolled the hide last night or mentioned it when Edward had rejoined them. A painful possibility popped into Virginia's mind.

"What if he thinks I did it on purpose? Because of his disagreement with Papa."

"You? Shush," Cameron murmured. "What could you possibly have to do with their quarrel?"

A chorus of "Yes, what's" sounded, but the question hung in the air long after the room grew quiet.

"It is my fault." Choked by self-loathing, Virginia moved away from Cameron and faced her family.

"You mustn't blame yourself," Agnes insisted. The baby burped loudly, and nervous laughter erupted.

"It's my fault because I'm the one who gave it to him."

"What?"

The prospect of confessing her role in the tragedy should have made Virginia feel better, but it did not. She hadn't even been home long enough to reacquaint herself with everyone in the family, and she'd already brought shame upon them.

Gathering courage, she said, "I admired him from the first word of that essay. For ten years, I read almost every copy of the *Virginia Gazette*, and never once did I read that possession of the document was punishable."

"It wasn't in America." Cameron wrapped an arm around her shoulder. "You couldn't know that."

"I should have known." What other rules would she break? "But life is so different over there."

"Tell us about it, Virginia," Cameron urged.

The need to unburden herself rose like a tide in Virginia. But hadn't she done enough?

"We are not strangers," he said softly.

"Not at all," Lottie said. "Look how much you've remembered already."

Strangers, family, friends. They didn't deserve to bear the responsibility of her mistakes.

Patting her child's back, Agnes said, "We'd love you, Virginia, even if you had remembered nothing more than the design on that keg."

Cameron squeezed Virginia. If he decided tomorrow to give his heart elsewhere, that small comfort would stay with her until God called her home.

She looked up at him. "Can your father truly help? When will he return from Italy?"

Like sunshine, his smile warmed her. "He'll return soon, and yes, he'll do everything in his power. We all will help."

"You're never alone, Virginia," Agnes declared. "You're never alone."

Between fretful sniffs, Lottie said, "Don't forget our father and David have friends at court."

"We'll need a barister," said sensible Sarah.

Edward nodded. "But not a Glaswegian. That fellow in Carlisle . . ." He turned to Agnes. "What's his name?"

"Aaron MacKale."

"Yes. I'll send for him today."

"Thank you." No sooner were the words out than another possibility occurred to Virginia. "Why not deport Redding to America?"

Cameron's smile turned bittersweet. "Because seditious material is outlawed. Our king is still tormented over the loss of his American colonies."

Edward rose and took the baby from Agnes. "Some say that's what drove him mad."

"Hoots! The pettiness and boredom of his own court is what's to blame."

Edward came over to Virginia. "Excuse me, Cunningham." When Cameron released her, Edward said, "Virginia, kiss your niece. 'Tis time to put her down for a nap."

Edward handed over the baby. Cradling her, gazing into her angelic face, Virginia felt her pain ease. This sweet child was Agnes's baby, named for Virginia's mother, the duchess of Ross.

So many dreams were coming true for Virginia and now this nightmare.

"You're a MacKenzie, lass," said Edward. "Never forget that."

The MacKenzies wielded great power in Scotland. Edward Napier was considered a national treasure. Cameron's father was a member of Parliament. *Hope is not lost,* a voice inside her said.

" 'Tis magic, no?" said Edward. "The way holding a baby can clear your mind."

National treasure didn't begin to describe Agnes's husband. "Yes."

"Good." He patted her shoulder. "So what is next?"

Possibilities flashed in her head. "We need a plan."

"She's right," Cameron said.

Looking around the room, Virginia reconsidered the situation. Putting herself in Redding's place was easy, for bondage was surely similar to jail. "First, for Mr. Redding," she said to all in the room. "We must look after his needs. He should not suffer humiliation or hunger."

With a look, Cameron urged her on. "I'll see to it today."

Lottie stood. "I'll supervise the preparing of a basket."

"Don't forget bed linens," Virginia said, remembering the nights of luxury she spent in the main house at Poplar Knoll prior to Cameron's arrival.

Agnes tapped a spoon against her glass. When she had everyone's attention, she stood. "Sarah, choose

279

some books from the library—nothing seditious, mind you. Fill a box, and get Mrs. Johnson to find a lamp and plenty of oil. And a comfortable chair."

More to himself than the crowd, Cameron said, "We'll need bribes for the guard."

"I have money," Virginia said, regretting the purchases she'd made in Norfolk. The remainder of her one hundred pounds would go far in ensuring Redding's comfort.

"I'll take care of it," Cameron offered.

"No." Pride urged her on. "I insist on using my money."

"Very well. You can pay me back later."

Virginia remembered meeting the constable of Glasgow last night. "Who arrested Redding? Was it Constable Jenkins?"

" 'Twould be his first arrest," Agnes grumbled.

Lottie said, "Agnes should be named constable."

Edward looked askance at that. "Countess of Cathcart is enough responsibility for me, thank you."

"Worry not," Cameron said. "I'll visit Constable Jenkins myself."

"Nay," snapped Edward. "You'll send a coach for him but show him no more courtesy than that."

Although Cameron still held Virginia, he faced Edward Napier. "Why should I welcome him when our cause will be better served if I happen upon him at the cordiner's guild."

"The cordiner's guild?"

"Aye, with luck and good planning, I should arrive just as he collects his stipend from them."

"He takes bribes?" Agnes shuddered in revulsion. "That's politics."

"I'll go with you, Cameron," Edward said.

"There you have it," Lottie declared. "The constable doesn't stand a chance. Just don't take Agnes along."

"I resent that!"

Virginia prayed the plan succeeded. "Redding cannot be punished for my mistake."

"Look at me, Virginia." Taking the baby, Cameron gave the child back to her father. "If it comes to it, I'll pluck him from that jail myself and take him back to America."

Agnes banged the table. "Hoots! I'll help. The locks must be old. Any awl will spring the mechanisms. We'll make a drawing of the building, noting every guard and exit. Notch can obtain a schedule of the guards—"

"Take the baby, Agnes," her husband said in a voice that dropped like stones into the conversation.

She looked him up and down, a challenge in her eyes. He lifted a brow, and to everyone's surprise, she capitulated.

Virginia's thoughts grew jumbled. "What if Redding wants to go to France?"

Cameron grinned. "Then you must learn to say *bonjour.*"

The urge to laugh brightened her soul. "Ireland?"

"Ireland?" Lottie chirped, a pinched expression on her face. "No one goes there. The food is more distasteful than Mary's husband."

Chuckling, Agnes said, "I hope he does not chose Spain for his place of sanctuary."

Lottie twitched her nose. "The Spaniards never bathe."

The playful chatter, combined with Cameron's strong presence, brought a normalcy to the occasion. But another dire consequence occurred to Virginia.

"That's it too. If Redding is not exonerated of the charges, he will lose his freedom."

"Virginia." At the urgency in Cameron's voice, her gaze snapped to his. "Only in America does freedom truly reign."

Confused, she studied him. "Why do you say that?"

"Because 'tis true. So long as there's land aplenty to be had in America, people will choose their own destiny. This island is tied to the past. Claims were laid on every furlong, every rock and tree, centuries before the *Mayflower* sailed."

Virginia hadn't thought of that. "But Glasgow is Redding's home."

"Truly?" he challenged. "After a time in jail, I think he'll be happy to see the last of Scotland."

"True," said Edward. "Redding confided to me that he was eager to return to Philadelphia."

"Are you sure?"

"Think about it."

For days, Virginia thought about little else. Her sisters tried to distract her; Edward even suspended his rules and invited her to view his laboratory.

Cameron visited Redding every morning, replenishing the supply of necessities and bringing new culinary delights from the Napier kitchen. Although Cameron objected, he'd taken her remaining money, eighty-two pounds and bribed the guards. The evenings he spent with Virginia at Napier House.

Afternoons were devoted to visits from the local gentry. Virginia excused herself during those times and wrote letters to Rowena; to Cameron's sister, Sibeal; to Merriweather and Mrs. Parker-Jones. She wrote to Horace Redding every day. In the first exchange, she'd apologized, and he had forgiven her. Not until he was free would she forgive herself.

Were it not for the danger to Redding clouding the happy atmosphere, Virginia felt as if she'd never been away from Cameron and her siblings. Familiar routines developed. Mornings with the children, all of whom vied for Auntie Virginia's attention. They shared stories about her as a child, stories told to them by her siblings and by Uncle Cameron. In their childish innocence, they admitted the general opinion that Virginia was with the angels. In a family portrait, Mary had even painted Virginia as an angel. Only Agnes had believed, but she felt responsible for Virginia's disappearance.

The barrister, Aaron MacKale, an apple-cheeked gentleman, arrived from nearby Carlisle with a staff of assistants. Cameron offered them the use of Cunningham Gardens, and Edward arranged for a dozen students from Glasgow University to aid MacKale.

A flurry of petitions and writs were exchanged. MacKale made no promises: The evidence was solid; the situation looked grim.

Virginia despaired.

Only Cameron brought her solace. He tried to ease her trepidation. At times she thought he could look into her mind and see the humiliation she'd suffered. He always understood the special place she kept in her heart for Redding. When she lost hope of righting the wrong she'd done to her mentor, Cameron told her in strict confidence about Redding's newest work, a secret piece on the fairness of American justice versus the oppression of the British courts. He planned to publish the essay under the title "Writings of an American Robbed of Freedom of Speech."

Every evening for a fortnight, meetings were held in the dining room of Napier House. They planned and schemed, theorized and sympathized.

On the fifteenth day, a friend of Agnes's, a man named Haskett Trimble, delivered the news that Lachlan MacKenzie was on his way home.

"What delayed him?" Agnes demanded. "Was there trouble? Is he ill? Has something happened to Juliet?"

Trimble said, "They are hale and hearty. His grace postponed his departure from Boston to await the arrival of an old friend." Looking pointedly at Cameron, he added, "A Moorish sea captain named Ali Kahn."

To Virginia's surprise, Cameron made a fist and triumphantly thrust up his arm. To Napier's dismay, Cameron smashed the chandelier as he said, "Sweet revenge."

Papa was coming home. The time to tell the truth was rapidly approaching. Upon Redding's release or her father's arrival, whichever came first, Virginia would bear her soul.

Later in the week Trimble returned with word from Italy. Cameron's sister, Sibeal, had borne her count a son. The happy grandparents, Myles and Suisan, would not return for another month. Trimble handed Virginia a stack of letters, two of which were from her brother, Kenneth, and her sister Cora, who had traveled with the Cunninghams. Virginia prayed that by the time they returned, Redding would be free.

A new round of activity began when Mary arrived, her children and husband in tow. Disproving Papa's belief that the sword always prevailed over the pen,

Mary took up a quill and, in a series of cartoons, made a mockery of Sir Constable Jenkins and the Glasgow courts.

Too tied to tradition, the *Courant* refused to print Mary's work. Seeing its chance to profit from the situation, the *Glasgow Mercury* not only printed the drawings, but paid Mary a stipend. Her husband, an influential member of the House of Lords, advised MacKale. But Constable Jenkins, a Glaswegian from birth, had publicly taken a stand. He would not reduce the charges against Redding.

After a joyous reunion with Mary, Virginia saw little of her artistic sister, but that had always been Mary's way when inspiration captured her.

A week later, Virginia and Edward each received a summons to court. Others at the reception had also been served. Three days hence, they must appear before the magistrate. What if Virginia were asked about the hide, about her past?

Cameron protested the summons. Edward tried to make light of it. Agnes fumed. Virginia trembled in fear of the court. Once she'd taken an oath, she must answer any question truthfully. Her time in bondage had been a private tragedy, and she balked at publicly speaking of the details of her life there. She must either lie or admit to strangers what she hadn't found the courage to confess to Cameron and her family.

On the evening before the trial, Agnes surprised everyone with a change of heart. She brushed off the importance of the summons and, with Notch as her helper, took the children to the May Fair. They returned with a guest—the vicar—who stayed for dinner.

* * *

Later that night, while the clergyman and the others played billiards, Virginia excused herself. In the library, an open and unread copy of *Humphry Clinker* in her lap, she fought hard to keep the melancholy away. During her indenture, she had grappled with the decision of what to do when her bondage ended. One day she convinced herself to stay in America, to move north and make a life there. On another day, she planned to rush home to her family. But the moment she'd drawn the hearts and arrow on the kegs, the decision was made.

She had feared risking a longer indenture on the slim hope that she'd be rescued, but had she not given Cameron the means to find her, she would not have known his love. Even now, in the safety of Napier's library, that realization tormented her.

"Whatever you are thinking, banish it from your mind." He leaned against the bookcase nearest the door, his arms folded over his chest, determination in his gaze.

As soon as she caught her breath, she closed the book. "I was thinking that popular fiction is much overrated."

He strolled toward her, resplendent in riding breeches and a brown velvet jacket. "Like resolve?"

Her heart took flight. "My last resolve vanished when you romanced me in the crow's nest."

Chuckling wickedly, he knelt beside her chair and reached for the book. Rather than take it from her, he traced the shape, the tip of his finger drawing a rectangle on her lap. Even beneath the layers of petticoats and skirt, her skin tingled and her senses grew keen. The look in his eyes turned positively dreamy.

The standing clock struck the first of ten chimes. By

the fourth clanging, Cameron took her in his arms; at the seventh peal, he was kissing her deeply. The sound of the last chime hung in the air, same as her senses dangled on the passion he inspired. In his arms, she floated above life and its troubles. Bliss captured her, and all she could think of was this man, her Cam, and the moment.

"I've missed you." He spoke against her mouth, and she felt rather than heard the words.

The yearning she'd spent weeks suppressing returned and, with it, a need for him that was both wild and tender at once. But she'd made a vow to herself. Weeks ago, when word of Redding's arrest had reached them, she'd vowed that before she and Cameron again succumbed to passion, she'd tell him the truth.

The moment was at hand.

Chapter

15

⁓

Virginia broke the kiss. "I have something to tell you, Cam." Catching his gaze and looking into his soul, she willed him to understand. "I have many things to tell you."

He studied her. At length, he shook his head. "Not tonight, Virginia." He took her hands and gave her a crooked smile. "We haven't had a moment to ourselves, and tonight is . . ."

"Is what?"

His gaze moved from the book to the clock. "Forget Redding. Forget your family. Tonight is for us. I want you like a newly wedded butcher wants his bride."

The coward in her grasped the reprieve. With that relief, her sense of humor returned. Inspired by his cockiness, she said, "In God's scheme, what makes you so different from a butcher?"

Her answer pleased him, for his eyes crinkled with mirth. "Nothing except you and the happiness you bring to me. Truth to tell, a butcher comes better prepared to love a woman."

On that bit of nonsense, she laughed. "I will not be baited."

Lamplight and innocence wreathed his face. "Baiting is the work of a fisherman. I aspire to butchery."

"How does one aspire to butchery?"

He jumped up and bolted the door, but his gait was lazy, determined, when he came back to her. Considering the tight fit of his buff-colored breeches, she knew what he had on his mind.

To bedevil him, she stared at his loins and said, "That's an interesting placket."

With a flair, he threw off his coat. "So kind of you to say so. Now where were we?"

"The elementals of butchery, I believe."

"Ah, yes. First, a good man o' the meat must learn the product of his craft." He sat on the floor, lifted her left foot, and removed her new slipper. Moving his hand up her leg, he stopped below her knee. "Here we have the calf, a well-turned one to be sure."

Laughter bubbled up inside her. "I've always heard it called the shank."

"See? We left the colonies alone for too long. No serious tradesman would ever name this graceful limb a shank." He feigned revulsion. "Dreadful word."

"In the field of butchery, what name do you give a stocking?"

Deviltry had him in its throes. "A stunning accoutrement."

She closed her eyes to savor the joy.

"So you do not wish to see the demonstration? Very well." He grasped her hips and eased her down in the chair. Tossing up her skirt and petticoats, he flipped them over her face. Then he spread her legs.

She gasped, blind to all but the feel of his hands.

"Hesitance is not allowed, Virginia. If I'm to serve out a butcher's apprenticeship, you must cooperate."

She knew he was teasing, trying to distract her. With her family and the vicar two rooms away, he couldn't possibly mean to love her here. "You have me on my haunches. How much more cooperative can I be?"

"We'll see, won't we, my clever lass?" Using both hands, he caressed her thighs. "Here we have the rounds, a favorite of English monarchs."

"What of the preferences of the Stewarts?"

"Ah, the Scots are much more discriminating." He touched her intimately. "We favor the loins but have a special preference for this tender morsel."

She sucked in a breath and couldn't keep her hips from rising to meet him. He encouraged her, murmuring sweet promises of what was to come. He worked her gently at first, and when she was primed and begging, he pulled her to the floor.

Through a storm of passion, reality surfaced. "What if someone comes looking for us?"

"No one will." Not stopping to undress himself, he opened the packet of his breeches.

His manhood popped free.

Feeling blissfully alive, she said, "Oh, so that's what you were hiding."

All pretense gone; he moved over her and, with a single thrust, made them one. She clutched him, called to him, and when he kissed her, he slipped his tongue into her mouth in a matching rhythm to the loving going on below.

The clock struck the half hour, but it could have been Sunday noon for all she cared. This man and his loving were her heart's desire. From the time she'd learned to collect memories, he'd been a keepsake, a treasure she intended to cherish. Time and circumstance had altered the path of their lives, but that was behind them. He'd set aside his mistress. Words had not been spoken, but it was as if he had said, *You have always been mine.*

She'd tell him the truth, and then she'd propose marriage. An instant later, all thoughts of that betrothal fled, and her mind stayed fixed on the here and the now and the pleasure he gave her.

When the rapture came, she felt caught up, reshaped, and her mind flung to the wind. He felt it too, for at the peak of his passion, he called out her name and God's in the same breath.

Neither moved, but the pounding of their hearts harmonized with the tick, ticking of the clock. He held her, and as she inhaled his familiar scent and languished in his arms, she thought this the most memorable time in her life.

When the clock struck the half hour, he rolled to his side.

"Ouch!" He'd banged his head on a table.

"Let me see." Ignoring her disheveled and wrinkled dress, she rose on her knees and examined his head. His thick hair cushioned her palms, and as she cupped his head, a knot rose beneath her fingers. "You've bumped yourself a good one, Cam."

"I care not." He buried his face in her bodice. "Curse me for a poor butcher," he lamented. "I never made it past the loins."

She chuckled. "I give you high marks for the parts you do know."

He jiggled his brows. "Shall we retire to your room and repair that slight?"

The truth clamored to be said. "No." She cleared

her throat, sat back, and fussed with her skirt. "I have something to tell you, and I don't want to be distracted."

"Sounds serious."

"It is."

As he righted his clothing, he glanced at the clock.

"It won't take long," she said, hoping that was true, for she feared her courage would flee.

Anticipation sharpened his gaze. "A brandy then?"

She nodded and waited for him to pour the drinks and return.

Handing her a glass, he held his up. "To you."

The dull thud of crystal against crystal sounded loud in her ears. Where to begin? She sipped the heady wine. As it spread over her tongue, she found a starting place.

"Do you know that this is only my second time to drink brandy?"

As serious as she'd ever seen him, he gave a slight shake of his head and waited.

"The first time was the occasion of Captain Brown's unexpected visit to Poplar Knoll. He came to say that he'd spoken with you in Glasgow. Mrs. Parker-Jones sent Merriweather to the hamlet to fetch me."

"The hamlet?"

Shame choked her. "Yes. That's where I lived."

"I love you." He reached for her.

She held up her hand. "I lied to you all the way 'round, Cam."

Compassion softened his gaze.

"I wasn't the housekeeper. I worked in the fields because . . ." The name of her villain tasted too bitter on her tongue.

"Because?"

Let it go, her heart said. "Because . . ." The words stalled in her throat.

"Take a sip," he encouraged.

She did, and the drink fortified her. "Because I tried to follow you to France. I planned to sneak aboard your ship, but—"

"But I'd already sailed to China."

"I didn't know that was your destination at the time. I thought you were going to France."

His smile was gentle, loving. "Sarah taught you French on the sly."

"She told you that?"

"Of course. For years, we spoke of little else save our misfortune in losing you."

She took strength from that love. "Let me go on. I must tell it all."

"I'm listening, love."

"When I learned you had sailed, I found another ship, captained by a man named—" Again, the named stalled on her tongue. She took a deep breath. "A man named Anthony MacGowan. He swore he was going to France. He said he knew you well and promised to take me to you."

"But he didn't take you to France."

Agony squeezed her chest. "No. He took me to Williamsburg and sold me to Mr. Moreland."

"Oh, sweetheart." Again he reached for her.

Again she held him off. "Wait." She must get on with it. "He called it an indenture and named the term ten years, but it doesn't change what they did to me."

"I hate them," Cameron swore through his teeth. "They are vile, and you were innocent."

Let him think that if he wished. At ten, she'd been mature enough to make the decision that had cost her a decade of her life. She would not place the blame elsewhere. "All of that changed."

"Oh, Virginia." He held out a trembling hand.

She slipped her fingers in his. "There's more. You must let me say it. I never fell from a horse. I wasn't allowed near a horse. My memory is perfectly intact, always has been. I lied because I hadn't the courage to tell you the truth about my life there."

"You thought to spare me and your family the guilt."

"Yes, and to give myself enough time to fit in here. I didn't always have shoes, and I slept on a pallet of hay." She gazed around the finely appointed room. "Life here is very grand."

His hand grew damp in hers. "You worked hard?"

She nodded. "I tried escape once but lost courage after that."

"Were you ever beaten?"

The frightened girl she'd once been now begged to be set free. "No, but other, more horrible things . . ."

"Have another sip of the brandy; 'twill ease the way."

The third swallow of the fiery drink cleared her throat and bolstered her courage.

His eyes were pools of kindness. "Who hurt you?"

The dark times hung on the edge of her mind, but she pushed them back. Cameron was here, and a happy future awaited them. "The doctor. Mr. Moreland had taken a slave for his mistress, but when she died bearing him a stillborn child, Mrs. Moreland assumed he'd take me. She had allowed him a slave, but she forbid him to move me into the house. He hadn't even spared a glance at me since he bought me from MacGowan. She didn't believe him. To assure herself that he'd left me alone, she had the doctor come 'round every month and—and . . ."

"Let it out, love."

"I didn't know at first what he was doing. I was four and ten at the time."

"Damn. That's enough, Virginia. You needn't—"

"Yes, I must. I had to lie on a table. It was so cold. He always told me to spread my legs." Quickly, she drank again. "He felt inside of me . . . for my maidenhead."

The glass slid to the floor, and she covered her face with her hands. Shame curled her spine, and she drew up her legs.

He held her then and rocked her, crooning words of comfort. When she quieted, he said, "How long did it go on?"

"Until two years ago when they sold the plantation to Mr. Parker-Jones."

"Bloody hell!" He squeezed her, as if in doing so he could drive out her demons.

But the horror was behind her. "That's why in Norfolk when we—"

"Made love?"

"Yes. That's why you thought I had been raped." In a way, she had been raped, often. Even now, she remembered the long walk to the main house, the icy table in the buttery, the cold look in the doctor's eyes. The relief that lasted for one turn of the moon. The next month, the doctor was back again.

"I'm sorry I lied to you, Cam, but I was ashamed."

"Oh, sweetheart. 'Tis in the past. We've only tomorrows ahead."

She felt cleansed. For the first time in a decade, her soul was unburdened. "I'll never lie to you again." Unfolding her hands, she help up her palms. "You have my word."

He twined his fingers with hers. "Put it behind you, love. Try never to think of those times again."

"I will as soon as I've told Papa and the others."

He held her at arms length, and she saw tears in his eyes. She attempted a smile to cheer him, but she failed.

"Must you tell them, Virginia?"

That surprised her. A full confession had always been part of her plan. "Yes, I must."

"Why? What good would it serve? They'll feel guilty if they know you were mistreated. As it stands, they are grateful to have you back, and they shoulder only the blame ignorance brings them."

"But I've never lied to Papa."

"Aye, you did. On many occasions we both lied to him."

"But we were children, and the lies were small."

Succinctly, he said, "And they hurt no one. Think of how Agnes will feel if she knows that you had no shoes." A tear slid down his cheek. "I gave up hope and went on with my life. Your father also did. You'll crush him with a confession. He's happy now. Why bring back his suffering?"

She wanted to believe him. Cameron Cunningham had been her dearest friend since before she knew the meaning of the word. But old beliefs brought doubts. "I owe him the truth."

Cameron searched for the words to convince her. Lachlan MacKenzie had found vengeance. Virginia need never know that Anthony MacGowan would spend his days rotting in the hold of a Moorish galley. Thinking of that well-deserved fate, Cameron said, "What is the truth? That you love your father well?"

"Yes."

"That you are glad to be back among those who love you?"

"Yes."

"That's truth enough. Our life together awaits. You cannot return to your father's house. We'll be married. You'll bear our children here or aboard our ship or where ever we find ourselves." He laid her hand over his heart. "Your place is here, with me, as we'd always planned."

Her smile was tentative at first; but reason won out. "All right. But what if Anthony MacGowan tells the truth?"

"What if Anthony MacGowan is dead? Shall I ask Trimble to find out?"

"Oh, please."

"I shall if you'll do something for me?"

She'd swim to France if it would ease the pain he didn't try to hide from her. "Anything."

"You must do this, true heart." He clutched her upper arms. "Please forgive me for giving up hope of finding you."

"That's easy. I love you." She moved into his arms and held on tight. "I have always loved you."

He breathed a sigh of relief. "And I you. 'Tis a pity we have to wait to wed until your father returns."

"Where is the betrothal agreement?"

He didn't answer for so long she thought he hadn't heard her. At length, he said, "That is the last truth. Your father and I burned it."

"Together?"

297

"Aye, we tapped a laird's keg and drank ourselves into a stupor. Drunk as Turks, we had a ceremony, although he recalls little of the night."

"You've never reminded him of it?"

"Nay, he has suffered enough."

"All of us have suffered."

"Aye, but no more," he said.

"I am at peace then."

"Good."

Without moving from the floor of Napier's library, they held each other, and a silent healing began.

Sometime later the peace was shattered by a knock at the door and the arrival of Constable Jenkins.

Cameron drilled Agnes with a curious gaze. When she winked, he breathed a sigh of relief. While Cameron had been in the library making love to Virginia, Agnes and Edward had engaged the vicar in a game of billiards. But Agnes had left them under the guise of soothing her fretful daughter. With the lad Notch for accomplice, Agnes had broken into the constable's office, stolen the hide, and destroyed the evidence.

Now she stepped forward. "Constable Sir Jenkins, are you acquainted with Father John? We've been playing billiards since after supper. When did you lose your evidence?"

Blustering, his chain of office crooked on his shoulders, he shook with anger. "Not above an hour ago."

"None of us is to blame."

All self-righteous servant of the law, Jenkins turned his hateful gaze on Cameron. "You're a thief, Cunningham. You stole that rabbit hide from my safe."

"Me? I couldn't have."

"Where were you?"

Virginia moved between them. "Cameron was with

me, sir." She paused, a blush flagging her cheeks. "We're betrothed, you know."

Cameron had expected as much, and he loved her for it. "You've told him enough, love."

With Virginia and the vicar to verify his alibi, Cameron could not be charged, and no other suspects were found. Without the key piece of evidence, Horace Redding was set free.

The next day, a cartoon appeared in the *Mercury*. In retaliation, Mary had depicted a dole-faced Constable Jenkins standing before a high court justice, his empty hands held out in supplication. MacKale was pictured off to the side, a smug look enhancing his striking features. A bewigged and stately justice glared down at poor Jenkins. The caption read, *"You've not seen hide nor hair of it?"*

A month later, Quinten Brown's ship arrived in Glasgow Harbor with the duke and duchess of Ross aboard. When word reached Napier House, everyone clamored to meet the ship. A caravan of carriages rumbled down Harbor Road, Napier's spherical conveyance in the lead.

The moment Lachlan stepped onto Scottish soil again, Lottie blurted the news that Virginia had taken up residence at Cunningham Gardens. Upon arrival at Napier House, Lachlan ordered Cameron into the study. An hour later they emerged, both smiling.

Virginia expected her father to call her into the study. Instead, he declared, "Do you truly want this half Englishman for your husband?"

"Yes, Papa. I love him well."

"Then we are twice blessed." He picked her up. "Worry not, lass, about those lost memories. You're back home and that's all that matters."

They adjourned to the nursery, where Sarah's daughter Isobel took her first wobbly steps—into the arms of a gloating Lachlan.

A special license was acquired, and on Saturday next, Virginia and Cameron fulfilled their destiny. As a private wedding gift, Cameron relayed a message to Virginia. Anthony MacGowan was dead.

"How? When?"

It served no purpose to tell her of her father's involvement. So he told a lie he thought would satisfy her. "Some time ago. His death was slow and painful."

"Good."

When they exited the Napier carriage and approached the dock to begin their honeymoon, Virginia noticed a canvas draped over the side of Cameron's ship. MacAdoo stood near the bow, and the crew stood at attention.

"What's that?"

"You'll see."

Holding her hand, he whistled to MacAdoo, who saluted, then tossed off the mysterious canvas. Cameron had again changed the name of his ship. Now it was called *True Heart*.

"For you," he said. "My dearest love."

Then he swept her into his arms and carried her aboard. As they waved good-bye to her family, Cameron said, "Where shall we go first?"

Feeling reckless and joyful, she said, "The crow's nest?"

Laughing, he held her close, and as they sailed away from Scotland, Virginia remembered the vow he'd spoken to her during their wedding.

Gazing up at him, love swelling inside her, she said, "Tomorrow is no dream, but our destiny."

"Aye, True Heart."

Epilogue

～

Rosshaven Castle
Scottish Highlands
Harvest, 1793

Harvest drummers and pipers heralded the return of the haywagons. Cameron scooted to the edge of the loft and peered through a knothole in the wall boards of the stable.

"Who's riding in the first wagon?"

Cameron gazed back at Virginia, who languished on the pallet. They'd spent the afternoon loving, napping, and enjoying being back in Scotland again.

For three years, they'd sailed the *True Heart* around the world. Only when Virginia had conceived had they returned to Scotland. But they hadn't gone to Cunningham Gardens in Glasgow, nor had they visited Cameron's parents. They'd come to Rosshaven Castle in Tain, principal residence of the ducal MacKenzies, the place where Cameron and Virginia had grown up together.

Now that the harvest was over, the celebration of the twenty-fifth anniversary of the duke and duchess of Ross would begin. With the exception of Cameron and Virginia, all of the MacKenzies, their spouses, and children had spent the day in the fields.

Only one member of the extended family was not here.

"Cameron Cunningham! Tell me who won."

The annual harvest race was over. In order of their finish, the wagons returned to Rosshaven.

Expecting her to gloat, Cameron said, "Edward Napier and Notch."

"I knew it. He never boasts. When he said his machine could harvest as much wheat as three men, you should have believed him. You owe me fifty pounds."

She rolled over and, on stiff arms, crawled toward Cameron, her breasts swaying in a hypnotic rhythm. Larger since the birth of their daughter, Virginia's womanly attributes never failed to rouse him. But then, with a saucy wink or a spicy rejoinder, she could as easily stir his desire.

"Where's Agnes?" she asked.

Peering through the opening, Cameron studied the line of approaching wagons. "Astride the lead horse pulling Napier's wagon, and Jamie's up before her. Hannah and little Juliet are perched atop the cargo."

"The next wagon?"

"Your father and Lily's husband, Sutherland."

"Third?"

"Lottie's husband, David, and Christopher Napier."

"Where's Lottie?"

Cameron chuckled. For her part in the celebration, Lottie had made dresses for all of the women. Except that each was a different color, the cotton dresses, designed for a day of frolicking in the field, were alike. The fabric of Virginia's gown was dyed a leafy green, and the contrasting apron was a darker hue. Lottie wore apple red with a crimson apron. "She's in that jaunty trap. Lily, Cora, Rowena, and Sarah are on horseback, carrying torches to light the way."

"Where's Mary?"

Cameron hesitated. Robert Spencer, the earl of Wiltshire, had met his death beneath the hooves of the leading pack at Avon Downs. Mary had buried him over a year ago. She had yet to forgive him. But neither had she forgiven herself for not giving him a son. Hamish Dundas, heir apparent to the constable of Scotland, was doing his considerable best to get Mary out of her mourning gown. Odds were running three to one that he'd succeed before Hogmanay next.

"Where?" Virginia repeated.

"In a cart with Hamish."

"Good." Content to have him narrate the order of finish, Virginia again lay on her back. "Who's next?"

"Kenneth and his rowdy nephews. Michael and MacAdoo are behind them."

Raising her arms over her head, Virginia stretched, effectively lifting her nipples into view. "MacAdoo should be playing the pipes."

"You should stop teasing me." Cameron shifted to ease the swelling in his loins. He winced at the movement.

"What's amiss?"

Shaking his head, he rolled his eyes. "I shouldn't want you again so soon."

All saucy female, she writhed. "Shall I show you the folly in that train of thought?"

He laughed.

She lifted her brows in warning and challenge. But the wagons had entered the yard. The din of dozens of familiar voices blended with the stamping of hooves and the rattling of harnesses.

Confident that they'd soon have company, Cameron folded his arms.

"I could change your mind," she threatened.

He smiled, taunting her. She lifted herself up and moved closer.

The stable doors opened, then closed. Footfalls sounded on the planked floor below.

Holding a finger to his mouth, Cameron whispered, "Shush," and eased to the edge of the loft. Virginia followed.

Arm in arm, the duke and duchess of Ross strolled toward the ladder. His hair was now liberally sprinkled with gray, but Lachlan MacKenzie could still hold his own with a man half his age. Juliet, serene and stately in a lavender dress and purple apron, smiled up at him. He stopped, drew her into his arms, and kissed her long and deeply.

Virginia leaned against Cameron and sighed. He had not longed for the devotion of his foster parents; he and Virginia had made their own.

When the kiss ended, the duchess said, "You didn't for a moment think I believed you asked me into the stables to show me a new horse. I've heard that before."

Lachlan reached for the ladder. "What I have in mind is infinitely more entertaining than a foal."

Cameron and Virginia giggled, and just as her

parents looked up, a storm of hay rained down on hem.

Sputtering, Lachlan declared, "You're time's up, Cunningham."

He looked at Virginia and spoke a solemn truth, 'Nay, 'tis just beginning."

**POCKET BOOKS
PROUDLY PRESENTS**

HIS FLAME
ARNETTE LAMB

**Coming Soon
from Pocket Books**

**The following is a preview of
His Flame. . . .**

Scottish Lowlands

"Gather your weapon and your tools, Robert. Your stepmother's put aside some bread and the last of the curd." Father pointed to the door of the one-room hut. " 'Tis time for you to go."

The breath in Jamie's lungs turned to fire as he watched his eldest brother get to his feet. Six-year-old Patrick, younger than Jamie by only a year, whimpered. The other children huddled in small groups, girls with girls, boys with boys. From a basket on the dirt floor, the new baby wailed. To Jamie the fresh cries served as a bitter reminder of a sad truth: Robert, as eldest, must leave to make room for the babe.

They were fifteen in all, counting father and stepmother, the MacNabbs of Salmon Burn. Soon they would number only fourteen. Robert was leaving. And all because of the arrival of that mewling baby. Summerlass, they'd named her. Bonny and bright, they'd said. But until the day he died, Jamie would hate her, for her coming marked the blackest day of his life.

Robert was only two and ten. Jamie wondered how his brother would survive on his own. "What will you do?" Jamie asked.

Father's stern gaze swung to Jamie. "Our Robert will not join a pack of rovers."

Their family was breaking up, same as the Hepburns on the hill and the Camerons near the low road. Highborn Scots didn't turn out their children. Only the poor sons must fend for themselves or join together in packs. Rovers, they were called, and they lived in the woods, found work when they could, bullied where they must, survived as they might.

Robert stood straighter. "I'll make my way to the city."

Father nodded solemnly. "See that you do."

Cold spring air whistled across the thatched roof and set the window flap to rattling. The peat fire smoldered. Yet Father would turn out his elder son.

Jamie couldn't see beyond the pain of the moment and forgot the future. He put Patrick down, ran to the door, and flung himself at Robert.

"Be of good cheer, Jamie," Robert said, his voice steady with maturity, his arms strong from hard work.

A sob broke through, and Jamie squeezed his eyes shut.

"Would you have me underfoot?"

Jamie spoke from the heart. "Aye, for all times, Rabby."

Robert shrugged. "I cannot bide here and wipe your skinny ass. 'Tis up to Wills now."

Eleven-year-old Wills would be the next to go. Then Richard and Ann.

The hands holding Jamie trembled, but the voice was cavalier. "There'll be more room on the sleeping pallet and extra peas in the porridge, don't you know."

Father cleared his throat. "Life makes room for life, Jamie. 'Tis the way of things."

Robert stepped back. "Aye, Jamie. I'll be about seeking my fortune now, and when I return on a fine white horse, I'll bring you a new top, straight from the toymaker in Glasgow proper."

Glasgow. A world away.

From the hearth, their stepmother said, "If the lad's so fashed, send him along with Robert."

Jamie's own mother had died giving birth to him. A second stepmother had come and gone, leaving three more wee ones as evidence of her presence among the MacNabbs of Salmon Burn.

"But then," his stepmother continued, "who will play the lute and help me grind the corn? Jamie's the best at that."

Stepmother walked two paces, the distance to the kitchen, which consisted of a kettle over a fire, a bread board, and two knives. But since this woman's arrival, dried herbs now hung from the rafters and the hut smelled fresh even in winter.

"Here," she ordered Jamie. "Take Summerlass. I'll get Rabby's food."

The babe's slight weight rested easily in Jamie's

arms. Her sunny little face glowed. Pumping her arms, she made hooting sounds of joy as she gazed up at Jamie. His anger toward her softened.

Robert kissed her brow, then winked. "She'll need you someday, Jamie."

As it happened, Summerlass would need Jamie, but at a time he least expected it and in a place he never dreamed to see.

Twenty-five years later

"You're stubborn, Miss Barklee," murmured the modiste around the pin pressed between her lips.

Was Eleanor stubborn? Every day, she had to confess. Why else would she be standing here arguing with a dressmaker over a length of lace? Because she wouldn't rest until she had things her way. How else could a well-bred yet poorly dowered girl expect to survive and secure a decent future? She'd spent her life at the Hanoverian court, except for summers at Bath and Tunbridge Wells, with excellent results.

She'd met her affianced at Bath, and acting stubborn and being well-bred had helped her land such a fine catch.

Visiting this provincial island, worlds away in the Caribbean Sea, had been a prenuptial necessity.

Her soon-to-be father-in-law was governor over all the islands in the Lesser Caribbean.

She wouldn't live here, though. As surviving heir to his uncle, the earl of Shelly, her betrothed would soon take his rightful place at the family holdings in Kent.

A fortnight from now, Edward Augustus Dearborne would sail into Society Bay and fetch his bride. Soon the Honorable Eleanor Barklee would become Lady Eleanor, countess of Shelly. While she had enjoyed her sojourn with his parents, Eleanor longed to return to England and begin the life for which she was destined.

But today, during a fourth and final fitting, she must convince the uncooperative modiste to put three rows of lace on the headpiece. The plain gray frock must give the appearance of one in servitude—a Spanish governess, to be precise.

Years ago the duchess of Marlborough had turned the court on its head by appearing in a similar costume. That had been Eleanor's first visit to court. She'd been six years old. So taken had the duchess been with Eleanor, she'd offered her a place in her household. Since Papa's remarriage and the birth of three sons, Eleanor had felt like a visitor in her own home.

"Be a clever girl," her grace had said. "Your dowry is small. You must depend on your beauty and charm to land a rich, titled husband. But not if you are stuck in the country."

With the duchess Eleanor had moved to court,

and in the years that followed, she proved an apt pupil. A stunning catch, they proclaimed. With the help of her mentor, Eleanor successfully navigated a sea of court intrigues and a storm of charming cavaliers.

Male voices sounded in the front room of the dressmaker's shop, drawing Eleanor from thoughts of the reasons behind her arrival on this island in the Caribbean.

This was to be a private fitting, all a part of Eleanor's plan to keep her costume a secret.

"Are you expecting someone?" she asked, ready to duck behind the worktable should anyone of importance enter.

Shaking her head, the modiste shrugged.

Eleanor relaxed and waved the mantilla. "More lace."

"No. It must be plain," the modiste insisted.

Eleanor wanted three rows of lace. Three rows of lace she would have. She intended to make a brilliant go of her role, and the occasion called for dashing and imagination. She even intended to speak Spanish. Counting to ten in that language had been easy enough to learn; the rest she would fake, but with a flair.

A scruffy man and an even scruffier youth appeared in the doorway.

"Go 'way, you rogues," the modiste spat.

Eleanor ignored the exchange. Holding up three fingers on one hand, she waved the headpiece in the other and forcefully declared, *"Tres mas."*

The scruffy fellow elbowed his friend and said, "Did ya hear her?"

On the edge of her vision, she saw the older of the two smile. Knowing he would be impressed, she murmured what she hoped sounded like a string of commands in Spanish.

"She'll do," he said, moving forward. "Take her."

"Say this to him. If he does not tell me who he is and why he is here, I will throw him to the crabs."

Eleanor bit back a stinging retort. She had been kidnapped, bullied with a wicked knife, and delivered to the scourge of the Caribbean: Captain Craven. Now, with a pummeled and bloodied man slumped in a chair nearby, Craven was ordering her—commanding as if she were one of his motley crew of pirates.

"Tell him, señorita."

Eleanor refused to say a word; silence had been her weapon of choice, but from the evil glint in her captor's green eyes, her resolve waned. If this bold blackheart wanted to play games, she would appease him. She'd spent her life playing games at court.

Noise sounded in the companionway. A servant, his arms laden with packages, stepped into the cabin. Thick brown hair, straight as a matron's spine, was swept back and held in place by a thick layer of pomade. Dressed in an odd uniform of gray with black piping and epaulets, and a pleated front shirt of pressed cotton, he looked like an upstairs usher in an Italian opera house.

From the corner of a package he carried peeked a string of cheap beads. Holding his burden at arm's length, he bowed from the waist, and said to the captain, "My lord, the pilot said the tide is outing."

At the address, the grandee laughed. One of her abductors cuffed him. The captain said, "Pay Stephens no mind."

Rumors of his heritage abounded. Some said he'd been raised by natives on an island named Crooked Arm Cay. Others said he'd been plucked as a babe from his mother's arms and reared by the notorious Captain Black. Still others said Craven had been caught in the wrong royal bed and transported for a crime of passion.

Eleanor thought him a bully.

"Señorita." Tried patience flavored his words. "Tell him."

Feigning boredom, she turned to the grandee. Beneath the bruises and a swollen eye, he resembled a man she'd seen the night before at the governor's palace. But with the ball coming up, the whole city teemed with strangers.

"Do it, *señorita.*"

"Sir, if you do not tell him—"

"In Portuguese!" her captor bellowed, and pounded the table. Dishes rattled. The flame in the lantern wavered. The air in the cabin grew close. "Tell him in Portuguese."

Enlightenment came to Eleanor. The modiste. The costume. Her poorly spoken Spanish. She eyed the two men in the doorway. Her captors. "She'll do," one of them had said before whisking her away. The pirate wanted an interpreter; that's why he'd had her kidnapped. Ravishment was not on his agenda for her. Neither was ransom. At that realization, relief mixed with new trepidation.

A hand grasped her chin, and she found herself nose to nose with the man who was rapidly exceeding his reputation. He smelled of mint, the flavor of wisdom. That notion made her smile.

"You find me amusing?" Craven asked.

Trapped beneath the glare of legendary green eyes, Eleanor stifled a shiver.

"Do you?"

"No."

"Then, tell him."

She wanted to tell him she'd as soon find amusement in the public stocks at Bartholomew Fair. Better judgment reigned.

She swallowed hard and, in her most refined court speech, said, "I cannot, for I do not speak Portuguese. I am English."

Stillness settled over him, and he closed his eyes.

The taller of Eleanor's kidnappers hurried into the cabin, ducking beneath the low entrance. "She's lying, Captain. I heard her with me own ears."

Craven's gaze again settled on Eleanor. Dressed as he was, in a cotton shirt, open at the neck, a vest, and knee britches in plain leather, he looked like an ordinary sailor rather than a blackheart. No, ordinary didn't fit. With his wavy black hair hanging loosely above his shoulders and his strong features poised in confusion, he looked like an adventurer. That's how his admirers, mostly women and impressionable lads, spoke of the infamous Captain Craven.

He reached for her hand. "Did Spanker hear you speaking Portuguese?"

The ship rocked, then began to move.

The grandee dashed for the door. Spanker intercepted him, returning him to the chair.

Eleanor tried to withdraw from the captain's grasp. He lifted his brows again, whether in query or in challenge, she wasn't sure, but somehow she knew she must tell the truth.

She would not show cowardice, though. With that in mind, she rested her elbow on the table and let him keep her hand. Catching his gaze, she said, " 'Twas part of my disguise, but I only told the modiste how many rows of lace I wanted on the mantilla."

His grip softened. "Repeat what you said . . . exactly."

To her surprise, her anxiety fled. *"Tres mas—"*

"Didn't I say so, Captain?" The man named Spanker slapped the table.

His accomplice beamed. "As I'm a man o' the seas, we didn't botch it."

A resigned grin gave the captain a cordial air. "Nay, you didn't."

Eleanor rushed to say, " 'Twas an unfortunate mistake."

"There's a pity for you, mistress." Spoken without malice, the admission held regret.

False regret, Eleanor knew. To defend herself, and convince him to let her go, she said, "I was at the modiste for a fitting."

Craven eyed her attire, then sighed. "A costume then."

He understood that she was in distress. "Yes, for the ball—the governor's ball."

"The ball," he said without emotion.

"Yes. Let me go, and I'm certain the governor will show you leniency."

His minions scoffed. The grandee cleared his throat. Stephens polished the brightwork on the bed frame. The captain ignored them all, his attention still fixed on Eleanor.

Sensing vulnerability in him, she said, "I'm to marry his son."

He gave her a sad smile and rose. "Not any time soon."

Look for
HIS FLAME
Wherever Paperback Books
Are Sold
Coming Soon from
Pocket Books

ARNETTE
LAMB

🍁   🍁

"Arnette Lamb ignites readers' imaginations with
her unforgettable love stories."

— *Romantic Times*